SNUGGLY TALES
OF FEMMES FATALES

Brian Stableford's scholarly work includes *New Atlantis: A Narrative History of Scientific Romance* (Wildside Press, 2016), *The Plurality of Imaginary Worlds: The Evolution of French roman scientifique* (Black Coat Press, 2017) and *Tales of Enchantment and Disenchantment: A History of Faerie* (Black Coat Press, 2019). He has translated more than three hundred volumes from the French, mostly in the genres of *roman scientifique, contes de fées* and Romantic and Symbolist fiction. His recent fiction includes the visionary science fiction novel *The Revelations of Time and Space* (2020) and its sequel *After the Revelation* (2021); the last in his long series of "Tales of the Genetic Revolution," *The Elusive Shadows* (2020); and the comedy fantasy *Meat on the Bone* (2021), all published by Snuggly Books.

I0591376

SNUGGLY BOOKS

SNUGGLY TALES
OF
FEMMES
FATALES

EDITED, TRANSLATED,
AND WITH AN INTRODUCTION BY
BRIAN STABLEFORD

THIS IS A SNUGGLY BOOK

ISBN: 978-1-64525-100-2

CONTENTS

INTRODUCTION

IN the jargon of modern mythology, a *femme fatale* is a woman who lures men to their doom by means of an intense beauty that inevitably inspires lust in male observers: "*la beauté du diable*," as another French phrase has it. The fact that such French terms are routinely reproduced in English parlance reflects the quaint protective desire of the English to think of un-English women as more likely than their own compatriots to inspire lust by calculation, and archetypes of the species featured in English literature are often Frenchified, as in John Keats' classic "La Belle Dame sans Merci," which refers to one of the "fées" [enchantresses] of French Medieval Romance.

Many literary *femmes fatales* are, indeed, merciless—which is not the same thing as being malevolent, although those who fall under their spell are not always appreciative of the difference—but that is a choice on their part, the whole point of the quasi-diabolical gift of exceptional beauty being that it is, to begin with, an unsolicited gift visited on the innocent-to-be as well as the incipiently culpable; the doom to which it frequently leads its victims is often unintended and sometimes regretted. There is no paradox in that—the *femme fatale* syndrome is merely a particularly glamorous instance of the universal and unavoidable problem of unrequited love—but the notion of a *femme fatale* adds a particular piquancy to a very commonplace tragedy, which gives it an exceptional gloss, and there is no literary or psychological market for bland tragedy, which is almost an oxymoron and has no role to play in drama, let alone melodrama.

Ancient mythology is by no means short of archetypal *femme fatales*, the most conspicuous one in Western culture being Eve, who offers an atypical but particularly graphic symbolism of the notion, in yielding to the temptation of the serpent prior to tempting Adam in her turn, and thus playing an instrumental role in the Fall of all Humankind. The extent of her culpability has been up for negotiation in religion and literature for millennia, as has the question of the extent to which all women can or ought to be considered "daughters of Eve" in the sense of reflecting her vulnerability to temptation and consequent tendency to turn temptress. The verdict has usually been severe, men having an inevitable tendency to blame women for their own failings when transported by lust and women tending to blame other women for men's failings in similar circumstances. Literary men, who often like to think of themselves as exceptionally sensitive, frequently criticize insensitive men in their creations, but one sometimes suspects that they do not always do so in good faith, especially when they invoke a *mea culpa*. Boys will be boys, as the saying has it, and hypocrites are naturally hypocritical, especially when they charge themselves with hypocrisy. In all fairness, though, women are routinely no less hypocritically severe in their criticism of feminine temptation than men are, and are sometimes more so.

That Eve and other Biblical *femmes fatales* co-opted into the Christian Mythos—notably Jezebel, Delilah and Salome—are scathingly stigmatized in much Western literature is unsurprising, given the misogynist tendencies of the Christian Churches (by no means not the only instance in which Churchmen do the opposite of what Jesus would do), but pagan mythology and literature does not seem to have been much more generous in its treatment of Pandora, Circe, Medea and the Sirens. Classical myth and literature, at least in the fraction of it bequeathed to later eras, does have other archetypes whose fatality is generally considered less culpable, most notably Helen of Troy, but its principal difference from the Christian tradition is that it displays a rich gallery of hapless victims of divine lust whose attractive beauty is only fatal to themselves: Persephone, Syrinx, Europa, Psyche and so on. Perhaps they should be excluded from the imaginative category of *femmes fatales*, but their own category is not entirely distinct, and—as is usual in matters of literary examination and reexamination—it is often in gray areas, where definitions dissolve or overlap, that original and intriguing specimens are to be found. In order to conserve variety in the present sampler, I have deliberately been a trifle lax in the matter of pedantic qualification.

The writers of the French Romantic Movement of the nineteenth century inevitably became obsessed with the idea of the *femme fatale*, and, in the spirit of reappraisal and extrapolation that their Movement demanded, which provided its impetus, its prophets and prose writers rapidly subjected the notion to a searching analysis and revaluation. As the Romantic Movement seemed to its observers to become Decadent, or to be refined in such derivatives as the Symbolist Movement, its *femmes fatales* were derived and refined too, and the examples included in this sampler illustrate that complex and multifaceted process of decadence and refinement, although they can only provide a collage of snapshots extracted from a much vaster panorama.

In developing and following that historical process, the writers of the Romantic Movement and its successors were aware, at least marginally, that some such process of reevaluation and refinement had begun in France more than a century before, when the substance of Medieval Romance had been deliberately reprocessed, with new agenda, by the feminist writers of the Parisian salons of the 1690s who had formulated *contes de fées*. What they probably did not realize, however, was the manner in which that genre had been suppressed and almost wiped out almost as soon as it had attained publication, by the refusal of the royal privileges required for the licit publication and sale of books. Sufficient time had elapsed, and that initial suppression had been so successful in the short term, that the awareness had been lost that the fugitive survival of *contes de fées* in the eighteenth century had been almost entirely due to illicit and initially-surreptitious publications, such as the one in which the sample included in the present collection first appeared.

The one author involved in the brief fad of the 1690s of whom the masters of the French Church did not disapprove, and who was therefore allowed to thrive while his contemporaries saw their works effectively strangled at birth, was Charles Perrault, a third-rate trader in stolen goods, who was falsely hailed as the pioneer of a genre on which his works were actually parasitic, but who was allowed to bequeath a new set of archetypal female figures to modern folklore, who were anything but *fatale*. Cinderella, the Sleeping Beauty and Little Red Riding Hood were all vaguely in tune with the prevailing misogyny of the era and the propaganda of meek chastity that the Church was intent to promoting, and were thus tolerated, while other images were quietly buried, only partially exhumed at a later date, and with difficulty.[1]

Because of that successful suppression, the influence of the genre of *contes de fées* on the writers of the Romantic Movement was both muted and perverted, but there is nevertheless a fragile continuity between that work and the kinds of fantastic fiction developed in the context of Romanticism. Although the French writers of the nineteenth century made a fresh start, they did not do so with a clean slate, and if their pens qualified, metaphorically speaking, as new brooms,

---

1 History still informs us stubbornly that Madame d'Aulnoy's works, which eventually came to be seen as archetypal of the genre of *contes de fées*, were first published in the 1690s. That is a lie; in fact, they were suppressed then; Madame d'Aulnoy was hounded out of Paris and did not live to see her *contes de fées* in print; the collections she prepared for publication then were only issued, belatedly and illicitly, after her death, and only became well-known after a further half-century.

they were mounted on the same sticks that the enchantresses of old had been slanderously accused of riding to Sabbats of diabolical debauchery. The Church that suppressed *contes de fées* had long been accustomed to stigmatizing enchantresses as witches tacitly or explicitly in league with the Devil, and the writers of the nineteenth century inherited that preconception, even if only to dissent from it; the conceptual categories of "witch" and *femme fatale* were confused by then in a complex fashion, and that confusion lies at the heart of much modern fiction dealing with the *femme fatale*.

A similar confusion—or an extension of the same one—links *femme fatales* with vampiric spirits of a kind to be found in many mythological traditions, including the lamias of Greek mythology, and such spirits acquired a particular importance in Romantic fantasy, often conflated or confused with *femmes fatales*, as in Théophile Gautier's "La Morte amoureuse," perhaps *the* classic Romantic *femme fatale* story, translated herein as "The Amorous Revenant," although Lafcadio Hearn's nineteenth-century translation is entitled "Clarimonde." Gautier's friend Alphone Karr, by contrast, employed a different version of the same idea in his account of "Les Willis," and the rich Romantic literature of Sirens reflects a wide range of moral positions, as illustrated in *The Snuggly Sirenicon*, none of whose inclusions are duplicated here, although some would have been prime candidates for inclusion if the companion volume did not exist.

It is not only in fantastic fiction, however, that the *femme fatale* thrived in nineteenth century French fiction; she made rapid strides in naturalistic fiction too, especially in a lush variety of historical fiction for which Théophile Gautier also provided an important archetype in "Une Nuit de Cléopâtre" (1838; tr. as "One of Cleopâtre's Nights). The classics of the antiquarian subgenre are novels, including Anatole France's *Thaïs* (1890) and Pierre Louÿs' *Aphrodite* (1896), because elaborate historical reconstruction does not lend itself readily to the short story formats, but naturalistic contemporary *femmes fatales* sometimes do, as in Charles Barbara's deliberately normalizing "Vieille histoire," and Gaston Danville's "Lisbeth," although the latter persists in resisting thoroughgoing mundanity. Classical variants can sometimes be normalized in an economical fashion, as in André Lebey's "Ennoia," which brings a legend featuring the inamorata of the magician Simon Magus, briefly featured in the *Acts of the Apostles*, down to earth.

Although naturalization of the *femme fatale* is certainly possible, however, and even attractive as a literary theme—especially to self-declared Naturalist writers—the impression made by such narratives is often disappointing, like most "debunking" narratives. The emotional engine of the notion and the mythology of the *femme fatale* is the fact that hormonally-generated lust, not being suspect of rational control, can easily give the impression of a supernatural force invading the psyche from outside, independently of and sometime in frank defiance of the conscious will. It is arguable, therefore, that the most sincere and most effective representations of that phenomenon in literature are the fantasies, the more extreme the better. In narratives in which there are tacit or explicit contests between real and supernatural women, the supernatural ones always have the odds stacked in their favor, even in cases where they suffer from an inconvenient lack of materiality, like the revenant in Catulle Mendès' "La Nuit de noces," and when such specters have no manifest competition, as if Maurice Renard's "Le Rendez-vous," their fatality is practically guaranteed, even in the absence of any malevolence.

Because the writers of the nineteenth century looked at the motif of the *femme fatale* from all possible angles, there is no single conclusion to be drawn from the collage assembled herein—fortunately, given that not all conundrums have solutions, and there are some that would surely be tragically diminished if they did. The item of popular "wisdom" that asserts that there are things that "men are not meant to know" is probably false, but it might well be more sustainable that there are some things that people are better off not understanding, at least without great effort and much meditation, and perhaps not even then.

After all, who, of either sex, really wants to believe that the fatality of *femmes* is merely a matter of humdrum hormones?

—Brian Stableford

SNUGGLY TALES
OF
FEMMES
FATALES

THE FAY LUBANTINE

by Catherine Durand

THERE was once a fay in Asia whose power had no limits; the likes of Circe and Armide did not come up to her waist. She loved her husband infinitely; destiny, which has always gone its own way, took him away from her in her early youth; nothing remained of him but a daughter so beautiful and so charming that her graces were infinite even in the cradle.

The young princess was seen from a very tender age to have an inclination for pleasure that astonished all those who approached her; no tears ever emerged from her eyes; her little mouth did not open to cries, its only usage being a gracious smile that inspired joy; games were invented for her; her little arms opened to embrace and thank the women who contributed to her amusement; violins, oboes, dances and spectacles made her delights; she showed a marked distaste for symphonies whose tones were melancholy, and anyone in the court who was sad did not appear before her with impunity; a delicate but piquant mockery made them sense the antipathy she had for them. Her mother, the fay, who had never seen anything like it, although she had seen everything, gave her a name that suited her character; she called her Lubantine, and that is how the ancients made their goddess Lubantine, known in their theology as the goddess of joy and liberty.

In fact, young Lubantine could not abide anything that constrained her; when her mother tried to moderate that violent love of liberty slightly, she sulked as prettily as anything in the world, but soon resumed a serene face, employing supplicant badinage to beg the fay not to exclude her from the only wealth one has in this life.

When she was fourteen years old and her person was formed, her mother consulted her books regarding the destiny of such an extraordinary young woman. She found that she would always live happily and amid pleasures, if she could avoid seeing a foreigner. That fatality appeared easy enough to deflect; we shall soon see what order her powerful mother brought to it.

Lubantine's stature was mediocre and slender; her arms were placed by the Graces, her feet were small and well-turned; her hair was a bright brown, her eyes had a dazzlingly brilliant finesse; her nose was small and made for the rest of her features, her face was round, her full, delicate and vivid cheeks each had a little dimple formed by the very hand of Amour; there was also one in her chin; her mouth was one of those that it has never been possible to depict, small, fashioned, red, laughing, ornamented by two rows of perfect teeth; her breasts were full, white and youthful.

She had intelligence; her imagination was sparkling, if one can speak thus, and one sensed a secret charm in her conversation, but she was libertine; she gave in to all her desires. Lubantine's mother, however, no sooner saw that she was at an age to be established than she proposed a very advantageous marriage to her. As you can imagine, that was not calculated to please her; she manifested such a strong opposition to it that her mother, who thought her the prettiest person in the world—as, in fact, she was—and who only thought of making her happy, established her with cheerful young people made to please her in a palace that has never had an equal. It was built of precious stones; the doors were never closed; there were magnificent baths, aviaries filled with birds, halls for spectacles; a regulated Opera whose inimitable actors never caught a cold; actors who never grew old; players of all sorts of instruments; gaming tables where the women became more beautiful and the men more gracious.

The general order of that court was to surprise Lubantine every day, and not to have any sad thought; malady and mortality were banished from that beautiful abode, amour made its pleasure felt, absolutely separated from its pain—for no one there believed that its pains were pleasures.

Four different gardens were seen from the four facades of the palace. In one of them there were swings of a particular form; Lubantine often availed herself of that amusement, and for the rest of the day her retinue performed plays. There were stakes planted with rings attached, and those who used the swings were obliged to carry away the rings; when they did not succeed, a penalty was ordered, which went no further than making up a garland of flowers for Lubantine or composing a madrigal in her honor. When hazard caused it to fall, one could laugh in safety, for then the previously beaten and solid terrain softened and became a padded mattress.

In the second garden there were acrobats, rope-dancers and jumpers, all so sure of their skill that no one was afflicted by the anxious attention caused by the fear of seeing them fall, even though they performed surprising feats.

The third garden was occupied by female bathers who worked in shifts incessantly. One pool of Cordovan water had, as well as the odor, the faculty of rendering skin whiter. Lubantine had a separate one in the palace, but she often went to amuse herself by pestering the bathers; teasingly, she tugged their bathing costumes, which were woven from nettle-cloth garnished with Malines lace; those women played countless different instruments on the edges of the pools; neat and elegant beds extended under magnificent tents served them for repose after that pleasant exercise. Men were excluded from the enclosure of that garden, but the walls were so low and people knew so little restraint in the place that they often violated the refuge with their gaze.

The fourth area was a park rather than a garden; it was filled with beautiful, clean and gentle wild beasts, which allowed themselves to be hunted by Lubantine and her court, and which enjoyed themselves afterwards with the same dogs that ran after them without doing them any harm; the hunting equipages were superb, and Lubantine's livery crimson and gold.

At the center of the palace there was a large court-yard surrounded by four facades. It was there that the ladies watched tourneys, jousts, ring-races and carousels, which the young princes admitted to Lubantine's court often put on in order to amuse her. Their skill was astonishing, and they received prizes from the hand of their sovereign when they merited them. She always had some new petty intrigue, but her heart was only engaged to the exact extent required to amuse her.

The three gardens I mentioned were, in any case, so beautiful, and everything that could render them delightful was so unsparing, that they were a spectacle themselves; as for the park designed for hunting, there were woods, streams, plains and a hill that was often preferred by arrangement to other places. Lubantine did not have to take the trouble to express a wish; her desires were always anticipated; but as she had a exquisite taste in everything, she treasured delicate cheer; never has there been anything to compare with what she was served at every meal; the white wines were chosen carefully, and I have even heard it said that champagne was often served, even though no mention of it in that century is known.

When the fay put her daughter in that place she made her this speech, or very nearly: "My age and my cares, my dear Lubantine, no longer permit me to savor the pleasures that suit you. I don't envy you them; on the contrary, I'm lavishing them upon you. Live happily, since I don't anticipate that your destiny can change, I'm going to retire to my manor in the woods; come to visit me there occasionally. Remember me and be a fay like your mother, since I've been able to allow you to participate in my art."

The savant fay refrained from prescribing to Lubatine never to receive any foreigner and not to leave the enclosure of her palace—that would have given birth to the desire to do so—but she extended that enclosure prodigiously. It did not have any appearance of a prison; one would have searched in vain elsewhere for what was found in that delightful abode, but there were stakes planted on all the roads that ended there on which the following inscription could be read:

> Refrain from having the desire
> To see the lovely Lubantine;
> Death would follow closely the dangerous pleasure
> Of contemplating her divine person.

Travelers, frightened by that warning, turned away from such a terrible path immediately, and Lubantine remained in the midst of delights for six years without ever experiencing any dolor or chagrin.

She sometimes went to see her mother. One day she found her bathed in tears; the young fay's first impulse was to flee an apparition so contrary to her humor; she had already taken a few backward steps when the afflicted mother said to her: "Come closer, Lubantine; your fate causes me compassion; you will soon be delivered to great misfortunes. I don't know yet what form they will take; it only depends on you to avoid them; it's necessary to deprive you of some pleasure; I can see that the fatal point is there, but as I can't disentangle which one will be deadly to you, deprive yourself of all those you take for a while; you'll discover more taste for them afterwards."

"Me, Madame," said Lubantine, "deprive myself of joy and liberty? I might as well be deprived of daylight. You're naturally sad," she added, "the situation of your humor might have made you dread imaginary perils, and I should deprive myself of real and imaginary possessions for that? No, no, rather . . ."

"Well, my daughter," said the sage fay, "the future is developing a little to my eyes; I can see that a hunt is going to cause you horrible misfortunes; don't go hunting for three months."

"Oh, Madame," said Lubantine, "you know that it's to liberty in particular that I attach my happiness. I might well have no desire to go hunting for ten years in succession, but the necessity of depriving myself of it would inconvenience me. I'll quit you, Madame," she added, "for fear of participating momentarily in the melancholy that I see in your eyes."

In fact, the free Lubantine went to leap into a carriage harnessed to six lions, which were meeker than lambs, and raced to the Palace of Pleasures.

She was embarrassed by a dream all that night. Until then the god of sleep, respectful of her repose, had only presented agreeable images to her, but this time she thought she saw an unknown individual whose appearance pleased her greatly; he had a little dart in his hand with which he teased her; she acquired a taste for that teasing; the dart had already inflicted a wound in the middle of her heart; she sensed her pleasures redoubling, but soon afterwards a beautiful woman whose features she did not know plunged it in so cruelly that she thought that she was falling, bathed in her own blood, and all that she could do was to kill the people who had just taken away her life.

She uttered a cry that woke her up and attracted her women; the agitation of the dream did not permit her to pull herself together until she had been awake for some time; then she started to laugh at her fear, and got up as quickly as possible, in order to dissipate that baleful imagination.

The pleasure she chose for that day was hunting; she even released the deer herself, which hurtled out of the park where the hunt usually concluded. It was the first time that had happened, for her journeys to see her mother were made by air; but destiny was conducting her, with the aid of her love of liberty.

Lubantine found herself somewhat fatigued; she suspended the hunt and dismounted from her horse. She sat down in a forest at the foot of a large tree that she chose.

"Go away," she said to the hunters. "I need repose; let me sleep."

Immediately, a bed of moss and flowers rose up beneath her; cushions of magnificent fabric were placed under her head, and an elegant awning was attached to the branches of the tree.

She had not yet savored the charms of slumber when she heard a man who was saying in a very agreeable tone of voice: "Is it possible that you can repent of having made me happy? Yes, divine Melisene, I am happy, since you have been good enough to confide yourself to my faith and have quit your father's kingdom to follow me. What my happiness lacks is essential enough, but I await your kindness with a respect with which you ought to be content. Don't be afflicted, then, and don't tarnish what you have done for me by an appearance of repentance."

"No," said a woman to whom the speech was addressed, "that isn't the subject of my tears. The fatal time is approaching when you are to endure proofs that frighten me. I only know you; will my feeble charms hold out against those of a . . ."

"Oh," interrupted the man who had spoken first, "don't alarm yourself ahead of time; the obscurity that encloses predictions might be hiding an agreeable verity from you, and whatever might happen, I shall belong as long as I live to my dear Melisene."

Lubantine thought that the man's promises were reckless, and that the woman to whom they were addressed was very imprudent to have followed a lover into such a solitary place: a severity that an unfamiliar impulse caused her.

Have these lovers come to spread the poison of amour in this locale? she wondered. *We only know its pleasures,* she added, *let them leave the places of my dependence.*

With those words she got up and soon found what she was seeking. A young blonde woman, pale and possessed of a perfect beauty, clad in an elegant but negligent costume, was sitting on the grass; a man was at her feet in a tender and respectful attitude. He was tall and handsome, with large dark eyes.

"Who are you," said Lubantine, "who come on to my land to talk about amour?"

The voice of the fay, her charms and her magnificence, attracted the gaze and the veneration of the lovers. They stood up diligently, and the man spoke. "We are, Madame, an unfortunate brother and sister seeking a refuge against the fury of a cruel and implacable family."

"A brother and a sister!" said the fay. "Who, then, said the passionate things that I have just heard you saying to one another?"

The young woman blushed; her lover threw himself at Lubantine's feet.

"It's necessary to admit to you, Madame," he said, "that I love the beautiful Melisene, whom you see here, passionately. Cruel relatives have forbidden us to see one another; a mutual love had made us seek means of never being apart, and we beg you, Madame," he added, "to suffer us in this place, where you apparently command."

The good looks and noble appearance of the man did not permit the fay to refuse his plea. I know not what impulse even gave her response a tender softness different from the joy that normally shone in her eyes. The beautiful young woman had no part in that mild welcome; on the contrary, she looked at her disdainfully. Then, turning back to the agreeable stranger, she said to him: "After having granted you what you request, don't refuse me your name. As for your birth, it would be difficult to hide it; the appearance you have is not encountered in ordinary people, and the title of king struck my ears when you were talking to this person." She pointed at Melisene.

"My name is Ciridor, Madame," he replied, "and my father is King Absolute, a name that has been imposed on him because he never yields to anyone, and everyone has always done his will. The princess you see is the daughter of the King of the Gentle Isle, and her mildness does not belie her origin."

"That's sufficient," Lubantine interrupted. "You can tell me the rest of your adventures at your leisure; not only will I receive you in my lands, but I'll take you to my palace; we'll seek there the means of rendering you happy, and prescribe for Princess Melisene a life a little less vagabond than she is leading at present."

With those words she sounded a small enameled gold hunting horn garnished with diamonds that she wore at her side, and the whole of her brilliant court soon gathered around her. Prince Ciridor's squire and Princess Melisene's governess came to mingle with that elegant troop. Ciridor aided Lubantine and his princess to mount their horses, and mounted his own with such grace that he attracted the attention of all the spectators. The deer that had rested in company with the pack gave a further hour of pleasure to the hunt, after which everyone returned to the palace.

The magnificence and the pleasures that were savored there gave Ciridor a sort of agreeable distraction, which cost the tender Melisene sighs. Lubantine allotted her an apartment whose views only overlooked the hunting park. She conducted her there personally and told her as she quit her that she would send ambassadors to her father's court to inform him that she had her in her power and was taking her under her protection; and that while awaiting his response she was obliged to keep her in a kind of solitude more appropriate to the estate of her destiny. With those words she embraced her and left her with her governess, in a kind of dolor that had something so piquant that tears soon covered her beautiful cheeks.

"Has anything ever been seen comparable to my misfortune, my dear Celinte?" she cried, as soon as she was alone with her. "What a bizarrerie of my star! You know everything that I have done for Ciridor; the virtue of which I make a profession ought to give him an eternal gratitude for the excess of my tenderness, and yet I see in him the deadly penchant of which a cruel prediction had warned me."

Celinte interrupted the dolorous reflections of the princess, and asked her what one could dread of a lover like Ciridor.

"What can I dread?" said Melisene. "Lubantine is charming; Lubantine is a fay; her power, her beauty, the pleasures that follow her everywhere and the fickleness of men all give me a mortal apprehension. And have I not seen Ciridor looking at her, admiring her and forgetting me momentarily?" she added, redoubling her sighs.

Celinte employed all her eloquence in consoling the princess, and promised to report to her faithfully what she knew, but the means were forbidden to her; she was not permitted to leave the apartment, where they were given in abundance, however, everything that might satisfy the senses.

Meanwhile, the prince, who was young, gallant and who loved pleasures, had an admiration for Lubantine that could already be called a liking; he spent the first days in a transport that made him forget Melisene. The fay had an inexplicable charm in all her actions; her fêtes were very extensive; the sighs that a commencement of amour was causing her to utter had a grace from which it was not possible for him to defend himself, and, as her sighs only marked the passion that gave birth to them, without having the sadness appropriate to them, her lovely smile followed close behind them.

Ciridor, heaped with joy by the effect of his merit, was more handsome and wittier than usual; Lubantine and he gave themselves gradually to amour and joy. The spectacles multiplied, the Palace of Pleasures finished new ones continually.

Lubantine went out on her own one day in order to stroll in the hunting park; her heart was already sensing the more impetuous movements of amour, but until then everything had passed in gazes. She plunged into the wood in order to dream at her ease. Ciridor, driven by the same desire, encountered her in that remote location.

"How I have wanted this moment," he said to the fay, "and how I have dreaded that it might not be favorable to me! You only like pleasures," he added, "I am not their enemy, but I am so jealous of them and I am audacious enough to wish that you only loved me."

That declaration was rather bold, but Lubantine was naturally too distant from the furious impulses of anger to invoke them on this occasion, and the tenderness that she felt added its effect to her temperament.

"Thus far, Prince," she replied, "you have no reason to complain of my rigors. I have not hidden the penchant I feel for you; I find pleasure in seeing you, I have an infinite one in hearing you. Let us love one another with ardor," she added, "since we are summoned to it. Is it not necessary to seize the opportunities that are presented to savor new felicities?"

That morality pleased Ciridor infinitely. He added further impetus to it in his fashion. They had a very long and very agreeable conversation. Lubantine agreed on emerging from the wood that only Ciridor could bring her pleasures to a culmination, and they plunged into sensual pleasures.

The fay's example gave birth to the countless new amours in her court; everyone was in love; everyone abandoned themselves to its delights, while the unhappy Melisene was dying of dolor and jealousy. She had seen her lover and her rival from her window emerging from the hunting park; their appearance was so contented and so amorous that she had no reason to doubt her misfortune. She abandoned herself to everything that a delicate soul is capable of suffering.

One day, losing the little patience that remained to her, she tried to force her way past her guards in order to go and reckon with the fay for her detention and her lover for his infidelity. Her emergence was opposed, but that action caused rumor; Ciridor was informed of it; a slight return to the past caused him to lament the situation of the princess. He tried to say something in her favor, but Lubantine, who did not want to be troubled by anything, replied that she would release her from her prison and that she even wanted to render her witness to their amusements.

"I have no fear," she added, "that she would dare to dispute anything with me, nor that you might return to her."

In fact, the fay went to fetch Melisene, in a gracious and mild manner. "Come, Princess," she said to her. "It is time that you had your part in our fêtes."

The sad Melisene left with her. But what a change! She no longer had the perfect beauty that might have been able to generate amour in the most insensible; her figure and the sound of her voice remained to her, but her face became so frightful, her features so irregular and her sort of ugliness so bizarre, that when Lubantine presented her to Ciridor he took several steps back, and even let an exclamation of disgust escape. The princess turned toward a large mirror, in which she saw herself as beautiful as usual, and became more indignant against her infidel lover; for the fay, in taking away her beauty and making her ugly for everyone else, had left her the slight satisfaction of appearing beautiful in her own eyes, and that was the origin of a self-esteem unknown before.

Celinte saw with astonishment the prodigious ugliness of the princess and forgave the prince his inconstancy. "Let us flee, Princess," she said to her. "Let us flee a court whose voluptuous mores cannot fail to corrupt; no one will try to stop us."

"Why flee?" replied Melisene, sadly. "Could I resolve myself to do it? Ciridor is fickle, but his fickleness will bring him back to me."

Then Celinte could not hide from her the degree to which she had become horrible; she was not sparing in the portrait she made of her. The princess, who still found herself beautiful, nearly became angry with her confidante, and flattered herself that her displeasures had only brought a slight change to her charms.

On the other hand, Ciridor, whose ingratitude was confirmed by Melisene's appearance, told Lubantine, laughing, that she had taken a strange path to make sure of his heart, and that even if she had changed nothing in the person of the princess, he would not have broken his new chains.

"I assure you," she said, "that that vengeance is not excessive; it is always necessary to take precautions against reversions. And then," she added, "what harm have I done her? She still believes herself to be beautiful; her imagination will always be satisfied."

"Good, Madame," said Ciridor. "Not content with having rendered her ugly, you also want to render her ridiculous, and the security she has regarding her attractions will make her play the part of a pretty woman."

They had the inhumanity to mock her for a long time because of a misfortune that she only had because of them, and when they wanted to enjoy their malevolence they made her appear, pompously adorned, to see the spectacles that were prepared for them.

The prince, intoxicated by amour, decided that he wanted to render an effective worship to the fay. "You are too charming," he told her, "only to merit adoration by virtue of your face. It's necessary to set up an altar to you, to burn incense to you, to immolate victims to you."

"Oh, as for bloody victims," Lubantine interjected, "I don't want any. People can offer them to me, but I shall give them liberty with my own hands."

That same day, an altar was constructed in a great hall of crystal; two thousand candles burned there incessantly before the figure of the fay, which was a single pearl with draperies of brilliant rose-colored diamonds. Behind the transparent walls of the hall, large hollow figures had been disposed, painted in perfection, which represented the peoples of all the continents of the world, adoring the beautiful Lubantine. Inextinguishable candles always made those bodies appear luminous. Each of them held an offering, which related to the character of the fay. There were pocket mirrors, diamonds, snuff-boxes, boxes of beauty-spots, ribbons and all the rest of the elegant equipment of ladies.

The interior of the hall, which had become a temple, was full of players of instruments and singers; sarabands and chaconnes were danced there in favor of tenderness or libertinage, and a perpetual commerce of love letters, gazes and pretty amorous larcenies was seen; a continual distribution was made of the most exquisite dishes and the most delectable liqueurs; the ice creams and chocolate there surpassed ambrosia, and if no one acquired immortality, at least the women there were always young and beautiful, and the men always well made and elegant.

A sofa with a golden back enriched with rubies was beside the altar, destined for the pretended goddess, when she wanted to receive her incense in person; a cushion of the same kind was below the sofa for the amorous Ciridor. The superb awning that covered the area descended in a curtain when it pleased Lubantine to disappear from the eyes of her subjects. Perfumes were lavished there. In sum, everything that luxury and adulation could invent was put to use in favor of the fay.

She had the cruelty of wanting the unfortunate Melisene to witness the consecration of the temple; she nearly died of dolor there. Her rival was as beautiful as Venus. Ciridor picked up a censer himself in order to be the first to adore her, and as he had the most beautiful voice in the world, he began this hymn, to which the chorus responded:

Alone you know the fine sensual pleasure,
Before you there were only feeble images,
Sweet joy with liberty
Are your gifts, receive our homages.
Queen of hearts, games and pleasures,
Who can drive away the ridiculous censors
And, braving remorse and scruples
Accord everything to your desires;
Goddess Lubantine, may our incense always
Rise above your altars;
Can we envy the fate of the immortals
When we contemplate your divine grace?

Alone you know the fine sensual pleasure,
Before you there were only feeble images,
Sweet joy with liberty
Are your gifts, receive our homages . . .

The hymn went on for a long time, but it is so pleasant to be praised, Ciridor's voice was so harmonious and the choir so marvelous, that Lubantine sensed what expression cannot represent; there was even something tragic in the ceremony, which did not spoil its savor at all.

The princess could not bear the bitterness of her affliction; she fainted in Celinte's arms. Ciridor turned his head in her direction, allowed himself to be carried away without admitting pain into his life and ran to throw himself at Lubantine's feet.

"Let everything perish, my goddess," he said, kissing one of her hands, which she held out to him, "provided that I adore you all my life."

That transport caused others in the fay.

When the ceremony had finished everyone went to occupy themselves with the customary pleasures. No one enquired about Melisene. She was suffering woes that would have given rise to pity in cruelty itself, but the fay only felt precisely what was necessary to make her suffer more—which is to say, that her life should be preserved and that she should be prevented from harming herself.

Several days passed in the worship of the new goddess. Amid that vaunted sensual pleasure the princess recovered in spite of herself, and, impelled by an unknown emotion, she ran once again to the fatal temple where all the objects renewed her dolor.

The high priest Ciridor was brilliant with gems and even more brilliant by virtue of his beauty; the fay was contemplating him with eyes in which amour was painted. Even the princess had more passion for him than when he was faithful; those sentiments furnished her with courage. Her voice was heard in the middle of the ceremony, which rose up to pronounce these words:

> *Charming Queen of Cythera,*
> *Whose wrath Psyche once ignited,*
> *Beautiful Venus, will you suffer*
> *The offense that a prince dares to make you in this*
>   *place?*
> *It is little that he violates his oath,*
> *That crime only injures me,*
> *But that ingrate, that reckless fool*
> *Profanes his incense for another than you;*
> *Render him forever the usage of his senses,*
> *Charming Queen of Cythera.*

When Melisene commenced that prayer to Venus everyone attempted to interrupt her, but no one was able to succeed in that; tongues were tied. Ciridor, the infidel Ciridor, opened his mouth in vain in order to impose silence; he could not articulate anything. Lubantine felt the same prodigy in herself, and that silence, which had a mysterious cause, was only broken after the princess had been seen to resume her original beauty.

Then the fay uttered a dolorous scream, and the assembly murmured a few words in praise of Melisene. As if recovering from an enchantment, Ciridor quit the worship of the false goddess and returned submissively to the feet of his first mistress.

Venus was recognized in those changes.

The temple was not destroyed; the statue of Lubantine remained standing; but the veritable Lubantine appeared ugly, with the same ugliness that she had previously given her rival, without the same consolation remaining to her. She found herself so frightful that, her love of pleasure changing into fury, and the goddess not having taken away her power of faerie, she no longer thought about anything but avenging herself on the innocent causes of her misfortune.

She had the princess imprisoned again, with terrible menaces. Ciridor, who wanted to repair his faults, opposed that with all his courage, but what could he do, alone against an absolute and sovereign fay?

Venus, the jealous Venus, had avenged her outrage; that alone was interesting for her; what did the success of the amours of Ciridor and Melisense matter to her? Lubantine went every day into a horrible prison where she had locked her up; there, with an unparalleled inhumanity, she disfigured her beautiful face with a diamond that she wore expressly; then she labored on her incomparable breasts, and did not quit that mortal exercise until the force of dolors had caused her death.

Celinte implored her at least to send her body back to the sovereign of the Gentle Isle; the fay granted her that.

The poor king had no sooner seen that sad spectacle than he died of affliction; before his death he ordered that a magnificent sepulcher be built for his daughter, for him and for Ciridor.

The fay attempted in vain to make Ciridor return to her; her ugliness and the repentance he felt excluded her from his heart. She applied herself to making him take a dose of poison every day, which weakened him gradually and often caused him furious pains; they only finished with his life, and the prediction of which Melisene had made mention was verified. No one has ever known the wording of it, but in essence, the prince was menaced with being unable to resist terrible ordeals, and then being exposed to a tragic end.

After that, Lubantine was tormented by remorse; she discovered too late that excessive sensual pleasure leads into profound abysms, and that, if one cannot have perfect happiness without amour, amour that is not regulated by virtue causes all the woes of life.

However, as the commencement of Lubantine's life presented a cheerful image, and the pagans sacrificed to much stranger divinities than Liberty and Joy, they erected temples to them under the name of the goddess Lubantine. But as no one was ever able to prescribe just limits to those two things, people only had imperfect ideas of them and always went beyond or fell short of joy and liberty.

THE SEMINARIST

by S. Henry Berthoud

There is no place that I would not like better with you, my sweet Henri, than the most beautiful palace in the world. Yes, my friend, it seems to me that I would prefer an eternity of dolor with you to Paradise without you. That is because, for me, you are more than repose, than happiness, than all the world. It is because I love you more than I can say, that I love you as you can love.

(Lettres d'amour.)

Is it not true that we shall no longer
be apart?
"Is the tomb not there?"
(Maurice Pteuginter, Contes allemands.)[1]

I want to make a bet of four gold pieces with you.
   I want to bet that none of you, good people of Paris, knows clearly and exactly what a collector of direct contributions does in a commune of two thou-

---

1 Fake, unsurprisingly.

sand souls under the ministries of Messieurs Villèle and Polignac.

Form a circle around me, then, and lend me your ears. I'll tell you simply and in my own fashion.

A rural tax-collector is a man to whom one gives fifty francs a year.

In order to obtain that large sum, he is enjoined to do various things, among which is collecting thirty or forty thousand francs in three hamlets, in which the richest of households never has two silver coins to rub together. If, on the appointed day, the said collector has not assembled the required sum in good coin, too bad for him; it is necessary that he put his hand in his pocket.

It is marvelous, also, to see a collector depart from his residence at daybreak, coiffed in a broad-brimmed hat if the weather is sunny, or wrapped up in a cloak if there is rain, wind, hail or snow.

As soon as he arrives in a village, woe betide the tax-payers—as he calls them—who are not "in measure," that being the official term. First he issues them with a summons without expenses, and then a summons with expenses, and then he threatens a collective garnishing.

It does them no good to protest: "I have nothing; I'm in the grip of poverty." The garnisher does not take long to come to their home, a brutal, devouring biped animal, drunk without ever losing his reason. The law, as you see, is delicate and good, squandering the meager possessions of its debtor recklessly, in order to assist him to pay.

Now, the man about whom I am speaking was a collector of contributions in a commune of three thousand souls. No one administered as well, or as honestly; never—and I mean never—was he ever found in remiss of a centime when the day came to transmit the funds to the receiver.

So, when evening came, he remained quietly at home, only daring to go out secretly, and equipped with loaded pistols. That did not always prevent him, nevertheless, from hearing whistles or feeling some large stone thrown by some unknown hand falling on his back.

Every Sunday, moreover, he was punctual in going reverently to hear mass, always at the moment when the sub-prefect came to say his prayers. A miscreant would have felt edified to see the worthy Christian on his knees, turning the pages of a Book of Hours and reciting litanies and psalms while moving his lips—not to mention the good *mea culpas* with which he struck his breast, and the white eyes that he turned to the heavens when the elevation bell rang.

One day, one of the sub-prefect's domestics brought the tax-collector a letter, and the collector omitted to gratify him with a tip. He had, however, traveled two leagues; it was election time, and in order to obtain goodwill, no one, as you know, neglects either the messages or the good care of tax-collectors.

Three days later, the same motive brought the said domestic back to the said tax-collector's abode. While awaiting a response, he went into the kitchen, where the lady of the house, good housekeeper as she was, was preparing a pullet of appetizing appearance.

At the sudden and unwelcome appearance of the administrative domestic, the pullet was immediately hidden, for it was Friday. But a glance had been sufficient for that benign individual; and even though the lady, when he left, doubled the usual tip, the sub-prefect nevertheless showed the poor tax-collector the most severe expression the following day.

The honest father of four did not get a wink of sleep that night.

The following day he went to confession and took communion solemnly; and as there was a procession he followed it bare-headed, singing high and clear, neither more nor less than a cantor, and responded more loudly that any other of the faithful *ora pro nobis* or *libera nos, Domine*.

Apparently, the work of piety, like the wood of Sganarelle, is salted by all the devils. For he, so orderly and of such edifying mores, spent the rest of the day in the café, drinking alone and in small sips a bottle of Burgundy wine.

Someone, by chance, uttered the celebrated word "consequent," then much in fashion.

The tax-collector—the Burgundy wine must have troubled his reason; God alone knows how he could have thought of such a thing—told the man that he was talking through his hat.

Alas, he realized instantly the immense error that he had just made. In order to recover his composure he picked up a newspaper, mechanically. Mercy! It was the *Courrier Français*.

He dropped it as if it were a fragment of red hot iron.

But it was too late. An honest Jesuit, who had long had his eye on the tax-collector's position for his own nephew, had seen everything. And without losing a moment he ran to ring the doorbell of the sub-prefect, whose house was opposite the café. He only came out again an hour later, so long had his report been, and listened to at leisure, and he went straight to vespers. You can imagine how ill the jubilation of that honest man made the tax-collector feel.

His destitution was infallible.

With death in his heart he slowly resumed the route to his village, and had no sooner arrived there than it was necessary for him to go to bed, for he was shivering with fever. His family, rendered anxious by the distress in his features, asked about the reasons that had produced it, but he attributed it to a sudden illness.

Alas, he thought, *the unfortunates will learn only too soon about the blow that will cast them into poverty.*

That day, I had been hunting since daybreak, and, more fatigued than I can say, I was doing my best to return to my village, from which two long leagues still separated me, when the village in which Monsieur Lefebre resides—that being the name of the tax-collector about whom I am talking—appeared to me, with its gray steeple, in the middle of a little wood.

Without intending to, I stopped walking, and my fatigue seemed greater than ever.

Then, I started thinking about a benevolent and jovial welcome, a large armchair next to a crackling fire, an abundant supper and a soft warm bed.

Madame de Staël has said that "the best means of getting rid of a temptation is to succumb to it." I followed Madame de Staël's advice, and I took the small side-path that began at my feet and which led to Monsieur Lefebre's house.

Having arrived at his door, I knocked on it with the butt of my rifle and shouted joyfully: "Hey! I've come to ask you for shelter." The door opened; Madame Lefebre gave me a good welcome, but, in spite of that, it as easy for me to see at the first glance that my arrival was an inconvenience.

I would have given anything in the world to get out of that false position and to be able to retrace my steps, but it was too late.

The good Madame Lebevre read in my face what I was thinking, for she hastened to explain the cause of her embarrassment.

"My husband fell ill on returning from the village," she said. "I fear that he has learned something troubling, for I believe that the malady is more anxiety than fever."

I asked to see him; I was taken to the bedroom where he was lying, and we were left alone. At the sight of me the poor fellow held out his hand, gripped mine convulsively and started to weep.

Then he told me what had happened to him and the fears that he had.

"Oh, my dear Monsieur," he added, as he concluded, "how frightful it is to have no other means of subsistence, for oneself and one's family, than a wretched position for which it is necessary to dread the loss incessantly, for which it is necessary to make the sacrifice of one's beliefs, opinions and honor every day. Better than anyone else, you know what I have done. Wretch! I have gone so far as to let my son, my poor Étienne, become a priest, drawn by an irreflective devotion and subjugated by insidious advice. Alas, how many chagrins that career is preparing for his weakness of character, his inconstant enthusiasms and his Romantic sensibility! I would have liked to oppose my paternal authority to that foolish resolution, but it was made known to me that if I opposed the slightest obstacle to what they called my son's vocation, I would immediately be destitute; it was necessary for me to curb my head and remain silent. Tomorrow he will be a priest.

"Ought I confess to you my weakness, and let you see the extremity to which poverty has reduced me? I have been cowardly enough to rejoice, in spite of myself, in that insensate resolution of my son, in the hope that its accomplishment might prevent my ruination. My God! What execrable thoughts poverty gives!"

I cannot tell you what I was caused to experience by that struggle of an honest man in the perpetual alternative of either offending his conscience or ruining his family.

I encouraged him as best I could; I enabled him to envisage things from a less depressing point of view, and succeeded in rendering him a measure of calm, and almost of hope.

His wife came to interrupt us, and I was very glad, for the heavy and unhealthy air that one respired in the invalid's little bedroom, combined with my extreme fatigue and the emotion caused by the tax-collector's confidences, was making my head ache severely and depriving my heart of vigor.

I hastened to go out into the fresh air, but it brought no relief to my malaise.

Black clouds had accumulated in the sky; flashes of lightning succeeded one another so promptly that my vision was fatigued by them; I could scarcely breathe, and there was I know not what impatience in all my nerves, mingled with agitation and depression.

I sat down at the entrance to a little shed at the bottom of the garden.

There, what the unfortunate collector had told me about his son Étienne returned to my imagination and took possession of it forcefully.

Étienne had been my comrade at school; for six years we had been inseparable; both sickly, both fonder of a work of fiction than a dance, we had not taken long to be united in the tender intimacy that takes such forceful possession of two young adolescents. Of a character weaker than mine, Étienne had allowed himself to be led, most of the time, by my advice, and his confidence in me was limitless. My affection for the excellent Étienne was no less, and I lent myself obligingly to the sidesteps of his strange and sometimes delirious imagination. Another might have mocked his bizarre ideas for their exaggeration and their eccentric impetuosity; exceedingly fond of everything related to the marvelous, I found in Étienne's conversation the attraction that one finds in a tale that makes one shiver.

It was eventually necessary for us to separate; and when, after ten years of absence, we met up again, I had become indolent, skeptical and disenchanted, while he was about to receive the tonsure.

I made a few observations to him; he responded bitterly, and since then we had seen one another rarely, and coldly, for we no longer understood one another.

Nevertheless, my relations with his family had not suffered, as you can see, and from time to time, as on that day, when hunting drew me too far, I went to seek shelter with Monsieur Lefebvre.

I was entirely occupied with those childhood memories; I was wondering, with no less anxiety than his father, what Étienne's despair might soon become in finding himself enchained by mystical vows that were so little in accord with his character when I saw a man dressed in black advancing toward me precipitately, with a gesture of mystery.

It was Étienne.

His clothing was in disorder, his head bare, and he attached a distraught gaze to me. He sat down beside me, covered his face with his hands, and made no response to my questions.

"Henri," he said, eventually, "I'm going to make you a strange confidence; I'm going to die soon." He placed a burning and fleshless hand on me. "Shh! Don't interrupt me, let me speak. I'm going to die soon, and I'm damned."

It was easy to see that it was a madman that was talking to me, and yet I could not help shivering.

"I wanted to visit my father's house once more," he continued, without noticing that movement. "I wanted to place my pale and hollow cheeks against the panes of his room, and see him, my mother and my sisters, but without them perceiving me, and without saying a word to them, for my moments are counted, and their despair will commence only too soon.

"I'm damned, Henri, damned for eternity. I have given my soul to an infernal spirit; it will only return it to me when I prefer Hell to Paradise; for I love it, that demon, and I love it more than an eternity of happiness. For it I have renounced the sacred character of a priest of Jesus Christ, I have renounced the happiness of giving alms, of reconciling sinners with God, the ecstasies of prayer! I am going to die today in order to be with it more quickly, in order never to quit it again.

"Listen, Henri. Two months ago, I was reciting my breviary; at first I prayed with fervor, but gradually, other thoughts preoccupied my imagination and drew it far away.

"I started thinking about a soul that responds to every thought of our soul, to the transports and tenderness of amour, to a burning bond of sublime affection that nothing can weaken or break. A sigh escaped me.

"I heard, beside me, a sigh respond to mine.

"There was a being there the sight of which made me feel ill and delighted, a being such as the most tender and fecund mind cannot imagine.

"Forms more ingenuous, more voluptuous, more delicate than those of a young woman; bare breasts, over which flowed long black hair; eyes simultaneously sparkling, soft and timid, whose gaze penetrated my soul.

"I dared not make a movement, I dared not let my breath escape. The apparition might have vanished!

"She sighed again, and the tears that were flowing from her eyes trickled down her cheeks like those of a sick child and came to fall upon her breast; and then she lowered her head as if she were afraid to show it to my gaze.

"'Étienne,' she murmured, finally, in a low voice full of emotion. 'Étienne!'

"I was beside myself; I extended my arms toward her.

"But she knelt down at my feet and said to me, in the tone of a young woman trying in vain to retain her sobs: 'Étienne, make the sign of the cross in order that I shall vanish.'

"'Oh, no! Stay, stay! Always! Always! You're so beautiful!'

"'Make it, the redoubtable sign, in order that I might return to the abode of malediction without having accomplished what Satan has demanded of me. Make it, I beg you, for I am an angel of darkness sent to earth to doom your soul.'

"She still remained there at my feet, her beautiful eyes raised toward me, her imploring hands joined together.

"'Étienne,' she continued, 'only tell me that you forgive me; tell me before I leave and I shall go without a murmur to offer myself to the chastisement of my irritated master; I shall not curse the horrible blows of his fiery whip, for you will not hate me, Étienne.

"'And then I will retain a sweet and sincere memory of you, a memory that will make me dream under the immense vaults reddened by the reflection of the eternal flames. Listen, I shall try to hide a drop of water, which I shall pour on to the lips of one of the damned. I shall say to him: *It's for love of Étienne that I'm soothing you*; and Hell will wax ecstatic on hearing its sad echoes repeat a benediction, for the damned soul will repeat: *Blessed be Étienne, forever.*

"'When you are in Paradise—for, Étienne, you have only a few days to live—when you are in Paradise, I shall try to approach its divine vaults; perhaps, in the midst of the eternal canticles, I shall be able to distinguish your voice. Then I shall return to my prison, and I shall say to myself: *I am alone, alone and unhappy for eternity, but Étienne is happy!*

"'Make the sign of the cross, Étienne, make it, that I might disappear.'

"And I, Henri, I listened, in an ineffable delight; I would have given my soul for her not to stop speaking.

"'Étienne,' she resumed, 'I imagined a kind of happiness for myself with you, but I no longer want it; it would cost me too dear, I would buy it at your expense. I said to myself: We will never be separated, a mysterious and indissoluble marriage will unite us for eternity, he and I, who will henceforth only be one. I shall carry him tenderly on my wings, in order that he does not feel the bite of the flames; with my breath I shall refresh his forehead; with my soft embrace, I shall cradle him softly in order that his eyes will be able to close in sleep. And while he alone is asleep in Hell, I shall repeat in whispers words of love and songs that will suspend the sufferings and cries of the reproved.'

"Henri, I could not resist those words; I surrounded the fallen angel with my arms and hugged her to my bosom. 'I want to be yours,' I said to her. 'I want to be yours, for you are able to love, as I am able to love, as I imagined love in the insensate dreams of my youth.'

"'No! Make the sign of the cross,' she interrupted me, 'there is also love in Paradise, and you will be loved by a cherub with a heart of flame. The torments of Asraelle will be increased by your happiness, but what does it matter? You will be happy.'

"'I want to be yours, to belong to you, who bear the sweet name of Asraelle, to be yours for eternity. I deny my God for you, I deny for you the salvation of my soul. Asraelle, Étienne belongs to you.'

"The naked arms of the angel were enlaced with mine; our lips met . . . and when I returned from a long ecstasy of amour, Asraelle started to weep, for I was damned.

"Every night, she has come to visit her husband; every night, she has come to rest her head on my shoulder, and surround me with her caressant arms.

"Yesterday, she seemed sad, and instead of covering my forehead with kisses, she folded her arms sadly over her breast and said: 'Étienne, tomorrow we shall no longer be apart.'

"I understood her meaning.

"'Tomorrow, Asraelle,' I replied, 'yes tomorrow, I consent to that; but let me see my mother and my sisters once more; let me see my father once more.'

"'You shall see them again,' she said, 'but without speaking to them.'

"This morning, I fled the seminary, and I hid in this garden, and just now I have seen them all. At present, Asraelle is waiting for m."

The storm had begun to rage violently, the wind was roaring, the rain falling in torrents, and the precipitate claps of thunder scarcely allowed me to hear Étienne's voice.

I cannot tell you the terror I experienced during my unfortunate friend's strange story.

"Don't allow yourself to be carried away like this by the whims of your imagination," I said to him, without paying overmuch heed to what I was saying.

A flash of lightning suddenly burst forth, and by its light I saw Étienne smile sadly; then he listened attentively, as if he had heard a noise. "Asraelle, my Asraelle," he cried, "there you are, my beloved. Come, come, I'm eager . . ."

The lightning fell at my feet, and when I recovered my senses, Étienne's cadaver was lying there.

Étienne's father has been rendered destitute, for having, according to the sub-prefect, engaged his son to flee the seminary.

The village curé, a young priest of twenty-five, preached a sermon, in which he proved clearly that God had struck Étienne with lightning to punish his apostasy.

Étienne's mother lost her reason. I am assured that, within his family, two other persons have also been afflicted by mental alienation.

THE AMOROUS REVENANT

by Théophile Gautier

YOU ask me, Brother, whether I have ever loved; yes. It is a singular and terrible story, and although I am sixty-six years old, I scarcely dare to stir the ashes of that memory. I cannot refuse you anything, but I would not tell such a story to a less proven soul. The events are so strange that I can hardly believe that they happened to me.

For more then three years I was the victim of a singular and diabolical illusion. Every night, I, a poor country priest, led in dream—please God that it was a dream!—a life of a damned soul, a worldly life of a Sardanapalus. A single glance too full of complaisance cast at a woman nearly caused the loss of my soul, but finally, with the aid of God and my saintly patron, I succeeded in repelling the evil spirit that had taken possession of me.

My existence was complicated by an entirely different nocturnal existence. By day I was a priest of the Lord, chaste, occupied with prayer and holy things; by night, as soon as I had closed my eyes, I became a young lord, a fine connoisseur of women, dogs and horses, playing dice, drinking and blaspheming; and when I woke up at dawn it seemed to me, on the contrary, that I was asleep and dreaming that I was a priest. Memories of objects and words of that somnambulistic life have remained to me, which I cannot forbid myself, and although I have never emerged from the walls of my presbytery, one might think, on hearing me, that I was a man returned from society worn away by everything, who has entered into religion and wants to end excessively agitated days in the bosom of the Lord, rather than a humble seminarian who has grown old in an unknown parish in the depth of woods, without any relationship with things of the present century.

Yes, I have loved, as no one else in the world has loved, an insensate and furious amour, so violent that I am astonished that it did not cause my heart to burst. Oh, what nights! What nights!

Since my earliest childhood I felt a vocation for the condition of a priest, so all my studies were in that direction, and my life, until the age of twenty-four, was nothing but a long novitiate. Having finished my theology I passed successively through all the petty orders, and my superiors judged me worthy, in spite of my great youth, to take the last redoubtable step. The day of my ordination was fixed for the week of Easter.

I had never gone into society; the world, for me, was the enclosure of the college of the seminary. I knew vaguely that there was something called "woman," but my thought did not pause thereon; I was perfectly innocent. I only saw my aged and infirm mother twice a year. That was the entirety of my relations with the outside world.

I did not regret anything; I did not feel the slightest hesitation before the irrevocable engagement; I was full of joy and impatience. No young fiancé had ever counted the hours with a more feverish ardor. I did not sleep without dreaming that I was saying mass; I could not imagine anything in the world finer than being a priest; I would have refused to be a king or a poet. My ambition could not conceive anything beyond.

What I am saying is to demonstrate to you the extent to which what happened to me should not have happened, and the inexplicable fascination of which I was the victim.

When the great day came I walked to the church with such a light step that it seemed to me that I was floating in the air, or that I had wings on my shoulders. I thought that I was an angel, and I was astonished by the somber and preoccupied physiognomy of my companions; for there were several of us. I had spent the night in prayer, and I was in a state almost akin to ecstasy. The bishop, a venerable old man, seemed to me to be God the Father inclined over his eternity, and I could see Heaven through the vault of the temple.

You know the details of the ceremony; the benediction, the communion under the two species, the anointing of the palms of the hands of the catechumens with oil, and finally, the holy sacrifice offered in concert with the bishop. I shall not dwell on that.

Oh, how right Job was, and how imprudent the man is who makes a pact with his eyes! I chanced to raise my head, which I had kept inclined until then, and I perceived in front of me, so close that I could have touched her, although she was in reality quite a long distance away and on the other side of the balustrade, a young woman of rare beauty, dressed with a regal magnificence.

It was as if scales fell from my eyes. I experienced the sensation of a blind man who suddenly recovers his sight. The bishop, so radiant a moment before, was suddenly extinguished; the candles paled in their golden candlesticks like the stars in the morning, and there was a complete obscurity throughout the church. The charming creature stood out against that background of shadow like an angelic revelation; she seemed self-illuminated, giving light rather than receiving it.

I lowered my eyelid, firmly resolved not to raise it again, in order to remove myself from the influence of external objects, for distraction was invading me increasingly, and I scarcely knew what I was doing.

A minute later, I opened me eyes again, for through my eyelashes I could see the colors of the prism sparkling, in a crimson penumbra, as when one gazes at the sun.

Oh, how beautiful she was! The greatest painters, when they pursued ideal beauty in Heaven and brought back to earth the divine portrait of the Madonna, did not even approach that fabulous reality. Neither the verses of the poet nor the palette of the painter could give an idea of it.

She was quite tall, with the figure and the deportment of a goddess. Her hair, of a soft blonde, was separated at the top of her head and flowed over her temples like two rivers of gold; one might have thought her a queen with her diadem. Her forehead, of a blue-tinted and transparent whiteness, extended broadly and serenely over two arcs of almost brown lashes, a singularity that added further to the effect of sea-green irises of an unsustainable vivacity and glare.

What eyes! In a flash, they decided the destiny of a man; they had a life, a limpidity, and an ardor and a brilliant humidity that I had never seen in a human eye; rays escaped from them like darts, which I distinctly saw terminating in my heart. I do not know whether the flame that illuminated them came from Heaven or Hell, but it surely came from one or the other. That woman was an angel or a demon, and perhaps both; she certainly did not emerge from the loins of Eve, the common mother.

Teeth of the most beautiful orient scintillated within her red smile, and little dimples were hollowed out with each inflexion of her mouth in the pink satin of her adorable cheeks. As for her nose, it had an entirely regal delicacy and pride, which revealed the noblest origin. Agate gleams played over the smooth and lustrous skin of her partly-uncovered shoulders, and rows of large blonde pearls, of a hue almost identical to the neck, descended over her breast. From time to time she straightened her head with an undulating movement of a snake or a strutting peacock and imprinted a slight frisson to the high frieze embroidered by daylight, which surrounded her like a silver trellis.

She was wearing a dress of nacarat velvet, and aristocratic hands of an infinite delicacy with long, plump fingers emerged from her broad ermine-lined sleeves, of such an ideal transparency that they let the daylight through, like Aurora's.

All those details are still as present to me as if they dated from yesterday, and although I was extremely troubled, nothing escaped me; I seized all the slightest nuances—the little black dot in the corner of the chin, the imperceptible down at the corners of the lips, the velvet of the forehead, the tremulous shadow of the eyelashes over the cheeks—with an astonishing lucidity.

As I gazed at her, I sensed doors opening within me that had been closed until then; obstructed ventilation shafts were cleared in all directions, allowing glimpses of unknown perspectives; life appeared to me in an entirely different aspect; I had just been born to a new order of ideas. A frightful anguish clawed my heart; every minute that went by seemed to be a second and a century.

The ceremony advanced, however, and I was carried far from the world whose entrance my nascent desires besieged furiously. Meanwhile, I said *yes* when I wanted to say *no*, while everything within me revolted and protested against the violence that my tongue was doing to my soul; an occult force wrenched the words from my throat involuntarily. That is perhaps what many young women do who march to the altar with the firm resolution to refuse in a striking manner the husband who is being imposed on them, not one of whom carries out her project. It is doubtless what many poor novices do when taking the veil, although they had decided to rip it into pieces at the moment of pronouncing their vows. One does not dare to cause a scandal before everyone or to deceive the expectations of so many people; all those wills and all those gazes seem to weigh upon you like a leaden cowl; and then, the measures have been so well taken, everything is so well regulated in advance, in a fashion so evidently irrevocable, that thought yields to the weight and collapses completely.

The gaze of the beautiful stranger changed expression in accordance with the progress of the ceremony. From the tender mildness that it had to begin with, it took on an air of disdain and discontentment, as if it had not been understood.

I made an effort sufficient to uproot a mountain, in order to shout that I did not want to be a priest, but I could not do it; my tongue remained nailed to my palate and it was impossible for me to translate my will by means of the slightest negative movement. While wide awake, I was in a state similar to that of a nightmare, in which one wants to cry out a word on which your life depends, without being able to do so.

She seemed to be aware of the martyrdom that I was experiencing, and as if to encourage me, she shot me a glance full of divine promises. Her eyes were a poem, every glance of which formed a song.

She said to me:

"If you want to be mine, I will make you happier than God himself in his paradise; the angels will be jealous of you. Tear apart the funereal shroud in which you are about to wrap yourself; I am Beauty, I am Youth, I am Life; come to me and we will be Amour. What could Jehovah offer you for compensation? Our existence will flow like a dream and will be nothing but an eternal kiss.

"Spill the wine in that chalice, and you are free. I will take you away to unknown isles; you will sleep on my breast, in a solid gold bed under a silver awning; for I love you, and I want to take you from your God, before whom so many noble hearts pour down floods of amour that never reach as far as him."

I seemed to hear those words to a rhythm of infinite softness, for her gaze almost had sonority, and the phrases that her eyes sent me resounded in the depths of my heart as if an invisible mouth had breathed them into my soul. I felt ready to renounce God, and yet my heart was accomplishing mechanically the formalities of the ceremony. The beauty darted a second glance at me so imploring and so desperate that sharp blades traversed by heart, and I felt more swords in my breast than the *mater dolorosa*.

It was done; I was a priest.

No human physiognomy had ever depicted an anguish so poignant. The young woman who sees her fiancé die suddenly beside her, the mother next to her child's empty cradle, Eve sitting on the doorstep of paradise, the miser who finds a stone in the place of his treasure, and the poet who has dropped the only manuscript of his most beautiful work in the fire do not have an expression more devastated and inconsolable. The blood abandoned her charming face completely and she became as white as marble. Her beautiful arms fell alongside her body, as if their muscles had been disconnected, and she leaned against a pillar, for her legs buckled and gave way beneath her. As for me, livid, my forehead inundated by a sweat bloodier than that of Calvary, I steered unsteadily for the door of the church; I was choking, the vaults flattened upon my shoulders, and it seemed to me that my head supported the entire weight of the cupola on its own.

As I was about to cross the threshold a hand took possession abruptly of mine; the hand of a woman! I had never touched one. It was as cold as the skin of a snake, and the imprint of it remained, burning like the mark of a red-hot iron. It was her. "Wretch," she said to me in a low voice. "Wretch, what have you done?" Then she disappeared into the crowd.

The aged bishop passed by; he looked at me with a severe expression. I had the strangest countenance in the world; I went pale; I blushed, I was dazzled. One of my comrades took pity on me. He took me and led me away; I would have been incapable of finding my way back to the seminary on my own.

At a street corner, while the young priest turned his head in another direction, a bizarrely-clad negro page approached me, and without pausing in his course, handed me a small portfolio with sculpted gold corners, making me a sign to hide it. I slid it into my sleeve and held it there until I was alone in my cell. I opened the clasp; it only contained two leaves with these words: *Clarimonde, at the Concini Palace.*

I was then so scantly acquainted with matters of life that I did not know Clarimonde, in spite of her celebrity, and I was completely ignorant of where the Concini Palace was situated. I made a thousand conjectures, each more extravagant than the last, but in truth, provided that I could see her again, I did not care in the least what she might be, great lady or courtesan.

That recently born amour had taken root indestructibly; I did not even think of trying to uproot it, so impossible did I sense it to be. That woman had taken possession of me completely; a single glance has sufficed to change me; she had breathed her will into me; I no longer lived within myself but in her and by means of her. I did a thousand extravagant things; I kissed the place on my hand where she had touched me, and I repeated her name for entire hours. I had only to close my eyes to see her as distinctly as if she were present in reality, and I repeated the words she had spoken to me under the portal of the church:

"Wretch, wretch, what have you done?"

I understood all the horror of my situation, and the funereal and terrible aspects of the condition I had just embraced were clearly revealed within me. To be a priest, which is to say, chaste, not to love, not to distinguish either sex or age, to turn away from all beauty, to put out one's eyes, to crawl under the glacial shadow of a cloister or a church, only to see the dying, to keep vigil over unknown cadavers and to wear mourning oneself under a black soutane, with the consequence that a drape for your coffin can be made of your costume!

And I sensed life rising within me like an interior lake, swelling and overflowing; my blood was beating forcefully in my arteries; my youth, so long compressed, suddenly burst forth like the aloes that take a hundred years to flower and which bloom like a thunderclap.

What could I do to see Clarimonde again? I had no pretext to leave the seminary, not knowing anyone in the city; I would not even remain there, and was only waiting for the parish to be indicated to me that I was to occupy. I tried to loosen the bars on the window, but it was frightfully high, and, having no ladder, it was necessary not to think about it. And then, I could only climb down by night, and how would I find my way through the inextricable labyrinth of streets?

All those difficulties, which might have been trivial for others, were immense for me, a poor seminarian, amorous since yesterday, devoid of experience, money and clothing.

Oh, if I had not been a priest, I would have been able to see her every day; I could have been her lover or her husband, I said to myself in my blindness. Instead of being enveloped in my sad shroud, I could have had garments of silk and velvet, gold chains, a sword and plumes, like the handsome young cavaliers. Instead of being dishonored by a large tonsure, my hair could play around my neck in undulating curls. I could have a beautiful waxed moustache, I would be valiant. But an hour spent before an altar, a few words scarcely articulated, had removed me forever from the number of the living and I had sealed my own tombstone, pushed the bolt of my prison with my own hand.

I stationed myself at the window. The sky was admirably blue, the trees had donned their spring robe, nature was putting on a display of ironic joy. The square was full of people; some were coming, others going; young fops and young beauties, in couples, were heading for the garden and the arbors. Companions went by singing drinking songs; there was a movement, a life, an enthusiasm and a gaiety that made my mourning and my solitude stand out painfully. A young mother was playing with her child on the doorstep; she kissed his little pink mouth, still pearled by droplets of milk, and made him, while teasing him, a thousand of the divine puerilities that only mothers are able to discover. The father, who was standing a short distance away, was smiling softly at that charming group, and his folded arms were pressing his joy to his heart.

I could not bear that spectacle; I closed the window and threw myself on to my bed with a frightful hatred and jealousy in my heart, biting my fingers and my blanket like a tiger that had gone hungry for three days.

I do not know how many days I remained like that, but when I turned round in a furious spasmodic movement, I perceived Abbot Serapion, who was standing in the middle of the room and considering me attentively. I was ashamed of myself, and, letting my head fall upon my breast, I veiled my eyes with my hands.

"Romuald, my friend, something extraordinary is happening within you," Serapion said to me after a few minutes of silence. "Your conduct is truly inexplicable! You, so pious, so calm and so mild, agitating in your cell like a wild beast! Be careful, Brother, and do not listen to the suggestions of the Devil; the evil spirit, irritated because you have consecrated yourself to the Lord forever, is prowling around you like an avid wolf making one last effort to draw you to him. Instead of allowing yourself to be defeated, my dear Romuald, make yourself an armor of prayers, a buckler of mortifications, and combat the enemy valiantly; you will vanquish him. Proof is necessary to virtue, and the gold emerges finer from the crucible. Do not be frightened or discouraged; the best protected and the firmest souls have these moments. Pray, fast and meditate, and the evil spirit will withdraw."

Abbot Serapion's speech caused me to reenter into myself, and I became a little calmer.

"I have come to inform you of your appointment to the parish of C***; the priest who possessed it has just died, and the bishop has charged me to go to install you there; be ready for tomorrow."

I responded with a sign of the head, and the abbot withdrew. I opened my missal and I commenced reading the prayers, but the lines were soon confused before my eyes; the thread of ideas became entangled in my brain, and the volume slid from my hands without my noticing.

To depart tomorrow without having seen her again! To add yet another impossibility to all those that were already between us! To lose the hope of encountering her again forever, barring a miracle! Write to her? By what means could I get my letter to her? Given the sacred character I had taken on, in whom could I confide, and who could I trust? I experienced a terrible anxiety.

Then, what Abbot Serapion had said to me about the artifices of the Devil returned to my memory. The strangeness of the adventure, the supernatural beauty of Clarimonde, the phosphoric gleam of her eyes, the burning impression of her hand, the disturbance into which she had cast me, the sudden change that had taken place within me, and in my piety, vanished in an instant, all proved clearly the presence of the Devil, and that satin hand was perhaps only the glove with which his claw was covered.

Those ideas threw me into a great fear; I picked up the missal that had fallen from my knees on to the floor and I resumed my prayers.

The next day, Serapion came to fetch me. Two mules were waiting for us at the door, charged with our meager valises; he mounted one and I the other, as best I could. While passing through the streets of the town I looked at all the windows and all the balconies in case

I could see Clarimonde, but it was too early and the eyes of the town had not yet opened. My gaze tried to plunge behind the blinds and through the curtains of all the palaces we passed. Serapion doubtless attributed that curiosity to the admiration caused by the beauty of the architecture, and he slowed the pace of his mount in order to give me the time to see.

Finally, we arrived at the gate of the town and began to climb the hill. When I was at the top I turned round in order to gaze once more at the places where Clarimonde lived. The shadow of a cloud covered the town entirely; the blue and red roofs were confounded in a general demi-tint, in which the smoke of the morning fires floated here and there like flecks of white foam. By virtue of a singular optical effect, one edifice that surpassed in height the neighboring constructions, completely drowned by the mist, stood out, blonde and gilded by a unique ray of light; although it was more than a league away, it seemed very close. The slightest details were distinguishable: the turrets, the platforms, the casements, and even the swallow-tail weathervanes.

"What is that palace I see down there, illuminated by a ray of sunlight?" I asked Serapion.

He put his hand above his eyes and, having looked, he replied: "It's the old palace that Prince Concini gave to the courtesan Clarimonde; terrible things happen there."

At that moment—I do not know whether it was a reality or an illusion—I thought I saw a svelte white form glide over the terrace, which glinted for a second and was then extinguished. It was Clarimonde!

Oh, did she know that, at that moment, from the height of the harsh road that was taking me away from her, which I would never descend again, ardent and unquiet, I was gazing fondly at the palace she inhabited, which a derisory play of the light seemed to draw nearer to me, as if to invite me to enter it as the master? Undoubtedly she did know it, for her soul was too sympathetically linked to mine not to sense its slightest shocks, and it was that sentiment which had driven her to go up to the height of the terrace in the glacial morning dew.

The shadow reached the palace, and there was no longer anything but an ocean of roofs and eaves, in which nothing could be distinguished but a hilly undulation. Serapion touched his mule, whose stride mine immediately matched, and a bend in the road hid the town of S*** from me forever, to which I was never to return.

After three days of travel through rather sad fields, we saw through the trees the weathervane on the steeple of the church that I was to serve, and after following a few tortuous streets bordered by cottages and gardens we found ourselves before the façade, which was of no great magnificence. A porch ornamented by a few ribs and two or three grossly-hewn sandstone pillars, a tile roof and buttresses of the same stone as the pillars: that was all. To the left was the cemetery, full of long grass, with a large iron cross in the middle; to the right and in the shadow of the church, the presbytery. It was a house of extreme simplicity and arid neatness. We went in; a few chickens were pecking rare oat grains scattered on the ground; apparently accustomed to the black coats of ecclesiastics, they were not frightened by our presence and scarcely moved aside to let us pass. A hoarse barking was heard, and we saw an old dog come running.

It was my predecessor's dog; it had dull eyes, gray fur and all the symptoms of the extreme old age that a dog can attain. I stroked it gently with my hand, and it immediately started walking beside me with an air of inexpressible satisfaction. An old woman, who had been the previous incumbent's housekeeper, also came to meet us, and after having taken me into a low-ceilinged room, she asked me whether it was my intention to keep her. I replied that I would keep her and the dog, and also the chickens, and all the furniture that her master had left her at his death, which caused her to enter a transport of joy, Abbot Serapion having immediately given her the price that she asked for it.

My installation completed, Abbot Serapion returned to the seminary. I therefore remained alone, with no other support than myself. The thought of Clarimonde began to obsess me again, and whatever efforts that I made to chase it away, I still could not succeed in it.

One evening, while walking in the paths of my little garden, bordered with box-trees, it seemed to me that I saw the form of a woman through the hedge, which followed all my movements, and two sea-green eyes between the leaves; but that was only an illusion, and having passed to the other side of the hedge I found nothing but a footprint in the sand, so small that one might have thought it a child's foot. The garden was surrounded by high walls; I visited all its corners and nooks; there was no one there. I have never been able to explain that circumstance, which, however, was nothing compared with the strange things that were to happen to me subsequently.

I lived like that for a year, fulfilling with exactitude all the duties of my position, praying, fasting, exhorting and assisting the sick, giving alms to the point of only retaining the most indispensable necessities for myself. But I felt within myself an extreme aridity, and the wellsprings of grace were closed to me. I did not enjoy the happiness that the accomplishment of a holy mission gives; my ideas were elsewhere, and Clarimonde's words often returned to my lips like a kind of involuntary refrain. O Brother, meditate this well: for having lifted my gaze to a woman once, for such a seemingly slight sin, I experienced for several years the most miserable agitations; my life was troubled forever.

I shall not dwell any longer on those interior failures and the victories that were always followed by more profound falls, and I shall pass directly to a decisive circumstance. One night, someone rang violently at my door. The old housekeeper went to open it, and a man with a coppery complexion, richly dressed but in a foreign fashion, with a long poniard, was outlined by the rays of Barbara's lantern. Her first movement was fearful, but the man reassured her and told her that he needed me immediately for a matter concerning my ministry. Barbara showed him upstairs; I was about to go to bed.

The man told me that his mistress, a great lady, was on the point of death and desired a priest. I replied that I was ready to follow him; I took with me what was necessary to administer extreme unction, and descended in haste. At the door, two horses as black as night were whinnying impatiently and breathing long trails of vapor over their breasts. He held the stirrup of one of them for me and helped me to mount, and then he leapt on to the other, only supporting himself with one hand on the saddle-horn. He tightened his knees and released the bridle of his horse, which set off like an arrow. Mine, the bridle of which he was holding, also started galloping and matched its pace perfectly.

We devoured the road; the ground fled beneath us, gray and striped, and the black silhouettes of the trees fled like an army in rout. We traversed a forest of a darkness so opaque and so glacial that I felt a frisson of superstitious terror running over my skin. The showers of sparks that our horses' shoes struck from the stones left a kind of fiery trail in our wake, and if anyone, at that hour of the night, had seen my guide and me, he would have taken us for two specters riding the nightmare.

Fire follets traversed the road from time to time, and jackdaws chirped piteously in the thickness of the woods, where the phosphoric eyes of a few wild cats gleamed from time to time. The manes of the horses became increasingly tangled, sweat streamed over their flanks, and their breath emerged noisily and urgently from their nostrils. When he saw them weakening, however, in order to reanimate them, the groom uttered a guttural cry that had nothing human about it, and the course recommenced furiously.

Finally, the whirlwind ceased; a black mass pricked by a few bright dots suddenly loomed up ahead of us; the footfalls of our mounts rang more loudly on and iron-studded floor, and we entered beneath a vault that opened its somber maw between two enormous towers. A great agitation reigned within the château; domestics with torches in hand were traversing the courtyard in all directions, and lanterns were going up and down from floor to floor. I caught confused glimpses of immense architectures, columns, arcades, perrons and staircases, a luxury of construction entirely regal and magical.

A negro page—the same one who had given me Clarimonde's note, whom I recognized immediately—helped me to descend, and a majordomo clad in black velvet with a golden chain around his neck and an ivory cane in his hand advanced toward me. Large tears were flowing from his eyes and running down his cheeks over his white beard.

"Too late!" he said, shaking his head. "Too late, Seigneur Priest; but if you have not been able to save her soul, come to keep vigil over the poor body."

He took me by the arm and led me to the funereal chamber; I was weeping as forcefully as him, for I had understood that the dead woman was none other than Clarimonde, so much and so madly loved.

A prie-Dieu was disposed beside the bed; a blue-tinted flame fluttering on a bronze paten cast a feeble and dubious light throughout the room, and caused to flicker here and there in the gloom from the projecting edge of some item of furniture or cornice. On the table, in a sculpted urn, a faded white rose was steeped, the petals of which, with the exception of a single one that was still holding, had fallen at the foot of the vase like odorous tears. A broken black mask, a fan, and disguises of every species, were trailing over

70

the armchairs, enabling the inference that death had arrived in that sumptuous dwelling unexpectedly and without being announced.

I knelt down without daring to cast my eyes upon the bed, and I started reciting the psalms with a great fervor, thanking God because he had put the tomb between the idea of that woman and me, in order that I might add her name, sanctified henceforth, to my prayers. Gradually, however, that fervor relented, and I fell into a reverie. That room had nothing of the mortuary chamber about it. Instead of the fetid and cadaverous air that I was accustomed to breathe in funereal vigils, a languorous smoke of Oriental essences and I know not what amorous feminine odor floated gently in the lukewarm atmosphere. The pale light gave the impression of a half-light contrived for voluptuousness rather than the yellow radiance that trembles near cadavers.

I thought about the singular hazard that had enabled me to rediscover Clarimonde at the moment when I was losing her forever, and a sigh of regret escaped my breast. It seemed to me that someone had also sighed behind me, and I turned round involuntarily. It was an echo.

In that movement my eyes fell upon the sumptuous bed that they had avoided until then. The red damask curtains with large flowers, lifted up by golden tassels, allowed the dead woman to be seen, lying full length, with her hands joined over her bosom. She was covered by a cotton veil of dazzling whiteness, which the dark crimson of the drapes brought out more emphatically, of such finesse that it hid nothing of the charming form of her body and permitted the beautiful undulating lines to be followed, like the neck of a swan that even death had not been able to stiffen. One might have thought it an alabaster statue made by some skillful sculptor in order to be placed on the tomb of a queen, or a sleeping young woman on whom snow had fallen.

I could not stand it any longer; the atmosphere of the alcove intoxicated me, the feverish scent of the faded rose went to my head and I strode back and forth in the room stopping at every circuit before the platform in order to consider the gracious corpse under the transparency of her shroud. Strange thoughts crossed my mind; I imagined that she was not really dead, and that it was only a feint that she had employed in order to attract me to her château and tell me about her amour. For an instant I thought I saw her foot stir under the whiteness of the veils and disturb the straight pleats of the shroud.

Then I said to myself: *Is this really Clarimonde? What proof do I have of that? Might that black page not have passed into the service of another woman? I'm truly mad to be so desolate and to agitate thus.*

But my heart replied to me with its beating: *It's really her; it's really her.*

I drew nearer to the bed and I gazed with increased attention at the object of my uncertainty. Shall I confess it to you? That perfection of forms, although purified and sanctified by the shadow of death, troubled me more voluptuously than it should have done, and that repose resembled sleep so closely that one might have been deceived by it. I forgot that I had come there for a funereal office, and I imagined that I was a young husband entering the chamber of his bride, who was hiding her face out of modesty and did not want to let it be seen. Distressed by grief, bewildered by joy, shivering with dread and pleasure, I leaned toward her and took hold of the corner of the sheet; I lifted it up slowly, holding my breath for fear of awakening her. My arteries were throbbing with such force that I felt them hissing in my temples, and my forehead was streaming with sweat, as if I had shifted a marble slab.

It was indeed Clarimonde, such as I had seen her in the church during my ordination; she was as charming, and in her, death seemed one more coquetry. The pallor of her cheeks, the less vivid rosiness of her lips, and her long lashes, lowered and cutting through that whiteness with their brown fringe, gave her an expression of melancholy chastity and pensive suffering, of an inexpressible power of seduction. Her long loose hair, with which a few little blue flowers were still mingled, made a pillow for her head and protected with its curls the nudity of her shoulders. Her beautiful hands, purer and more diaphanous than hosts, were crossed in an attitude of pious repose and tacit prayer, which corrected what might have been too seductive, even in death, in the exquisite roundness and ivory polish of her bare arms, from which the pearl bracelets had not been removed.

I remained absorbed in mute contemplation for a long time, and the more I looked at her, the less I was able to believe that life had abandoned that beautiful body forever. I do not know whether it was an illusion or a reflection of the lamplight, but one might have thought that the blood had begun to circulate again beneath that mat pallor. However, she still maintained the most perfect immobility. I touched her arm lightly; it was cold, but not as cold as her hand on the day when it had brushed mine under the portal of the church.

I resumed my position, inclining my face over hers, allowing the warm dew of my tears to rain down in her cheeks. Oh, what a bitter sentiment of despair and impotence! What agony that vigil was! I would have liked to be able to pick up my life in a heap in order to give it to her and blow over her icy remains the flame that was devouring me.

The night was advancing and, sensing the approach of the moment of eternal separation, I could not refuse myself the sad and supreme tenderness of depositing a kiss on the dead lips of the woman who had had all of my amour.

O prodigy! A light breath was mingled with my breath, and Clarimonde's mouth responded to the pressure of mine; her eyes opened and resumed a slight luster; she uttered a sigh, and, uncrossing her arms, she passed them around my neck with an expression of ineffable rapture.

"Ah, it's you, Romuald," she said, in a voice as languid and soft as the last vibrations of a harp. "What are you doing? I waited for you for such a long time that I died; but now that we are betrothed, I shall be able to see you and come to your home. Adieu, Romuald, adieu! I love you; that is all that I wanted to tell you, and I render to you the life, a minute of which that you have recalled to me with your kiss; I shall see you soon."

Her head fell backwards, but she was still surrounding me with her arms, as if to retain me. A furious whirlwind smashed the window and entered into the room; the last petal of the white rose fluttered for some time at the end of its stem, like a wing; then it was detached and flew away through the open window, bearing Clarimonde's soul with it. The lamp went out and I fell in a faint on the breast of the beautiful dead woman.

When I came round I was lying on my bed in my little room in the presbytery, and the former curé's old dog was licking my hand, which was dangling outside the blanket. Barbara was agitating in the room with a senile tremor, opening and closing drawers and stirring powders into glasses. On seeing me open my eyes the old woman uttered a cry of joy, while the dog yapped and wagged its tail; but I was so weak that I could not pronounce a single word or make any movement.

I found out subsequently that I had remained thus for three days, giving no other sign of life than an almost insensible respiration. Those three days are not counted in my life and I do not know where my spirit had gone during all that time; I have not retained any memory of it. Barbara told me that the same man with the coppery complexion who had come to fetch me during the night had brought me back in the morning in a closed litter and had gone away again immediately.

As soon as I was able to recover my ideas, I reiterated internally all the circumstances of that fatal night. At first I thought that I had been the victim of a magical illusion, but real and palpable circumstances soon destroyed that supposition. I could not believe that I had been dreaming, since Barbara had seen the man with the two black horses, as I had, and she described their equipment and appearance exactly. However, no one in the surrounding area knew of a château fitting the description of the château where I had rediscovered Clarimonde.

One morning, I saw Abbot Serapion come in. Barbara had sent word to him that I was ill, and he had come in all haste. Although that urgency demonstrated his affection and interest in my person, his visit did not give me the pleasure that it should have done. Abbot Serapion had something penetrating and inquisitorial in his gaze that troubled me. I felt embarrassed and culpable in his presence. He had been the first to discover my interior turmoil, and I held his clear-sightedness against him.

While asking for news of my health in a hypocritically honeyed tone, he fixed his two yellow leonine eyes upon me and plunged his gaze like a sound into my soul. Then he asked a few questions about the way in which I directed my parish, if I was happy there, how I spent the free time that my ministry left me, whether I had made any acquaintances among the local inhabitants, what my favorite reading was, and a thousand similar details. I responded to all that as briefly as possible, and he passed on to something else without waiting for me to finish. That conversation evidently had no relation to what he wanted to say. Then, without any preparation, as if he had just remembered an item of news and feared that he might forget it subsequently, he said to me in a clear and vibrant voice that resonated in my ears like the trumpets of the Last Judgment:

"The great courtesan Clarimonde died recently, after an orgy that lasted eight days and eight nights. It was something infernally splendid. The abominations of the feasts of Belshazzar and Cleopatra were renewed there. In what century are we living, good God! The guests were served by bronzed slaves speaking an unknown language, and seemed to me to have the appearance of true demons; the livery of the least of them could have served for the gala costume of an emperor. Many strange stories regarding Clarimonde had been running around for some time, and all her lovers ended in a wretched or violent fashion. It was said that she was a ghoul, a female vampire, but I believe that she was Beelzebub in person."

He fell silent and observed me more attentively than ever, in order to see the effect that his words had produced in me. I had been unable to forbid myself a movement on hearing Clarimonde named, and that news of her death, in addition to the pain it caused me by virtue of the nocturnal scene I had witnessed, threw me into a disturbance and a fear that appeared in my face, although I did what I could to master it. Serapion darted an anxious and severe gaze at me, and then said to me: "My son, I must warn you that you have one foot raised above the abyss; be careful that you do not fall into it. Satan has long claws, and tombs are not always reliable. Clarimonde's stone ought to be sealed with a triple seal, for it is said that this is not the first time that she has died. May God watch over you, Romuald."

Having said those words, Serapion went back to the door at a slow pace, and I did not see him again, for he left for S*** almost immediately.

I had recovered completely and resumed my habitual functions. The memory of Clarimonde and the old abbot's words were still present in my mind; however, no extraordinary event had come to confirm the funereal anticipations of Serapion, and I began to believe that his apprehensions and my terrors were over-exaggerated; but one night, I had a dream.

I had scarcely savored the first draughts of slumber than I heard the curtains of my bed open and the rings slide over the rails with a loud noise. I raised myself up on my elbow abruptly, and I saw the shadow of a woman standing before me. I recognized Clarimonde instantly. In her hand she was carrying a little lamp of the form of those that are placed on tombs, the light of which gave her slender fingers a rosy transparency that was prolonged by an insensible gradation as far as the opaque and milky whiteness of her bare arm.

Her only garment was the linen shroud that had covered her on her sumptuous bed, the pleats of which she retained over her bosom, as if ashamed to be so scantily dressed, but her small hand was not sufficient for that; it was so white that the color of the drapery was confounded with that of her flesh under the pale radiance of the lamplight. Enveloped in that delicate fabric, which betrayed all the contours of her body, she resembled a marble statue of an antique bather rather than a woman endowed with life.

Dead or alive, statue or woman, shadow or body, her beauty was still the same, except that the green glow of her eyes was deadened slightly, and her mouth, once so vermilion, was only tinted any longer by a faint and pale pink, similar to that of her cheeks. The little blue flowers that I had noticed in her hair were entirely desiccated and had lost almost all their petals—which did not prevent her from being charming: so charming that, in spite of the singularity of the adventure and the inexplicable fashion in which she had entered the room, I was not frightened for an instant.

She placed the lamp on the table and sat down on the foot of my bed; then she leaned toward me and said, in the voice, silvery and velvety at the same time, that I had only known in her: "I have waited for some time, my dear Romuald, and you must have thought that I had forgotten you. But I have come from far away, from a place from which no one else has yet returned. There is neither moonlight nor sunlight in the place from which I have come; there is only space and shadow; no road nor path, no ground for the feet, no air for a wing; and yet, here I am, for love is stronger than death, and it will finish by vanquishing it. Oh, the bleak faces and the terrible things I have seen during my voyage! How much trouble my soul has had, having reentered this world by virtue of the power of the will, in rediscovering its body and reinstalling itself therein! How much effort it was necessary for me to make before raising the slab with which I was covered! Look—the palms of my hands are all bruised by it! Kiss them in order to heal them, dear amour."

She applied the cold palms of her hands, one after another, to my mouth; I did indeed kiss them several times, and she watched me do it with a smile of ineffable complaisance.

I confess, to my shame, that I had completely forgotten the opinion of Abbot Serapion and the character that I had taken on. I had fallen without resistance at the first assault. I had not even tried to repel the tempter; the freshness of Clarimonde's skin penetrated mine, and I felt voluptuous frissons running over my body. Poor child! In spite of all that I had seen, I could not believe that she was a demon; at least, she did not have the appearance of it, and Satan has never concealed his claws and his horns more effectively. She had folded her claws back beneath her and was crouched on the edge of the bed in a posture full of nonchalant coquetry. From time to time she passed her little hand through my hair, and rolled it into curls as if to try out a new hairstyle for my visage. I let her do it with the most culpable complaisance, and she accompanied all that with the most charming babble. One remarkable thing is that I did not experience any astonishment at such an extraordinary adventure, and with the facility that one has in a vision of admitting the most bizarre events as quite simple, I did not see anything in it that was not perfectly natural.

"I loved you for a long time before having seen you. my dear Romuald, and I searched for you everywhere. You were my dream, and I perceived you in the church at the fatal moment; I said immediately: 'It's him!' I darted a gaze at you into which I put all the amour that I had had, that I had and that I would have for you: a gaze to damn a cardinal, to make a king kneel at my feet before his entire court. You remained impassive, and you preferred your God to me. Oh, how jealous I am of God, whom you loved and still love more than me!

"Unfortunate woman that I am, I shall never have your heart entirely to myself, I whom you have resuscitated with a kiss, Clarimonde the revenant, who has forced the doors of the tomb because of you and who has come to consecrate to you a life that she has only resumed in order to render you happy!"

All those words were punctuated with deliriant caresses that stunned my senses and my reason, to the point that I did not hesitate to console her by proffering a frightful blasphemy and telling her that I loved her as much as God.

Her eyes became vivid again and shone like chrysoprases.

"Truly? Really and truly? As much as God!" she said, enlacing me with her beautiful arms. "Since it is thus, you'll come with me, you'll follow me wherever I wish. You'll leave behind your vile black coats. You'll be the proudest and most envied of cavaliers, you'll be my lover. To be the admitted lover of Clarimonde, who has refused a Pope, is a fine thing. Oh, the good, happy life, the beautiful gilded existence we shall lead! When shall we depart, my gentleman?"

"Tomorrow, tomorrow!" I cried in my delirium.

"Tomorrow, so be it," she said. "I shall have time to change costume, for this one is a trifle succinct and worthless for the voyage. It's also necessary that I go to inform my people, who believe me to be seriously dead and are desolate, to the extent that they can be. Money, clothes, carriages, everything will be ready; I shall collect you at the same time as this. Adieu, dear heart."

And she brushed my forehead with the edges of her lips. The lamp went out, the curtains closed again, and I saw nothing more; a leaden slumber, a dreamless sleep, weighed upon me and held me in a torpor until the next morning.

I woke up later than usual, and the memory of the singular vision agitated me all day long; I ended up persuading myself that it was only a vapor of my heated imagination. However, the sensations had been so vivid that it was difficult to believe that they were not real, and it was not without some apprehension of what might happen that I went to bed, after having prayed to God to distance evil thoughts from me and to protect the chastity of my slumber.

I soon fell profoundly asleep, and my dream continued. The curtains parted, and I saw Clarimonde, not, as the first time, pale in her pale shroud with the violets of death on her cheeks, but cheerful, brisk and sprightly, with a superb traveling costume in green velvet, ornamented with golden braid and tucked up at the side to allow the sight of a satin skirt. Her blonde hair escaped in large waves from beneath a large black velvet hat charged with capriciously contorted white feathers. In her hand she was holding a small riding crop terminated by a golden whistle. She touched me with it lightly and said: "Well, handsome sleeper, is this how you make your preparations? I expected to find you on your feet. Get up quickly, we have no time to lose."

I leapt out of bed.

"Come on, get dressed and let's go," she said, pointing her finger at a little package she had brought. "The horses are getting bored and chewing the bit at the door. We ought to be ten leagues away from here already."

I got dressed in haste, and she handed the garments to me herself, laughing in bursts at my awkwardness and indicating their usage to me when I made a mistake. She combed my hair, and when that was done she handed me a little pocket mirror in Venetian crystal bordered with silver filigree and said: "How do you like it? Would you like to take me into your service as a valet de chambre?"

I was no longer the same, and I did not recognize myself. I did not resemble myself any more than a finished statue resembles a block of stone. I had the impression that my old face had only been a crude sketch of the one reflected in the mirror. I was handsome, and my vanity was sensibly tickled by that metamorphosis. Those elegant clothes, that rich embroidered jacket, made me an entirely different person, and I admired the power of a few ells of cloth tailored in a certain manner. The spirit of my costume penetrated my skin, and after ten minutes I was passably conceited.

I made a few tours of the room in order to put myself at ease. Clarimonde watched me with an air of maternal complaisance, and seemed very content with her work.

"That's enough childishness; let's go, my dear Romuald. We have a long way to go and we won't get there."

She took me by the hand and drew me away. All the doors opened before her as soon as she touched them, and we went past the dog without waking it.

At the door we found Margheritone; that was the groom that had conducted me before. He was holding the bridles of three horses as black as the others, one for me, one for him and one for Clarimonde. Those horses must have been Spanish genets born of mares fecundated by the zephyr, for they went as fast as the wind, and the moon, which had risen at our departure to light our way, was rolling in the sky like a wheel detached from its cart; we saw it to our right leaping from tree to tree and getting out of breath in order to run after us.

We soon arrived in a plain where, next to a clump of trees, a carriage was waiting for us, harnessed to four vigorous beasts; we climbed into it and the postillions made them take an insensate gallop. I had one arm around Clarimonde's waist and one of her hands folded in mine; she leaned her head on my shoulder and I felt her semi-naked cleavage brushing my arm. Never had I experienced such an intense happiness. I had forgotten everything at that moment, and I did not remember having been a priest any more than what I had done in my mother's womb, so great was the fascination that the evil spirit exercised upon me.

From that night on my nature was, in a sense, duplicated, and there were two men in me, one of whom did not know the other. Sometimes I thought I was a priest who dreamed every evening that he was a gentleman, sometimes a gentleman who dreamed that he was a priest. I could no longer distinguish the dream of the previous day, and I did not know where reality commenced and illusion ended. The conceited and libertine young man mocked the priest, the priest detested the dissolution of the young lord. Two spirals, entangled with one another and confounded without ever touching, represent very well the bicephalous life that was mine.

In spite of the strangeness of that situation, I do not believe that I touched madness for an instant. I always conserved very clearly the perceptions of my two existences. However, there was one absurd fact that I could not explain, which was that the sentiment of the same self existed in two such different men. That was an anomaly of which I could not take account, whether I believed that I was the curé of the little village of *** or *il signor Romualdo*, the lover in title of Clarimonde.

At any rate, I was—or at least believed that I was—in Venice; I have not yet been able fully to disentangle what was illusion and reality in that bizarre adventure. We lived in a grand marble palace on the Canaleio, full of frescos and statues, with two Titians of great days in Clarimonde's bedroom: a palace worthy of a king. We each had our gondola and our liveried singer of barcarolles, our music room and our poet. Clarimonde understood life in a grand manner, and there was a little of Cleopatra in her nature.

As for me, I led the life of a son of a prince and I kicked up dust as if I had been of the family of one of the twelve apostles or the four evangelists of the Most Serene Republic; I would not have turned aside from my route in order to let the doge pass, and I do not believe that, since Satan had fallen from Heaven, anyone had been prouder and more insolent than me. I went to the Rialto where I played an infernal game. I saw the best society in the world, the sons of ruined families, women of the theater, crooks, parasites and assassins for hire.

In spite of the dissipation of that life, however, I remained faithful to Clarimonde. I loved her madly. She would have reawakened satiety itself, and fixed inconstancy. To have Clarimonde was to have twenty mistresses, it was to have all women, so versatile was she, changing and dissimilar to herself: a true chameleon. She enabled you to commit with her the infidelity that you might have committed with others, by taking on completely the character, the manner and the genre of beauty of the woman who appeared to please you.

She rendered my amour a hundredfold, and it was in vain that young patricians and even the old men of the Council of Ten made her the most magnificent propositions. A Foscari went as far as proposing marriage to her; she refused everything. She had enough gold; she no longer wanted anything but amour, a young, pure amour awakened by her, which would be the first and the last.

I would have been perfectly happy but for an accursed nightmare that returned every night, in which I believed myself to be a village curé, mortifying myself and doing penance for my diurnal excesses. Reassured by the habitude of being with her, I hardly ever thought any longer about the strange fashion in which I had made Clarimonde's acquaintance. However, what Abbot Serapion had said about her sometimes returned to memory and did not leave without causing me anxiety.

For some time, Clarimonde's health had not been as good; her complexion deteriorated from day to day. The physicians who were summoned did not understand her malady and did not know what to do about it. They prescribed a few insignificant remedies and did not return. Meanwhile, she became visibly paler and gradually colder. She was almost as white and as dead as on the famous night in the unknown château. I was desolate to see her perishing slowly thus.

Touched by my dolor, she smiled at me tenderly and sadly, with the fatal smile of people who know that they are going to die.

One morning, I was sitting next to her bed, and having breakfast at a little table in order not to quit her for a minute. While slicing a fruit I chanced to inflict a rather deep cut on my finger. Blood immediately emerged in a crimson trickle, and a few drops fell upon Clarimonde.

Her eyes brightened, and her physiognomy took on an expression of ferocious and savage joy that I had never seen before. She leapt out of bed with an animal agility, the agility of a monkey or a cat, and pounced upon my wound, which she began sucking with an expression of unspeakable voluptuousness. She swallowed the blood in little sips, slowly and preciously, like a gourmet savoring a wine from Xeres or Syracuse; she half-closed her eyes, and the pupils of her green eyes became rectangular instead of round.

From time to time she interrupted herself in order to kiss my hand, and then she recommenced pressing her lips to the lips of the wound in order to make a few more red droplets emerge therefrom. When she saw that the blood was no longer coming, she raised her eyes again, humble and brilliant, rosier than a dawn in May, her face full, her hand warm and moist—in sum, more beautiful than ever and in a perfect state of health.

"I shan't die! I shan't die!" she said, half mad with joy, hanging from my neck. "I can love you for a long time yet. My life is in yours, and everything that I am comes from you. A few drops of your rich and noble blood, more precious and more efficacious than all the elixirs in the world, have rendered life to me."

That scene preoccupied me for a long time and inspired strange doubts in Clarimonde's regard; that very evening, when sleep returned me to my presbytery, I saw Abbot Serapion, graver and more careworn than ever. He looked at me attentively and said: "Not content with dooming your soul, you also want to lose your body. Unfortunate young man, into what trap have you fallen?"

The tone in which he pronounced those few words struck me vividly, but, in spite of its vivacity, the impression was soon dissipated, and a thousand cares effaced it from my mind.

One evening, however, I saw Clarimonde in my mirror, the perfidious position of which she had not calculated, pouring a powder into the cup of spiced wine that she had the custom of preparing after the meal. I took the cup, pretended to bear it to my lips, and I put it down on a table as if to finish it later at my leisure; then, taking advantage of a moment when the beauty's back was turned, I emptied its contents under the table—after which I returned to my room and went to bed, determined not to sleep and to see everything that happened.

I did not have long to wait. Clarimonde entered in a night-dress, and, having removed her veils, lay down in the bed beside me. When she was sure that I was asleep, she uncovered my arm and took a golden pin from her hair; then she started murmuring in a low voice:

"One drop, nothing but a little red drop, a ruby at the tip of my needle! Since you still love me, it's not necessary that I die. Oh, poor love, his beautiful blood, of such a bright crimson color, I shall drink it. Sleep, my only wealth; sleep, my god, my child; I shall not do you any harm, I shall only take as much of your life as is necessary for mine not to be extinguished. If I did not love you so much, I could resolve myself to having other lovers, whose veins I would drain, but since I have known you, I hold everyone else in horror . . . Oh, the beautiful arm! How round it is! How white it is! I would never dare to prick that pretty blue vein."

And while saying that, she wept, and I felt her tears dripping on to my arm, which she was holding in her hands. Finally, she made up her mind, made a little puncture with her needle, and started sucking the blood that flowed from it. Although she had only drunk a few drops, the dread of draining me gripped her; carefully, she surrounded my arm with a small bandage after having rubbed the wound with an unguent that caused it to scar immediately.

I could no longer have any doubt; Abbot Serapion was right. In spite of that certainty, however, I could not help loving Clarimonde, and I would gladly have given her all the blood she needed to sustain her artificial existence. In any case, I had no great fear; the woman answered to me for the vampire, and what I had heard and seen reassured me completely. I had lush veins then, which would not soon be exhausted, and I would not haggle over my life drop by drop. I would have opened my arm myself and said to her: "Drink! And may my amour infiltrate into your body with my blood!"

I avoided making the slightest allusion to the narcotic that she had poured for me and the scene of the

89

needle, and we lived in the most perfect accord. My priestly scruples, however, tormented me more than ever, and I did not know what new infliction to invent in order to master and mortify my flesh. Although all those visions were involuntary and I did not have any participation in them, I dared not touch the Christ with hands so impure and a spirit soiled by such debaucheries, real or imaginary.

In order to avoid falling into those fatiguing hallucination, I tried to prevent myself from sleeping. I held my eyelids open with my fingers and I remained standing against the wall, struggling against slumber with all my might; but the sand of somnolence soon fell into my eyes, and, seeing that all struggle was futile, I let my arms fall in discouragement and lassitude, and the current drew me back toward perfidious shores.

Serapion made me the most vehement exhortations, and reproached me harshly for my slackness and my lack of fervor. One day, when I had been more agitated than usual, he said to me: "In order to rid you of this obsession there is only one means, and, although it is extreme, it is necessary to employ it: great evils require great remedies. I know where Clarimonde has been buried; it is necessary for us to disinter her, and for you to see the pitiful state that the object of your amour is in; you will no longer be tempted to doom your soul for a filthy cadaver devoured by worms and ready to fall into dust; that will assuredly render you to yourself."

For myself, I was so fatigued by that double life that I accepted; wanting to know, once and for all, whether the priest or the gentleman was the dupe of an illusion, I had decided to kill, to the profit of one or the other, one of the two men who was within me, or to kill both of them, for such a life could not endure.

Abbot Serapion equipped himself with a pickax, a lever and a lantern, and at midnight we headed for the cemetery of ***, of which he knew the lie and the disposition perfectly. After having run the light of the muted lantern over several tombs, we eventually arrived at a stone half-hidden by long grass and devoured by moss and parasitic plants, on which we deciphered the commencement of an inscription:

Here lies Clarimonde
Who was when alive
The most beautiful woman in the world

. . . .

"This is it," said Serapion; and, placing his lantern on the ground, he slid the lever into the interstice of the stone and began to lift it up. The stone yielded, and he set to work with the pickax. I watched him do it, blacker and more silent than the night itself. As for him, bent over his funereal work, he was streaming with sweat; he was breathing heavily, and his hasty breath gave the impression of a death-rattle.

It was a strange spectacle, and anyone who had seen us would have taken us for profaners and thieves of shrouds rather than priests of God. Serapion's zeal had something harsh and savage about it, which made him resemble a demon rather than an apostle or an angel, and his face, with great austere features, profoundly outlined by the reflections of the lamplight, had nothing reassuring about it.

I felt a glacial sweat pearling on my limbs, and my hair was standing up dolorously on my head. Deep down I regarded the action of the severe Serapion as an abominable sacrilege, and I would have liked a bolt of lightning to emerge from the somber clouds that were rolling heavily overhead and reduce him to dust. The owls perched in the cypresses, disturbed by the light of the lantern, came to whip the glass heavily with their dusty wings, uttering plaintive moans; foxes were yapping in the distance, and a thousand sinister sounds emerged from the silence.

Finally, Serapion's pick collided with the coffin, the planks of which resounded with a dull and sonorous noise, the terrible noise than annihilates when one touches it. He tipped back the lid, and I perceived Clarimonde, as pale as marble, her hands joined; her white shroud only made a single pleat from her head to her feet. A little red droplet glistened like a rose in the corner of her colorless mouth.

At that sight, Serapion entered into a fury. "Ah! There you are, demon, indecent courtesan, drinker of blood and gold!" And he sprinkled the corpse and the coffin with holy water, tracing the form of a cross with his aspergillum.

Poor Clarimonde had no sooner been touched by the holy dew than her beautiful body fell into dust; she was no longer anything but a frightful formless mass of ash and semi-calcined bones.

"Behold your mistress, Seigneur Romuald," said the inexorable priest, showing me those sad remains. "Will you still be tempted to walk at the Lido and at Fusine with your beauty?"

I lowered my head; a great ruination had just been effected inside me. I returned to my presbytery, and Seigneur Romuald, Clarimonde's lover, was separated from the poor priest with whom he had kept such strange company for such a long time—except that the following night, I saw Clarimonde; she spoke to me, as she had the first time under the portal of the church.

"Wretch! Wretch, what have you done? Why did you listen to that imbecile priest? Were you not happy? And what have I done to you, for my poor tomb to be violated and the misery of my annihilation laid bare? All communication between our souls and our bodies is broken henceforth. Adieu; you will regret my loss."

She dissipated in the air like smoke, and I never saw her again.

Alas, what she said was true. I regretted her loss more than once, and I regret it still. The peace of my soul has been dearly bought; the love of God was not enough to replace hers.

That, Brother, is the story of my youth. Never gaze at a woman, and always walk with your eyes fixed on the ground, for, chaste and calm as you are, it only requires a minute for you to lose eternity.

THE WILLIS

by Alphonse Karr

A T the end of an autumn day, outside the house of the guard general Wilhelm Gulf, young women and men were waltzing joyfully; one young man was playing a violin, another the horn. The forest became even more silent; a light wind that had made the foliage stir from time to time had ceased to agitate the trees; the sun only left a crimson reflection on the horizon at present, which still illuminated the clearing in which people were dancing obliquely, and colored the faces of the dancers with a vivid roseate tint.

After a waltz finished, Anna Gulf spoke out. "It isn't just," she said, "that poor Henry should spend all evening blowing into his horn, without waltzing at least once. Conrad can play alone for a while, and Henry can take part in the dance."

"And to recompense the fatigue that he's acquired in enabling us to waltz," added the pretty Genevieve, "we'll declare that, to the scorn of all engagements made in advance, he has the right to choose whichever one of us appears to him to be the most beautiful, and to waltz with her twice in succession."

Anna Gulf became utterly tremulous. She was to marry Henry; it was a project formed a long time ago between the two families; but Henry, thus far, had almost never seemed to distinguish the daughter of the general of the guard.

Anna Gulf loved Henry. Who would not have loved him? He was the handsomest and the best young man in the region; there was no hunter more adroit or more audacious; the prince had promised to raise him to the rank of guard general as soon as his father-in-law had resigned, when he was married.

For her part, Anna was a good and pretty girl, who had been at the head of the general's household since the death of her mother had left him a widower with two children, Anna and Conrad. No other house appeared as clean and well-kept; not one, with a limited income, offered such an appearance of ease and good fortune. Anna was the idol of her father and her brother; they called her their good angel, and she had, in fact, something of the angels about her: her body was slender and flexible, her pretty face a trifle pale, her long black hair secured in a headband over her brow, and her dark blue eyes full of tenderness and melancholy seemed, by virtue of a secret instinct, to foresee that Anna Gulf, angel of heaven, had only been lent to the earth, and that, after having given life and wellbeing to everything that surrounded her, like a beneficent dew, she would spread her wings and return to her celestial homeland, leaving in the hearts of those who had loved her the bitterness that seems to be a necessary condition of any human happiness.

Without hesitation, Henry came to take Anna's hand; her heart was scarcely beating, so much was it oppressed by dread and pleasure. Conrad made his bow resonate, playing a waltz that Henry had composed, and the waltzers set forth.

But the moon was beginning to rise behind the trees, and its white light appeared above their summits. At that moment there was so much calm and so much solemnity in the meditation of nature that people ceased waltzing and, moving closer to the door of the house, where old Gulf was smoking tranquilly while watching the young folk, all the dancers yielded to a graver and more intimate conversation.

Suddenly, Henry and Anna, who had remained in the rear, approached the old man, and Henry said to him: "Father, we love one another, give us your blessing." Both of them knelt down. Wilhelm Gulf blessed them and requested on their behalf the most powerful benedictions of heaven.

Conrad came to shake Henry's hand. Henry gave Anna Gulf a bouquet of heather that he was holding in his hand. Anna went into the house abruptly, and took refuge in her room, where she was able to give free rein to the tears of joy that were choking her. From that day on they were promised to one another, and people occupied themselves with the preparations for the marriage.

But one day, Henry arrived at the general's house somber and sad, and showed him a crumpled letter that he had received; an uncle dying in Mayence had asked him to come and close his eyes.

Anna said to him: "Don't forget me, and come back very quickly." She did not say another word, for she had begged him not to go; that news had squeezed her heart; the darkest thoughts presented themselves in a host to her imagination. Happiness is such a fragile thing; there is so little of it reserved for human beings that it cannot help but seem, always, to be taken from the share of others; one hides it like a thief in order to enjoy it, and only dares to be happy in a whisper.

Father Gulf received the news without emotion. He said to Henry: "Bon voyage, my son, and come back to me as soon as you have decently acquitted the duties that nature imposes on you. When are you leaving?"

"I'll leave tonight," said Henry, "in order to join the coach that passes along the road eight leagues from here tomorrow morning."

"Take your carbine," added the old man.

At midnight, in fact, Henry set forth, with his knapsack on his back and his rifle under his arm. He made a detour, because, being obliged to quit the locale, he wanted to see Anna's house one last time, and the glimmer of the nightlight that was burning in her bedroom.

As he approached it, he plucked a few sprigs of white heather and wove a wreath with them, to hang on his beloved's window. Gently, he parted the branches of the hazel trees that surrounded the house and placed the wreath; through the curtains, the nightlight illuminated the little room with a mysterious glow. Henry broke a branch from the hazel trees that touched the window most closely, and took it with him.

Then he drew away slowly, sometimes looking back; he paused for some time at the place where the bend in the path was about to hide the moonlit path, and then disappeared.

The following morning, as soon as the sun slid its first roseate rays into the little room, Anna opened her window; her hair was in disorder and her dress was crumpled; she had wept all evening, and had been lulled to sleep by lassitude, without undressing. She found the white wreath, raised it to her lips and pressed it against her heart.

At each relay, Henry sent a letter, but whatever his chagrin was, the bitterness of absence is greater for the one who remains behind, and in very little time Anna lost the rosy tint from her face. A moment came when the letters became rarer, and then no more were received at all. Anna did not complain, but her cheeks and her eyes hollowed out, and she wept in silence in her room. She became somber and grim, and even fled the society of her father and her brother Conrad.

Eventually, she fell very ill. Conrad had written to Henry four times without receiving any response. One morning, he departed for Mayence.

Two months later he returned on a cart, pale and wounded. A few days after that, he died, killed by Henry.

This is what had happened.

On arriving in Mayence, the uncle had proved to be less ill than Henry expected. Henry's resemblance to his father had filled that relative with joy, who attributed his imminent convalescence to the arrival of his nephew. That uncle was very rich, and of his numerous children, the only one that remained to him was a very beautiful daughter whom he imagined marrying to Henry. The latter dared not refuse at first, asked for time to obtain the consent of his mother and wrote to her asking her to refuse it; but in the time that the response took to arrive, he became habituated to his cousin and her fortune, and he was not a little delighted, instead of the letter he had asked his mother to write, to receive one in which she depicted all the advantages of the union that he ought to contract.

In the midst of the pleasures of a great city, he contrived to forget Anna, and to regard the sacred engagement that he had made with her as a childish game that a reasonable man ought to renounce.

Conrad had arrived on the day of Henry's marriage to his cousin; he had made sharp reproaches to his former friend and, exasperated by being unable to change his mind by means of the depiction of the sadness and sufferings of his sister, he had insulted and provoked him in public. They had fought, and Henry had struck him with his sword.

Anna did not weep, but her tears fell back upon her heart and burned it. From that moment on she devoted herself entirely to caring for Father Gulf, who was very downcast since the death of his son, and to prayer. Prayer is the refuge of the unhappy; it is a last support when all other supports and broken; it is a sacred link between humans and the divinity.

Henry found himself master of a large fortune and the husband of the prettiest young woman in the city of Mayence; everything was new for him in the life of luxury and pleasure that he led in the city. A year after his marriage, however, his father-in-law died and his wife, newly a mother, wanted to retire to the country for a while. Henry bought a country house a few leagues from the abode of Father Gulf, and spent the entire summer there. During that time, Anna completed her extinction and died without any apparent dolor; she was buried with the white wreath that Henry had attached to her window on the night of her departure.

One evening, as Henry was returning from a long hunting party, he went astray in the forest and could not imagine any better means of recovering his route than to find his mother's house; from there it would be easy to get his bearings. The first half of his life had been spent in that part of the forest, and there was no path, however small, that was unknown to him.

It was necessary to pass by the house where old Gulf remained alone with an old maidservant. It was another beautiful autumn evening, the light of the sun was once again illuminating the clearing obliquely. Henry sighed and increased his pace; he would have walked even more rapidly if he had been able to hear the old man who was up late, praying for his son and his daughter, and saying: "Henry, Henry, you who have killed my two children, be accursed!"

The forest was more silent and more mysterious than ever. In the path that Henry was following, it became darker and denser at every moment; the moon scarcely slid a pale and furtive ray of light through the branches from time to time; in vain Henry tried to chase away the painful impressions that were reawakened in his mind; in vain he recalled his wife, his child and all the pleasures that surrounded him; the memory of Anna and the days of his love for her, so happy and so pure, threw a funeral crepe over all his other thoughts.

At moments, a light wind brought from afar the perfume of honeysuckle flowering in the forest; as he continued marching, it seemed to him that the wind also brought, in gusts, a few vague and singular measures of a song that was not unknown to him.

He went on, but stopped suddenly, shivering.

It required an extraordinary danger to make Henry, the bravest of the hunters of that forest, tremble thus; and yet, he did not load his rifle, for what had frightened him had nothing human about it; it was a few quite distinct measures of the waltz that he had once composed, and which Conrad had played, on the day when old Gulf had blessed Henry and his daughter.

He made the sign of the cross, and advanced.

Then he no longer lost anything of the songs: they were the voices of women, pure, suave, fugitive voices. He stopped and held his breath in order to listen. It was still the waltz that was being sung, and the friction of measured footsteps was also audible, but so light and so faint that no human foot could have produced anything similar.

His hair was bristling on his head; his legs were buckling beneath him; nevertheless, he went forward, still listening. Words were being sung; they were words that he remembered having composed himself for that tune, on the night when he had gone away from Anna. He had never told them to anyone, and yet they were being sung:

> *For a few moments, the deserted forest*
> *Becomes for me alone a rich and splendid palace;*
> *The leafy oak forms a green tent*
> *And we are two beneath that cool and perfumed roof.*

Proud sign of sovereign grandeur
Red turban folded over the head of kings,
No, you do not have the gleam of the ebon tresses
That crown her forehead, which my fingers braid.

I have often seen, at fêtes less fine,
Shining in a dark-eyed woman's hair,
Diamonds with vivid glints
Like stars in the somber evening sky.

And I prefer the desiccated wild rose
With which her hair was bound all day,
And I prefer the moss still depressed
Whose velvet keeps the imprint of her feet.

Those words, devised by Henry on his route, had never been written down; he had all but forgotten them himself, but he heard them without the singer mistaking a single word. He took a few more paces, and at a bend in the path, he found a clearing surrounded by tall chestnut trees and mysteriously illuminated by the moon.

He stepped into a bush, and was able to contemplate a strange spectacle. Young women, clad in white robes and crowned with flowers, were waltzing and singing on the moss; but their white robes were whiter than any fabric ever seen, and their floral crowns seemed luminous; their footsteps were so light that it was impossible to tell whether they were really touching the ground; their suave and mysterious voices did not appear to be hindered at all by the movement of the waltz; their faces, above all, had a frightful pallor.

Henry then recalled the tradition of the round-dance of the willis,[1] young women abandoned by those to whom they were promised and who had died unwed, who danced with one another by night, by moonlight, in the woods. The waltz stopped for a moment, and Henry heard the beating of his heart. A few moments passed in the readjustment of the floral crowns, and then the song was resumed: and it was still Henry's waltz that was being sung.

The white women enlaced one another, two by two, for the waltz; one remained alone and cast a long glance around in search of a companion; her figure was supple and slender; her black hair was held by a headband above her brow; her dark blue eyes had a tender and melancholy gaze; she was crowned with white heather.

It was Anna.

Henry thought that he was going to die.

Anna advanced toward the bush in which Henry was hiding, and took him by the hand. Anna's hand was as cold as marble. Henry did not have the strength to follow her, but a supernatural power carried him.

They sang; the waltz recommenced, and Henry, still drawn involuntarily, waltzed with his fiancée.

---

1 The legend Karr has in mind is that of the Slavic version of Greek nymphs, more often known as *vila*, although the spellings *wilis* or *wiles* are also found in Slavic languages. They are ghostly females who play the role of temptresses sometimes attributed to fays of the supernatural variety, and are fond of dancing. They were popularized in French consciousness by Adoph Adam's ballet *Giselle* (1841), based on a prose interlude in a poem by Heinrich Heine which stresses their alleged vampiric tendencies, making them more closely akin to lamias. Puccini's *Le Villi* (1884) is a later ballet based on the same source.

Then another phantom came to take Henry, and waltzed with him in her turn; that one was succeeded by a third, and then a fourth. Henry was worn out; cold sweat was trickling over his forehead, and he was as pale as the dead.

A fifth dead woman took him, and then a sixth, and, the movement of the waltz always accelerating, the exhausted Henry, half-dead as much from fatigue as fear, wanted to let himself fall on to the grass, but he could not do it; an invincible force drew him away, and he waltzed on.

The air could no longer enter or exit his lungs; he was stifling; he tried to cry out, but he had no voice. Then Anna took him again in her turn, and the movement of the waltz was accelerated again; but Henry sensed that the white robe was no longer filled by anything but the bones of a skeleton; Anna's hand, placed on his shoulder, entered into his flesh. He looked at her; she no longer had her black hair in a headband; he could no longer see anything but a hideous skull, still crowned by white heather.

He struggled, and the phantom hugged him in its arms, and dragged him into a waltz movement, the rapidity of which nothing can give any idea . . .

The next day, Henry's cadaver was found in the forest.

AN OLD STORY

by Charles Barbara

". . . A month later, they were married. *Finis coronat opus.*[1] The wedding celebrations lasted a week . . . And bring on the violins!" cried Prosper, out of breath, throwing his manuscript on the table.

That manner of concluding a tale made some smile and scandalized others. Anselme, whose turn had come to amuse or bore the circle, as they might wish, put an end to the scandal with this beginning:

As might happen to anyone, I returned from a voyage. I was welcomed with an item of news that made me prick up my ears. During my absence, a tenant of the house, a young man, had hanged himself from his window, and that because of a woman who was almost my neighbor. I had some difficulty at first in remembering the young man, a Monsieur Paul, it was said, a chubby

---

1 "The end crowns the work," traditionally attributed to Ovid.

young man whom a word succeeded in rendering red in the face. As for the woman, Madame Clémence, by an ironic hazard, I remembered very well having crossed paths with her frequently on the stairway, and even having remarked more than once her bright eyes, her dark hair, her shoulders, her stature, and her youthful and cheerful expression . . .

That denouement, not only tragic but also singular, would have stimulated the most dormant curiosity. The house, at the corner of a square and a street, had five stories. The wall of the last two, slightly oblique in order to facilitate the flow of water, was covered with slates. At intervals, one of the iron hooks emerged from it that serve to attach the scaffolds of roofers. It was from one of those crampons, solidly sealed into the woodwork, that the young man had hanged himself, during the night. From my apartment, without a support bar, by reaching out with my arm, I could have touched that hook. It was to my right, a little below me, between one of Madame Clémence's windows and that of the room occupied by young Paul.

The difficulty alone of suspending oneself from it caused a shiver. He must first have passed the rope around his neck, then successively climbed out of his widow, walked along a very narrow lead gutter, reached the hook by standing up on tiptoe, hoisted himself up to a certain height by the strength of his wrists, maintaining himself in that position with one hand, and fixing the loose end of the rope to the curved iron with the other, and then let go. Was that not fabulous? What a steady gaze, what sang-froid, it must have required! A slightly bigger man would not have been able to hang himself. The death of the unfortunate fellow had only depended on a few inches.

Who knows? Without that hook, perhaps he would never have thought of suicide. The traces of his feet were still visible on the wall, and the broken slates that testified to the efforts of his death-throes, were still in the gutter . . .

I had not ceased to be importuned by the desire to know the story of that catastrophe when, one morning, I saw Madame Clémence come into my apartment. I was all the more surprised because that lady, until then, had hardly seemed concerned to make my acquaintance. The day before, between eleven o'clock and midnight, I had found her, all dressed up, chatting on the first steps of the staircase with the sergeant-major of a line regiment. I cannot describe the extent to which I was amazed. She had moved aside to let me pass and had returned my greeting while studying my expression slyly . . .

Her presence caused me a considerable disturbance.

"My God, Monsieur," she said, in a wheedling tone, "I've come to ask you if you'd be good enough to write a letter for me."

I had no sooner replied affirmatively than she sat down, took a letter out of her pocket, and added; "But first, I beg you to reread this letter for me, because I can't read very well, especially not handwriting."

It was only then that I perceived her drawling and common accent. Under the elegant exterior of the woman, I discovered a Norman peasant.

The letter, three pages of stilted writing in a grotesque style, unsteady in its orthography, of mediocre interest, in sum, was from the sergeant-major whose mature age, enormous moustache and chevron I had clearly remarked the day before. I no longer remember very clearly what it contained, except that there were charges laid at full tilt against the bourgeoisie, which collided with protestations of amour, making a noise comparable to that of twenty sabers clashing, and in the middle, a proposal of marriage resounded like a cannon shot.

I also know that, at that proposal of marriage, Madame Clémence, who was listening with the most serious expression, burst out laughing. I asked her what response she desired me to make. "Anything you like," she said, with vivacity, "provided that I never see him again. The monsieur has lost his head. Can you see me as a camp follower? It's quite enough to have had dinner with him. If *Monsieur* learned that I had had dealings with a soldier, he wouldn't be pleased, for sure."

We chatted, and in response to my plea, she explained to me how she had met the sergeant-major.

"I have a friend," she said, "whose suitor is in the regiment. They invited me to dinner and I found that sergeant with them, who seemed at first to be very amiable. He paid court to me and escorted me back to my door in the evening. I didn't know how to get rid of him. He never finished telling me stories and swearing that he adored me. I was bored to death, asleep standing up, when you saw us together. That's it."

The response that I promised Madame Clémence required another visit the following day. I had no need of any pretext to retain her; she sat down and talked to me about herself without being asked, with a complete abandon. She told me that *Monsieur* was a tall, stout man of thirty-eight who, in addition to a personal fortune and great expectations in regard to his mother, also received five or six thousand francs as a professor in a faculté. He was mad about her and gave her everything in profusion. With a view to distracting her and teaching her about society, which he was keen to do, he had taken her to respectable houses several times, but she had shown herself so gauche, and had committed so many gaffes, that he had been obliged to renounce that system of education. He had demanded that she take lessons in French, dancing and music, and had, to that effect, bought a piano. It was as much sterile expense; by her own admission, she did not understand anything; she was too stupid. *Monsieur*'s mother, very proud of her son, was thinking of marrying him off, but she, Clémence, would not hear of it. At the first rumor of a marriage, she had decided to make a scandal such that its conclusion would become impossible.

While listening to her, I got up to close the window, because the noise of carriages sometimes prevented me from hearing her. She stopped me. "Leave it open," she said. "If everything were closed, your neighbor would be able to hear what we're saying."

Encouraged by that benevolence, I tried to broach the subject of her amours with Paul. Her obstinacy in not understanding my allusions to that subject ended up making me impatient. At the risk of appearing brutal, I took her by the hand and tried to draw her to the window with the objective of placing the nail before her eyes. I don't know how it happened, but she divined my intention.

"Oh," she said, recoiling in a fearful manner, "what horror!"

I had a fit of repentance.

"I see what it is," she added. "Someone has told you that frightful story."

"Yes," I said, "but in passing. I'd like to have more details."

"Another time, we'll see," said Madame Clémence. "For now, close the window."

She was standing up and had resolved to go.

"You didn't want that just now," I observed.

"I want it now," she replied, going toward the door.

"What harm can it do you?" I said.

She became extremely animated. "What!" she cried. "You don't know that I've had my window on that side sealed up! You don't know that I feel ill and have attacks of nerves simply on looking at that hook."

I closed my window.

That awkwardness did not prevent Madame Clémence from making me regular visits of a sort from that day on. I was scarcely any further forward. She eluded my questions, or replied with impatience that I knew everything, that she had nothing new to tell me. On the other hand, about herself, her past and her family, she never shut up.

She came from Normandy, where there are so many beautiful women and magnificent blood. She was the eldest of three daughters of a worthy man who made full value of a small farm of which he was the tenant, in the vicinity of Caen. Decried in her village because of a few adventures, she had come to seek her fortune in Paris. From time to time, in order that she would be remembered, she sent money to her father and gifts to her sisters. They, moreover, came to see her once a year. For a fortnight, she gorged them with pleasures and then sent them back charged with all the toilette items capable of flattering their taste. So, not content with sending her baskets of big red apples for the winter, her younger sisters had created a reputation for her in the region of supernatural beauty, and it was necessary to admit that she was provided, with a fabulous luxury, with everything that could excuse such an enthusiasm. Her splendid hair would have been a burden for a frail woman. Thick eyebrows designed a dark and expressive line above her dark eyes. Her pallor did not prevent her from being fresh. She had the most beautiful teeth in the world; her body seemed as firm as marble; her feet were well made and not too large, a notable thing in a girl who had been brought up in the fields. In addition to that, she had an instinct for dresses that suited her as sitting on eggs suited a chicken.

By dint of looking at the woman, I had come to dream about her often. I recognized her footsteps by my sudden palpitations. If a day went by without her coming, I experienced a profound ennui, but, curiously enough, as soon as she was present, I became preoccupied and sad.

She questioned me about that sadness. I responded evasively. I no longer talked to her about young Paul, at first out of lassitude, and then because of personal sentiments that absorbed me. It was at one of those times that Madame Clémence, to my great surprise, told me at length a story that I had requested fruitlessly many times. My curiosity had tied her tongue, it seemed that my indifference had loosened it.

At this point, Prosper, who was thought to be asleep, suddenly repeated, in a low voice, the unsuitable exclamation with which he had concluded his own story. All eyes turned in his direction. Several people raised their voices at the same time to reproach him. Once again, Anselme drowned out the rumor by resuming his reading thus:

By combining her story with what I had learned elsewhere, I understood the drama precisely as if it had passed before my eyes. I had succeeded in recovering from my memory the exact image of the young man. He was of medium height and somewhat replete. Twenty years of life had not yet affected the vivid red of his cheeks. Chestnut hair, long and neglected, was turned up over his nape like a bird's tail. His blue-gray eyes, buried under ever-lowered eyelids, rarely dared look anyone in the face, and his humble manner and the sadness of his garments bore the indelible imprints that seminary life engraves on every individual.

With a view to utilizing the time that separated him from the age when he would be able to purchase an advocate's office, he had come to Paris to study law. Devoid of friends and relationships, reluctant in addition to make any, by virtue of taciturnity and mistrust, he lived in a complete isolation and scarcely appeared to suspect that women, cafés, dance-halls and theaters existed. He did not love anything in the world profoundly except for his mother, an aged widow with a heart of gold, whose unique weakness he caressed by means of heroic economies and weekly reports of his expenditure. His neighbor, whom he encountered every day, seemed not to exist for him. He paid no heed to her.

That was not to the liking of the young woman, who was offended by the indifference of a young man bursting with health, who edified and embalmed the entire house, so to speak, by virtue of his tranquil life and his laborious habits. She had taken it into her head to force his attention. She succeeded only too well in that. Her beauty and her bold and provocative gaze inundated the young man's breast with disturbance, where a profound and incurable amour soon germinated.

But Clémence had to struggle against prejudices all the more tenacious because they grew roots of a new and robust nature. Timidity and ignorance immured the mind of the student more fully than his eyelids veiled his eyes. He had formed of women, whom he judged by his mother, an idea so noble and so elevated that he could not think of his unworthiness without blushing. His neighbor finished crushing him under the prestige of a pitiless coquetry. He was obstinate in believing her to have a nature far superior to his own.

Although he allowed amour to grow within him and enabled it to prosper in his dreams, it was without hope. Passion, which is almost a law, multiplied his pusillanimity tenfold and dictated fashions of acting to him that one might have thought inspired by hatred. If Clémence jogged his elbow in passing, he turned his head away; if she greeted him in a loud voice he turned a deaf ear; if, by chance, she saw him in the concierge's lodge and went in, he picked up his hat and escaped, with an abruptness that bordered on impoliteness.

The extravagance of his conduct, which she could not explain, would inevitably have put her off, if she had not had the presentiment of new and keen pleasures in the education of the young savage. Her stubbornness increased by reason of the obstinacy of her neighbor. Bold in her weakness, she knocked on his door and solicited insignificant services. Under the pretext of thanking him, she went into his room and hung on there with the aid of a conversation of which she bore the expense. At other times, she drew him into her apartment, where she kept him prisoner for entire hours. The student kept his head down and his eyes lowered, like a wolf trapped in a ditch. Clémence teased him about his girlish mannerisms, and reproached him for living like a bear—and for hating women, with whom she set out to reconcile him.

All of that turned the young man's head. He began to open his eyes wide and to go away pensive. The significance of those provocations began to penetrate his mind. It was only an imperceptible glimmer, but that gleam, like a drop of oil on a piece of cloth, spread so rapidly that it invaded his entire body.

To be loved by her—him! He had transports in his brain and nearly went mad. The shock that he felt is more easily conceivable because the blood was burning in his veins, his calm attitude hid a passionate soul, and it was his first amour. Clémence, by that time, could read his heart more easily than a book. Fatigued by three months of the comedy and resolved to end it, she finally extracted from his soul the secret of his passion, and then mocked him because he had not divined sooner that she also loved him . . .

An inexpressible happiness, dolorous by virtue of being intense, filled the student's days. His physiognomy took on an entirely new expression. He was incessantly penetrated by such joy that his entire body was radiant. The beauty of his mistress maintained a perpetual hearth of enthusiasm within him. He had surges of passion of a stunning impetuosity. Inexhaustible follies, of which Clémence did not sense the facility, emerged from his lips, electrified by the fire of embraces. The poor fellow had alienated all the treasures of his soul to her, exclusively and irrevocably. More taciturn than ever with strangers, even his filial love descended rapidly to the level of a banal respect. His mother's letters importuned him; he no longer had time to read them; he did not reply to them. He had even lost the memory of the good woman's weaknesses, or, at least, those weaknesses no longer appeared to merit anything but disdain, for at present, he spent more money in a month than he previously had in a year.

That rapid analysis, I ought to warn you, only exists in view of a denouement that, in the very old and ever-new story of the affinity of men of soul for statues in living flesh, only offers curious particularities. The student's amour was bound to follow the irresistible slope of these abnormal passions. Already, that amour, which was desiccating within him the roots of his oldest affections, no longer had the security of the first days. Jealous and umbrageous, he was alarmed by trivia, and

Clémence did not always take the trouble to reassure him. So, for fear of losing her, or merely of seeing her cool, he exhausted all the resources he judged to be capable of attaching her to him.

A new eccentricity of intention or action marked each of his days. For instance, he wanted to realize his fortune and go to live with his beloved mistress in a forgotten corner of the world. Clémence smiled. Another time, in a paroxysm of excitement, he proposed resolutely that they die in one another's arms. The woman frowned and became icy. Paul, in despair at having saddened her, accused her of having no soul and offered nothing less than to jump out of the window in order to rid her of him. She only succeeded in calming him down by composing a laughing face.

To complete the measure, he nearly killed himself in front of her one day. They were having breakfast together. The young man, playing with his knife, affirmed that he would wound himself if she demanded that proof of his amour. She challenged him to do it, as a joke, and he stabbed himself in the chest. Clémence, frightened by the blood that was flowing from the wound, nearly fell backwards. She ran to fetch a doctor, who, after inspecting the wound, declared that a rib had fortunately caused the blade to deviate.

Such scenes went directly contrary to the student's objective. Clémence, very pleased in the beginning to inspire such an exclusive passion, did not take long to weary of it as a yoke. She was already seized by fits of ennui that she was unable to overcome. Paul reproached her for them as the equivalent of a crime. That was the point of departure of endless quarrels, which exasperated the woman and increased her distaste. She did not fail, on such occasions, to exaggerate the expression of her repugnance. The young man's passionate transport soon buckled under that implacability. He fell to his knees and begged for mercy. His pallor, his tearful eyes, and the irresistible eloquence that his passion produced, triumphed again over the rigors of his mistress.

It was in the aftermath of one of those reconciliations that he threatened her with a horrible vengeance. Beside one another at the window they were gazing vaguely into the street. Raising his eyes, Paul suddenly perceived the iron crampon that projected between Clémence's window and his own. He indicated it to his mistress with his finger and said, in an energetic tone: "You see that nail . . . well, if the time comes when you no longer love me, I swear to hang myself from it, in order that, when you open your window in the morning, you'll find me dead."

"That threat made me laugh out loud," Madame Clémence added. "However, I was paid for knowing it . . ."

Their sentiments with regard to one another had not ceased to be modified in an inverse direction, to the extent that one could say that the temperature of the woman's heart descended to zero while the student's rose to boiling point. The result of that was that Paul, without being more exigent than in the beginning, appeared to be excessively demanding. Twenty times she had warned him, refusing the door to *Monsieur* of her own accord. Presently, she took no account of a pretention that she could not even imagine. It was the jealousy of a young man who had previously amused

117

her, but of whom she could not now even bear the appearance.

She told me that with a naïve cynicism that chilled me to the bone. "Oh, God in Heaven, I have no reproaches to make to myself. I loved him for three months as much as possible. By virtue of no longer quitting me, any more than my shadow, he ended up being taken in horror. I was bored, I had the desire to yawn; it made me feel ill. If I tried to talk reason to him, there were cries, tears and nervous twitches, just like a cat that has eaten arsenic pellets. I was wasting my time. I was a thousand feet over his head, and all those stupidities, I ask you, what do they mean? What's the point of hurting oneself? Because a woman no longer loves you! Love is like nails, one drives out another. Then again, I don't know how many times I annoyed *Monsieur*, who ended up having doubts about my relationship with Paul. Imagine, monsieur, if I'd lost my estate! I couldn't, however, be unfortunate for him!"

For a long time already, Madame Clémence had been slyly meditating introducing a new actor on to the stage. As a prelude to that *coup d'état* she closed her door to the student from time to time. Unable to recover the key that she had confided to him, she drew the bolts, and Paul, in spite of the scandal with which he filled the house, in spite of passionate letters, eloquent merely by virtue of the tears with which they were stained, could not always succeed in opening it. From her alcove she heard him sobbing or writhing in convulsions, or proffering death threats against her. It was no longer sufficient to have an aversion for him; now she was afraid of him and thought seriously about assuring herself of a solid arm, in view of the violence she thought she had to fear.

Long before knowing Paul, she assured me, she had not ceased to have a penchant for the artiste who enjoyed the exclusive privilege of dressing her hair. For some time she had been going to see him more frequently than usual. He was a fellow of twenty-eight, tall and robust, with a fresh and pretty face, always well groomed and perfumed. His name was Achille. His sign bore a Greek translation of his name and profession, because a few Hellenes were shaved in his establishment. He was implacably cheerful. His quips and puns made Madame Clémence roar with laughter. The attraction she felt toward the fellow developed rapidly under the influence of the ennui and fear that Paul caused her.

It did not take long for her to have in hand something analogous to those scarecrows that are used to frighten birds. The devotion of the hairdresser could not be put in doubt. However, what had more charm for him than anything else in the adventure was having the opportunity, knowing Latin as well as Greek, to parody Caesar's saying: *Veni, vidi, vici.*

From then on, Clémence broke entirely with the student and refused obstinately to receive him. In vain he begged her, spent nights at her door, wrote her ardent letters; she remained inflexible. Paul was drowning in tears; he was as fleshless as an old man; his hollow eyes had a strange fixity, and momentary flashes that presaged something terrible . . .

❋

At this point, the incorrigible Prosper put the lid on his impertinence with an ambiguous observation that revolted people of the most moderate character. A grave man told him hotly that no one was forcing him to listen to the reading, which was tantamount to telling him that he ought to keep quiet or go away. Sensible to the reprimand, Prosper did not say another word, and Anselme finished his story in the midst of the utmost calm.

The student put himself incessantly in the path of his mistress. Clémence, no longer daring to go home alone, had herself escorted by Monsieur Achille, who, with an air of sovereign scorn, limited himself to pushing his rival aside with his hand.

One evening, Paul changed tactics. In the absence of his mistress, instead of waiting for her on the landing, he penetrated into her apartment with the aid of the key that he was obstinate in retaining, and hid in a closet next to the alcove. It would be difficult to specify his motive, unless he hoped to find himself alone with Clémence and, in that case, to extract a little pity from her. Previously, he had gone downstairs to give the concierge a letter for Madame Clémence.

At about eleven o'clock, from the place where he was, the young man must have heard the footsteps of his mistress. Unfortunately, as usual, she was returning home accompanied by the hairdresser. She was holding Paul's letter in her hand. Glad not to have encountered the student at her door, she said to Monsieur Achille:

"It's another letter from the madman; read it to me. We'll have a good laugh . . ."

She lay down. Monsieur Achille sat down next to the bed and opened the letter.

"In all my life," Clémence said to me. "I had never heard anything so extravagant . . . I didn't know he was there . . . I laughed like a lunatic, especially because of Achille's comical remarks. I'm sure, Monsieur, that you would have done the same."

I asked Madame Clémence abruptly if, by chance, she still had that letter.

"I think so, yes," she replied. "Are you really curious to see it?"

"Very curious, I swear to you," I said.

"Wait," she said. "I'll go down and fetch it for you."

She soon came up again and said: "Here, read it yourself and see whether I'm not right . . ."

Very slowly, because tears had dampened the ink in a number of places, I deciphered this letter:

> *I have a body full of tears. Sobs are stifling me. The warm and bitter tears that are falling in large drops on my fingers, would hollow out stone but have no effect on your heart. You no longer want to see me or speak to me; you hate me. I could die without extracting a tear from you; perhaps my death would give you pleasure. But was it me who sought you out? Why did you not leave me to my mother, to my books? Who jogged my elbow? Who said to me:* Look at me? *Who said to me:* Love me, I love you? *Who lit*

the inferno in my breast? Who poured the poison into my veins? Who stifled my filial sentiments? Who riveted me to a woman, so firmly that I can no longer think about anything else? Who has absorbed, devoured, annihilated me? I find you strange. You grip like a vice my limbs, my mind, my will, my soul, and you say: Let me go. *You have covered me with an incurable leprosy and you say:* Get rid of it. *Do you imagine that I can fold my arms, that I can stiffen myself against the invasion of evil? Do you think, then, that it is so sweet to love you? It would be necessary to know you less. I have only stirred the mud in your soul, I have only displeased you by opposing your crapulous habits; morally, you are more a monster than a woman. I am scorned because of this amour, and rightly so. If misfortune overtakes me, they will say*: That's good; why love such a creature? Why did he not reject that infamous amour? *They speak about it at their ease. They blush for me, and they do not know that I blush even more for myself, that the scorn in which I hold myself only equals in depth and extent my monstrous passion. Amour is not a coat that one puts on and takes off at will. I would soon have uprooted it and trampled it underfoot. It is a coat of flame stuck to my skin; the shreds that I tear off are full of my flesh and my blood, and my body is no longer anything but a wound. I have at least the right to pity. I did not have much, but I have given you everything. What have I harvested from that? Endless tortures. The further I go, the more I suffer. It seems that the saying was made for me:* Either suffer, or die. *I spend nights at your door; I am on the floor, my ear to the wall, while you are in another's arms, and I hear you say to him what you said to me, and kiss him as you kissed me. I have red-hot coals in my entrails. Those caresses, which you lavish on anyone who does not care about them, you refuse to me, to whom they are life. In sum, for having loved you too much, my life is only hanging by a thread, and I hope that it will soon break. No, it is not for vain ostentation that I allow these horrible pains to accumulate within me, which are burning and killing me. I frighten those who see me. The neighbors no longer recognize me. The woman downstairs said to another:* What's the matter with that fellow? I've seen him as chubby as a cherub; now one can see daylight through his body. *My legs can no longer support me. One might think that I were dissolving in water. And I fear that only the sight of you can return me to life. Your love was my breath, and you know whether it will ever return. I only ask to see you. If you have anything dear to you in the world, I implore you, let me see you one last time; one last time, do you hear? To those condemned to death nothing is refused. Will you be more pitiless than an executioner?*

Monsieur Achille's clowning and Clémence's bursts of laughter were suddenly interrupted by the fall of a body that made the partition creak. The woman shuddered and uttered a scream simultaneously. The hairdresser, who had not heard anything, asked her whether she was mad.

"No," said Clémence, pale with terror. "I'm sure there's someone hiding in there." She indicated the partition separating the closet from the alcove.

Bewildered by such an energetic assertion, Monsieur Achille picked up the candle and went into the closet. He was struck by stupor on perceiving his rival there, who, collapsed against the wall, seemed devoid of life. A few moments later, he cried, brutally: "What are you doing here?" but Paul did not move, any more than a dead man.

Clémence had ice in her veins. "Who is it?" she asked, in a faint voice.

The hairdresser seized Paul by the arm and dragged him into the room. A little compassion mitigated the woman's fear, for, as she said, the student was a sorry sight. His face had holes big enough to contain a fist. His paltry limbs, which had the mechanical mobility of a child's toy, were floating in overly large garments as if in a sack. One could not say, at that moment, where dolor had drawn his soul.

The voice of his mistress suddenly extracted him from his lethargy. Raising toward her a gaze from which floods of melancholy flowed, and extending his imploring arms, he said with sobs in his throat and his soul on his lips: "Don't you want me to talk to you?"

Monsieur Achille interposed himself. He felt brave. Apart from the fact that Paul was small in stature, he was at that point so thin and so weak that it appeared that a breath could knock him over. At the moment when he took a step toward Clémence, the hairdresser grabbed him by the collar of his coat and shoved him with so much force that the poor lover fell to the floor against a piece of furniture. The woman made a gesture of pity.

Paul came to his knees and said, in a tearful voice that would have stirred the entrails of a hyena: "I'm meek, you see; I allow myself to be beaten." He added, animatedly: "It's not that I'm a coward, at least. One word, one gesture, oh, and you'd see my strength!"

Monsieur Achille, outraged by the threat, closed his fists and ran toward Paul. The latter, with the bound of a wild beast, was on his feet in the blink of an eye. Throwing his fists backwards like two menacing slings, he nailed the hairdresser to the spot with a magnetic gaze comparable to two red-hot sword-points. But that superhuman muscular tension only lasted for a few moments. The flames he had in his eyes were immediately extinguished by the indifference of his mistress.

"Come on," said the latter, "be reasonable, Monsieur Paul, and go away."

Then there was a scene of ignoble pathos. Monsieur Achille, ashamed of having been afraid, took hold of the student bodily and tried to throw him out. The resistance that the amorous individual opposed, by clinging on to the furniture, rendered him furious, and Clémence completed exasperating him by addressing Paul two or three times with tenderness. He struck his frail adversary indignantly. After a quarter of an hour of that revolting fight, if it can be called a fight, he finally succeeded in pushing the student outside, bruised by punches, like an inert mass.

"Nothing was moving any longer," Madame Clémence added. "I thought Paul was already unconscious or dead, when I heard him going back into his room and turning the key in the lock. I thought I could finally sleep tranquilly. Sleep was already overtaking me.

"Suddenly, Paul opened his window, the one alongside the room where we were. I shoved Achille, who was asleep, and said to him: 'Listen!' By the sound, he was sure that Paul had climbed out of his window and was walking along the gutter. I was afraid. I imagined that he had heard me barricading my door and that he was coming back through the window. I was also afraid that he would fall into the street. I had all the trouble in the world holding back Achille, who wanted to get up. What do you expect? I was a thousand leagues away from the thing . . .

"But we couldn't hear anything any longer. There was a silence to make you shiver. The blood froze in my veins. We were still listening. Then something extraordinary and frightful happened. I can't think about it without my hair standing on end and my heart lurching. It still seems to me that it was only yesterday. At first one would have sworn that Paul was climbing along the slates. Then, for perhaps two minutes, he didn't budge at all. Then he fell like a stone, and started jigging about so forcefully that one might have thought that he was trying to demolish the wall. It was a rumble that went on and on. My windows trembled and slates flew to the right and left as if in a big wind. I leave you to imagine the state I was in. I stuck out my neck and opened my eyes. Not to mention that the sweat was flowing over my face like water. I could have been punched in the chest and I wouldn't have suffered so much. I was more than half dead. Achille's arm bore the mark of my fingernails for a long time . . ."

"And you didn't suspect, after his threat . . . ?" I exclaimed, suddenly.

"Yes," she interrupted, "you're astonished today, because you know that he's dead. But I didn't even remember his threat any longer. I only thought of it afterwards. At the time I was so far from the truth that I used all my strength to prevent Achille from going to see what it all meant. I squeezed his neck so tightly with my arm that I strangled him.

"We heard a man who stuck his head out of the window and said: 'Will they soon have finished knocking, whoever it is?' Unfortunately, the sky was so cloudy that he couldn't see anything. He went back inside almost immediately. In any case, the noise had stopped suddenly. One could only hear the thumps at longer and longer intervals. But it had all been finished for at least half an hour when we were still there, like statues, listening. Achille went back to sleep, though. As for me, it was impossible to close an eye. I didn't suspect anything, I swear to you! Only, without knowing why, I was devoured by anxieties; I felt something like two leaden hands on my breast, which were weighing on me and stifling me.

"It was only after dawn that I went . . . not to sleep but, so to speak, to float between two slumbers. When he woke up, Achille didn't take long to make me open my eyes. He had no sooner gone than a horrible dread took possession of me. I made great efforts to chase it away. I would have liked to have some laudanum to drink. I shifted in my bed as if it were a sack full of thorns. Not being able to stand it any longer I got up. An invincible force drew me toward the widow. I opened it . . .

"Oh, what I saw . . . I'll never, ever forget it. I uttered a scream that must have been heard a league away, and I fell backwards . . ."

Madame Clémence drew breath and concluded thus: "Oh, that Paul knew very well what he was doing. I can't count the nights I've spent without sleeping, and the bad dreams I've had. In the early days I couldn't remain alone for a minute. Even now, even though I make arrangements in such a fashion that I never see the frightful nail, it sometimes enters into my eyes and wakes me up at night. I see Paul again as I saw him when I opened my window, hanged, with his face stuck to the wall. I can only hope to have repose when I've quit this house. And the gossip of all the neighbors! And the scenes I've had with *Monsieur*! Don't you find that abominable? Yes, that's what I've reaped for my excessive generosity. But what do you expect? I'm made that way; I'll never correct myself, I'll always be the same fool of the good Lord . . ."

Etc., etc.

Everyone knows the ardor with which we ordinarily lay claim to the faculties that we lack. After that speech, it was necessary not to doubt that Madame Clémence would have applied to herself the dictum, if she had known it, that sensitive people are fatally unhappy. Their hearts are too voluminous for the space in which they beat; one bumps, bruises and wounds them without noticing, as one detaches a wisp of straw in going past a laden cart; and if they complain and protest, one turns round and asks, with surprise: "Why are you screeching like that?"

Prey to a dull irritation, I quarreled with Madame Clémence one day, I don't know on what subject. She quit me, throwing in my face the original epithet, and never came back.

Three years later, from Saint-Germain, where hazard had taken me, I was going to Passy through the forest to see a person of my acquaintance. I sat down outside the railway station just as a passenger train went by, going from Paris to Rouen. The noise of the machine made by the steam did not prevent me from hearing someone calling. I raised my head and I perceived the smiling face of Madame Clémence in the frame of a window.

I approached. Her health was more flourishing than ever. She had filled out. With her milky whiteness, her ample bosom, the finesse of her linen, the necklace of hair she had around her neck, fastened with a miniature portrait of a man, she gave the impression of a rich bourgeoise, or, even better, a beautiful and worthy mother of a family. She seemed charmed to see me again. The train was about to pull away again, so we scarcely had time to chat, and she brought me up to date with her affairs in a few words.

"Monsieur is established," she said. "He gave me thirty thousand francs. I've married in my homeland a worthy man who adores me. We've bought a pretty house where we live on our income. You can see that I'm as healthy as a charm. I have a magnificent child. I'm happy."

I'm happy. What was so strange, then, about those few syllables, that they resonated in my ear like an unexpected drumbeat, and threw me into a whirlwind of sad ideas? *I'm happy . . .*

After all, why not? Where there is neither knowledge nor intention, there cannot be any crime. A person who meditates a murder silently is nevertheless culpable even if, thinking of the talion, he does not combine action with the thought. But can one cry *assassin* at a roofer who falls from a roof and conserves his life at the expense of a passer-by that he crushes?

Once and for all, it is for those whose jealous souls have the privilege of durable affection and exclusive devotions to beware of these mechanical dolls, full of seduction but cold, treacherous and cruel, who, in the fashion of the gears of a mill, hook on to your coat-tails and then, stupidly and fatally, break your legs, arms, body and head.

The audience protested somewhat against the taste and ambition of that final image. Nevertheless there was unanimous agreement that, all things considered, it was no worse than the concluding sentence of the turbulent Prosper. After which, in view of the advanced hour, the other story-tellers were adjourned until the next session.

THE TITANESS[1]

by Jules Lermina

I had never seen her handwriting, and yet, when her letter was handed to me, I didn't hesitate for a moment. The letter came from *her*, the woman I had not seen for three long years, since she had, in ignorance of the profound love I had conceived for her, become the wife of Frédéric Wertheim, the scientist whose works were honored by all the Academies, and whom I admired too much myself to dare to envy.

I gazed at the letter without opening it and, I don't know why, an inexpressible anguish depressed me. Strangely enough, the paper seemed pale to me, and the slender black letters that were traced thereon seemed to have an unhealthy and painful thinness.

I had been Paula's childhood companion; I had known her cheerful, slightly wild, with flashes of enthusiasm—the irradiation of naïve hearts! Oh, she

---

1 The French title of this story is *Titane*, which normally refers in modern French to the metal titanium, but when the story was first published, that would have been as esoteric as the specification of a female Titan.

would not have written in this manner then! Like her capriciously-curled hair, the strokes designed by her childish hand would have had a joyful flirtatiousness and merry flourishes—but on this envelope, the jet of the pen had the abruptness of a summons, and the characters of my name stood out like a clamor.

Feverishly, I broke the seal. One single word: *Come!*

For her to address that plea to me, which was a command, not knowing what rights she had over me— rights that I had reserved permanently to the mystery of my consciousness—must not some quasi-divinatory power have revealed the secret of her power to her?

I did not hesitate for a minute. Paula lived with her husband in a large property about six leagues from the town where I was resident. I never went that way any longer, fearful of causing my dream—so carefully respected—to wither before some absurd and discouraging reality. I had never pronounced her name, in order not to trouble the soft echo that remained to me, vibrant and crystalline, of the farewell in which, amorously, I had caused to resonate one last time, for me alone, the two exquisite syllables.

It was the first month of Autumn: that ambiguous period in which one already feels sepulchral gusts from the tomb of winter.

It is true, however, that the heavy moroseness that darkened my soul was even more mournful than nature—and it seemed to me that to continue going forward, I had to struggle through the tangled network of an immense and impenetrable spider-web.

How much time it took me to travel that distance it is impossible for me o say.

The château in which Paula dwelt was situated at the extremity of an exceedingly long drive-way lined with chestnut trees, whose branches interlaced and whose rectitude, progressively diminished by perspective, gave rise to the suggestion of a funnel. At the moment when I launched forth into it, it seemed to me—a rapid hallucination superimposed on my anxieties—that at the far end, in the narrow circle that resembled the lair of a funnel-web spider, something was waiting for me in the form of a lugubriously laughing animal mask composed of mist, which both attracted and threatened me.

And the sinister impression of that mirage was so powerful that I threw myself backwards, tightening the reins, while, leaning over the neck of my disconcerted house, I plunged my fearful gaze into that profundity.

Then, with a cry, I dug my spurs into the beast's flanks, launching it into a furious gallop, charging into the unknown.

I almost collided with the gate, whose bizarre torsions—the masterpiece of some unknown artist—caused me to understand the illusory nature of what I had glimpsed and, better still, explained it. Then, standing in front of those jaws of iron and bronze and their sharp-pointed projecting spirals, I saw the white and slender form of Paula, who was waiting for me, holding a pink infant in her arms.

✳

You say what she was; I cannot. A woman's beauty is merely the result of the emotion of whoever is looking at her. As for me when my eyes alighted on Paula, I sensed a surge of admiration and love throughout my entire being. Was that for her hair, as black as a Lycian vulture,[1] which separated in two wings from a white line traced by a bird's claw, for her slightly high and bulging forehead, where the grey radiance of her faded eyes was extinguished, or for that mouth, whose red-dened lips alone set a ruddy gleam within that white face? What do I know? I said nothing; I bowed and, shivering, kissed the hem of her dress.

Without replying to that silence in which she doubtless understood adoration, she addressed a sign to me.

I followed her along a drive whose white pebbles crackled beneath my feet, but were silent beneath her ethereal step. When we reached the front steps, she leaned forward momentarily, cocking an ear.

Doubtless she heard nothing, for she pushed the ebony door deliberately, which slid over a thick car-pet—and a few moments later, we were in a small draw-ing-room, illuminated by stained-glass windows that set glimmers of ruby and emerald upon our garments.

And she said: "Listen to me!"

They were the first words she had pronounced, and her somber voice, indolently sad, struck me as if it had emerged from some immeasurable abyss. When I was almost touching her hand, she spoke to me as if from

---

1 Lermina has *le Iagatès de Lycie*, which I am assuming to be a reference to the Eurasian black vulture *Aegypius*.

afar. And my eyes undoubtedly expressed my saddened amazement, for she continued hurriedly.

"I have summoned you. You were my childhood friend, perhaps more. There is a link between our hearts that is stretched, but not broken. That's true, isn't it?"

I answered her with an eye-blink.

"Three years ago," she said, without pausing over the preliminaries that are the cowardice of confession, "I became Frédéric's wife. In my childish mind, that man, who was already called a Master, was one of those whom no one can resist. He took possession of me with a word. His gaze conquered me and I felt gripped by his will.

"My weakness was proud to be supported by that strength: I dreamed of proud submission to that energy, which dominated everything. I mention all this because I know—I *know*, you hear—that you loved me, that you love me still, and that you will always love me, as I love and will love you . . ."

"Paula!"

"Don't mistake the meaning of my words. No guilty thought can or must occur to us. We are united with one another by the very debility of our desires. We are made to march side by side, giving one another mutual support. Of the two of us, neither can have ascendancy over the other. That is why I have summoned you, like my other half, because my weakness has need of support, in order to recover its equilibrium . . ."

"But what has happened, then? Is it Frédéric?"

"Frédéric is good. Frédéric loves me. Frédéric is the foremost among us, the husband and father!"

"I don't understand, then," I said, a trifle put out.

135

She reproached me for that unjust irritation with a gesture, and her voice, which rang like a village bell heard on the horizon, continued: "Don't interrupt, I beg you. A single word will explain everything to you. I'm afraid: afraid of everything, especially of him. Why? Oh, if I could tell you that, if I could divine it myself . . . but the terror that overwhelms me every day, and more so every night, is all the sharper because it is inexplicable . . ."

I started laughing.

"Fear! Terror! Words."

"Words that resonate in our heads, without our reason grasping their meaning, have funereal echoes. Why are you smiling? Don't you know that *mystery* is stronger than reason, and that fatal anguish emerges from the unknown?"

Involuntarily, and although I desired, in my vanity, to retain the appearance of scepticism, I felt wretchedly anxious. Lowering my voice, I interrogated her more gently, apprehensive with regard to the words that were about to give substance to that ambient fear.

This is what she told me.

For about six months—which is to say, since the birth of his child—Frédéric, who had until then carried his head high, like a warrior anticipating victory, had suddenly become depressed. Of what problem was he pursuing the solution? In what battle had he dared to engage? Taciturn, he remained silent, and only replied to his wife's questions with haggard glances, as if he were begging her not to reawaken some distressing memory.

Day and night he remained shut up in a greenhouse built at considerable expense, in the depths of the grounds. Weeks passed without him appearing at the château, although he sometimes slipped into his wife's room by night. She had seen him do so, while he thought that she was asleep. She had seen him sitting in a chair, his eyes staring, fascinated by some frightful vision.

He had on his twisted face an indescribable expression of *horror*. His entire being shivered, and his hands, agitated by convulsive movements, appeared to be pushing back some invisible enemy. Then—oh, she had studied him carefully during those few moments—he made a gesture of commanding, triumphant resolution . . . and, getting abruptly to his feet, he fled . . .

Paula had run to the window, and had seen him running toward the greenhouse, whose lamps, never extinguished, shone like a lighthouse.

Frankly and boldly, she had interrogated him. What was going on out there, in that isolated corner of the grounds? Why did he refuse obstinately to let anyone into it?

And with the same shiver, he had pushed her away harshly.

Then, courageously hypocritical, she had attempted to discover the truth—and she had learned something strange. Every day, Frédéric had his assistant purchase several pounds of fresh meat and bring them to the greenhouse every evening. Never had the slightest detritus been discovered in the vicinity of the outbuilding!

What, therefore, was it nourishing? Was it some dangerous, unknown animal to which he was obliged to give its daily rations in person? A creature with which he was resigned to live in the isolation of a scientific enquiry? And was that, then, the struggle of which his rebellions in nocturnal solitude gave evidence?

Was he going mad?

That thought had pierced Paula's tortured soul like a dagger of ice.

She had not dared to interrogate him further, as anguish hollowed out his face profoundly; he distanced himself from her. He never came any longer, as he had formerly done, to rest in the intimacy of conversation from his tiring labors. Sometimes, though, she caught glimpses of him, looking haggard, prowling through the tall bushes, bare-headed, shaking his fists at the sky.

Finally—and this surpassed the supreme torment—one night, while she was asleep, he had come into her room, his steps raising no echoes. She had sensed that someone was there, and had opened her eyes abruptly. Frédéric, upright, was darting crazed glances into the child's crib, and his hands were undergoing supplicatory spasms.

"Frédéric! Frédéric! What are you doing at his hour?"

He had uttered a brutal imprecation, and, once again, had fled!

That was what Paula told me, and as she spoke, I felt a reassuring coolness descend into my breast. What was she describing after all, but a morbid state of excessive excitement caused by overwork?

I had once been Frédéric's friend and pupil, and I had often had occasion to listen to him when he had plunged into the realm of Hypothesis in a surge of marvelous audacity. Was I not a physician, and had I not looked into the face of the enemy, Fever?

I reassured myself in that fashion as best I could—and, sure of my eloquence and the law of reason, I disappeared into the grounds in search of Frédéric.

Night was falling, but I had shaken off my first impression. I straightened myself up, feeling an inexpressible pride in my mission of protection and salvation. I went along the crepuscular pathways, becoming firmer in my duty with every step.

Soon I perceived the greenhouse that Paula had mentioned to me. It was vast and solidly-constructed, composed of a series of adjacent sections with rounded domes, like the cupolas of a Turkish bath. In the last glimmer of twilight, their window-panes were like gleaming plates of steel.

There was the mystery. In truth, I was almost laughing at these childish dreads. Was I not familiar with the exhausting, all-consuming influence of scientific research?

As I thought of that, I heard precipitate footsteps behind me.

I turned around abruptly.

In the veiled gloom of the bushes, I saw—or, rather, divined the presence of—Frédéric. Boldly, I went toward him.

"My friend," I said, "don't you recognize me?"

He stopped dead.

"It's me, Frédéric," I continued. I was holding out my hand, and was astonished not to feel the grip of his.

139

Guided, or so it seemed to me, more by the sound of my voice than by sight, he leaned forward and said, in a raucous, hoarse voice that resembled the cracking of a branch bent too roughly: "You! What do you want with me? Go away!"

"What! Is that how you greet me after such a long absence? Don't you remember our old friendship?"

He was indecisive, stamping his feet. I saw then that he had a basket on his arm, which seemed quite heavy.

"I can't stop," he said. "Let me pass."

"Of course you can pass," I replied, "but you won't prevent me, I assume, from following you, so that we can have a pleasant chat, as we used to do."

He laughed in a singularly sardonic fashion. "Follow me—you! Let's go, then."

"Upon my soul, what are you hiding in this glass palace? Some treasure of which you're exceedingly jealous?"

He seized my arm with his free hand, and, as I fell silent, he leaned forward, cocking an ear. It seemed to me that I perceived a strange sound, something like the slithering of a snake.

"She's waiting for me!" he said, in a tone in which I discerned a barely-suppressed terror. "I *must* go."

"Once again, let's go together."

He seemed to hesitate again. Then, with a decisive gesture, he said: "Come on, then. Perhaps you're the only one who will be able defend me, if . . ."

He did not finish—but as his hand gripped mine, I felt that it was icy, like compacted snow.

He was dragging me now.

We arrived at the door of the greenhouse. He took a key from his pocket and opened the glass panel—and as I went forward, still unable to distinguish anything around me, he pulled me back in a violent manner.

"For the sake of your life," he whispered, "don't move!"

In spite of my self-assurance, I felt a singular malaise invading me. Then I heard that bizarre rustling, which had struck me a little while before. It was a slow slithering, a sound similar to that of a piece of paper drawn over a marble slab.

Suddenly, without my being able to see what Frédéric had done, a dazzling glare lit up the greenhouse . . . and, horrified, my hair standing up on my head, I plastered myself against the door, my hands clenched on its iron frame.

Looming up in the middle of an open space, entirely carpeted with fantastically-formed plants, was a creature of nightmare, a Thing. A hydra? An octopus? A squid? Who could have put a name to it? It was hideously crouched on the ground, in an enormous shallow bowl filled with spongy and sticky mosses. It was shaped like a colossal leather bottle, and from the edges of that bottle extended innumerable long arms, at the tips of which were bulbous spheres, as glaucous as eyeballs. The bottle was green; the arms were streaked with dark red, and as they tapered toward those atrocious eyes the blood-red was mingled with the greenness of putrefied flesh.

And I shut my eyes, feeling a sinister constriction in my heart.

Except that I could still hear the slithering I mentioned, and I deduced that it was made by the arms, stretching out or recoiling.

However, surprised by not having been seized by that something, so hideous and so powerful, I made a superhuman effort and I looked.

Frédéric, livid, had taken a piece of meat from the basket he was holding, and, with infinite precaution—perched on tiptoe as if he feared that his hand might be touched by those horrible tentacles—he placed it on the extremity of one the bobbing arms.

Suddenly, as if by the effect of a spring, the arm snapped back, snatching the piece of meat, which was thus conveyed to other, shorter arms, which I then saw protruding from a further, inner circle—and the latter, having seized the flesh, transmitted it—if I might employ such an expression—to other arms further in toward the center. All the arms folded back over the center grabbed the morsel simultaneously, and I was no longer able to see it.

Shuddering, with my throat taut, I fixed my eyes on Frédéric.

His forehead was streaming with sweat; his teeth were chattering. The demonic beast was immobile now, intent on its monstrous absorption.

"She eats!" he cried. "She eats! The Titaness is feeding!"

"Titaness?" I repeated, staring at him in amazement.

"Oh, you don't know anything! You don't understand anything! Don't you recognize her? Look, look! For the moment, she's subdued . . ."

And in a sudden burst of comprehension, I realized what the beast was . . .

✳

It was a gigantic *Drosera*:[1] a carnivorous plant grown to fabulous dimensions, a vegetable colossus, and unprecedented creation . . . and I shouted out its name.

"She'll be like that for about an hour," Frédéric told me. "Oh, I know why you've come. People think I'm mad! No, it's not true! Mad, the man, who, by a miracle of perseverance, by means of a masterpiece of selection, has magnified a Drosera to that formidable stature? You see her, the monster . . . in a little while, she will extend her avid tentacles toward me again . . . and I shall have to feed her . . . it's necessary that I stuff her . . . or else . . ."

He looked around, fearfully.

"Or else?" I asked.

"Listen," he said. "You shall know my secret. You know how ardently I've studied the discoveries of Nitschke, Warming and Darwin[2] regarding these strange plants, intermediate between the vegetable and the animal, which catch insects, enslime them, stifle

---

1 I have transcribed Lermina's *Drosera* directly, although that Latin term is more familiar in French than it is in English; the English common name of the plant in question, sundew, is, however, also echoed in the French *rossolis*, which Lermina could have employed had he desired.

2 Charles Darwin published a book entitled *Insectivorous Plants* (1875), which was translated into French in 1877. It refers to work done on *Drosera* by Theodor Nitschke (1834-1883) and Eugenius Warming (1841-1924), and was presumably the source from which Lermina took his inspiration for the story.

them and slowly nourish themselves upon them. Oh, I understood the consequences of those bizarre studies! I never doubted it for an instant . . . and I told myself that *Drosera, Dionaea* and *Drosophyllum*[1] are—listen closely—degenerations of monstrous animals whose terrifying forms remain in the memory of primitive peoples: hydras, chimeras, wyverns, dragons . . .

"All those things existed; human imagination has created nothing. By virtue of climacteric[2] adaptations, however, and geological upheavals, these creatures of abominable form, deprived of the nourishment necessary to them, have fallen back by virtue of a retrograde atavism to vegetal form, immobilized and attached to the soil by roots. Because they were obliged to seek their primary alimentation in the earth, they have become plants again . . . conserving only one sole vestige of their past life, the supreme aptitude of animal nutrition . . .

"Well, I wanted to reconstitute the atrophied creature . . . I wanted the plant to become an animal again. Oh, how many experiments failed! Finally, chance—for our science is nothing but chance—delivered a *Drosera* of exceptional size . . . and I've nourished it,

1 *Dionaea* is the Venus fly-trap. *Drosophyllum* is a genus of carnivorous plants closely resembling *Drosera*, limited to a single species found in Portugal.
2 I have transcribed Lermina's *climatérique* directly; a climacteric is a critical period in human life (or, by analogy, life in general) at which some crucial change takes place—puberty, for instance. Within the theory of the Earth's evolution popularized by Georges Cuvier, still familiar in France when Lermina wrote this story, the history of the Earth was conceived as a series of distinct epochs separated by large-scale catastrophes, which tempted analogical description as planetary climacterics.

and impregnated it with animal secretions. Gradually, it developed. A triumph of deduction! The hydra, the dragon, lives again!

"Do you see her, my enormous and sublime Titaness? Do you see her, ferocious in the hunger that I can never sate?"

At that moment, he threw a new piece of food on to two tentacles that were reaching out.

"But you don't know everything," he told me, in a low voice. "If the Titaness is hungry . . . I've deduced this . . . in the phase of strength and growth that she has now reached, she will tear herself away from the retaining link that binds her to the soil, in the depths of the moss. And then, an execrable and victorious animal, she will escape from here. She will make her way across country, dragging her viscous enormity . . . and my masterpiece will become my crime!

"And I shall be accursed!

"I don't want her to escape. I want her to remain a prisoner. And, attentive in the dread that she might get hungry, I watch . . .

"A few minutes' delay, and I *know* that she would launch herself forth, like an odious squid, into the world . . . menacing my wife, my child! My child!

"How she eats! How she eats! She must—in order that she doesn't *want* to escape!"

And again, I saw him throw the haunches of meat. And through the fibers of the atrocious plant passed crimson waves of discharged blood.

※

At that moment, as I stood there mute, overwhelmed by the intensity of my revulsion, the door of the greenhouse, which I had not closed properly, opened abruptly—and Paula appeared!

Her courage had been stronger than her fear. Now she knew that I was there, she had had the audacity to violate the secret of the greenhouse.

"Frédéric!" she cried.

To that appeal, however, a horrible clamor replied.

As he took an abrupt step backwards, heedless of the danger, Frédéric had touched the tentacles of the Titaness with his hand . . . and with a formidable rapidity, all the hideous trunks had fallen upon that hand, grasping the wrist, and the forearm . . .

Horror! I saw him imbibed by that irresistible suction. I seized him round the waist, striving to snatch him back from the terrible embrace of the Titaness . . . but the beast was stronger than I was . . .

Then my eyes fell upon a hatchet that was lying on the ground . . .

"The base! The base!" I shouted to Paula. "Cut it! Slice it!"

Did she understand? I don't know—but she did as she was bid. Weak as she was, she picked up the steel implement, nervously, and struck . . . so accurately that she cut through the mosses and the root of the plant.

It seemed to make an effort to stand up, perhaps to launch itself forth, but, suddenly impotent, collapsed with a flaccid sound, like wet clothing—and, at the same instant, I snatched the unfortunate victim from its extended tentacles . . .

And I saw—a horrible sight!—that his hand and arm were already reduced to a bloody pulp.

He opened his eyes and, fixing them on me in a final spasm, was only able to say: "Murderer! You've killed the Titaness!"

And he fell backwards, dead.

I have remained a brother to Paula, and have adopted the child.

THE WIDOWHOOD OF SCHEHERAZADE

by Henri de Régnier

> Speech is not its language . . .
> *Madame de Staël*

SCHEHERAZADE had slept badly that night. The day had been weighed down by blazing sunlight, and the air had been so penetrated by it that it felt as if one were breathing in a kind of burn, whose ill-effects nothing could temper. The lightness of the most transparent muslins seemed an unwelcome burden, and the winged caress of fans remained powerless to refresh the overheated shade.

In vain Scheherazade had stripped off, one by one, the veils not demanded by decency. In vain she had freed herself of the inconvenience imposed by her necklaces and bracelets. In vain she had let her most precious rings slip on to trays, with a clink of gold and a click of gems, including the magic ring that Sultan Shariar had placed on her finger himself on the evening of the thousand-and-first night, as a testimony of love and a guarantee of security: the ring whose sacred talisman rendered her henceforth inviolable and set aside forever the threat of the trenchant blade of the sword and the mortal grip of the silken cord.

Having retreated to the most secret and best-ventilated summer-house in the gardens—the one that was made entirely of crystal and above which intersected the flexible plumes of three great water jets, which ornamented it with a sparkling fluid crown—Scheherazade had seen the hours of that torrid day go by ponderously, in the regular tears of clepsydras and the successive grains of sand-glasses, without anything bringing relief to the overwhelming languor of her impatient lassitude. Even her favorite white doves with the crimson throats, in brushing her weary face with their amorous wings, had scarcely caused her mouth and eyes to smile momentarily.

Exhausted by that torpor, Scheherazade had not even had the strength to think about the marvelous story that she would relate to Sultan Shariar that evening, when, the sun having set, they would meet on the highest terrace of the palace in order to savor the furtive nocturnal alleviation beneath the starry sky.

Just as the day had been unbearable, the evening had been scarcely less so, and Scheherazade, before trying to obtain a little sleep, had recalled its disagreeable circumstances without any pleasure. Not the least of them had been the indifferent and distracted fashion in which the Sultan Shariar had listened to the quotidian tale. Scarcely had Scheherazade begun to speak than Shariar had turned his attention away from the storyteller's words to his own thoughts.

By the manner in which the Sultan passed his hand through his black beard, which was beginning to be streaked with silver threads, it was obvious that those thoughts could not be offering any enjoyment to Shariar's mind. Scheherazade had seen the Sultan's dark eyebrows frown. Several times, he had even put his hand impatiently upon the ruby-studded hilt of his sword and fidgeted with the agate hilt of his dagger. In spite of the ingenious twists and turns of Scheherazade's tale, which was the story of a genie enclosed in a bottle, Shariar's face had remained taciturn beneath his diamond-bedecked turban. Not only had he not reached out to Scheherazade, as he normally did, to thank her for her tale, but he had even neglected to have her brought the customary cup of snow so that she might quench her thirst. Was that forgetfulness not proof, in Sultan Shariar, of great preoccupation?

Shariar's attitude had afflicted Scheherazade's vanity. Scheherazade was proud of her prowess as a storyteller and of the artistry she brought to her stories, whose renown had spread beyond the limits of Bagdad throughout the world. The name of Scheherazade was universally famous, and her celebrated adventure was related everywhere. Women, especially, professed an enthusiastic admiration for her. Was she not the honor and the pearl of their sex, and the marvel of their intelligence? Had she not been able, by virtue of her talent, to impose herself on Shariar's cruel whims and put an end to them? By her delightful ruse, by her ingenious cunning, she had thwarted the mortal trap to which she had been exposed. Was she not a magnificent and charming example of feminine superiority? All that had earned her a renown to which she was not insensible.

And that evening, Shariar had wounded her susceptibility. He had been negligent. He had forgotten to thank her for all that she had done for him. When one has the privilege and the good fortune to hear a Scheherazade tell a story, one ought to be all ears. How can one risk missing the least of her words? What was the meaning of the pensive expression, the frown beneath his turban, the fidgeting with the sword and the dagger, the adoption of a distracted and preoccupied appearance?

That was a veritable insult, and, like all authors. Scheherazade was irritable and rancorous. She had been extremely vexed by Shariar's behavior, but what had completed her irritation was that Shariar, when she had stopped speaking, had not asked her the questions that he never failed to address to her concerning the events and characters in her tales. Decidedly, Shariar had been a recalcitrant listener, and when the tale was finished, without paying any further heed to Scheherazade, he had surrounded himself with spirals of smoke from his long pipe, while from the depths of the garden, beneath the stars, came the plaint of fountains, and mischievously furtive bats fluttered around his somber turbaned face.

The silence of Sultan Shariar had lasted until the appearance on the terrace of the grand vizier Kerendar. Kerendar was an individual that Scheherazade did not like at all. Shariar listened to him, and more than once, he had opposed Scheherazade's costly fantasies. For example, he had criticized the construction of the famous crystal summer-house crowned with water-jets, and various other amusements of the Sultana.

Kerendar explained these oppositions and criticisms by reasons of State. The great and glorious wars waged by Sultan Shariar had cost a great many men and a great deal of money. The kingdom was decimated and the treasury had run dry. All that had not made Shariar very popular. He was accused of not being sufficiently sparing with either the gold or blood of his subjects, and squandering them to satisfy his ambitions and his pleasures. The people of Bagdad were murmuring and complaining.

Kerendar had been alerted to these murmurs and complaints, for he maintained a powerful and perspicacious police force. It kept him up to date with what was going on in the kingdom, and also in the city and the palace. Scheherazade's actions and gestures did not escape Kerendar's investigations. The surveillance that Kerendar carried out reassured Shariar's jealousy, but made Scheherazade's hair prickle. Not that she had any intention of being unfaithful to Shariar, but it had not displeased her to be surrounded by tender tributes and sweet words. Now, the vigilance of Kerendar deterred the most audacious; no one dared look at her in his presence. The sight of a handsome face is an innocent pleasure, however, and Scheherazade had liked to see a few of them demonstrating that they were charmed by her beauty. Shariar's somber face was not extremely diverting, so far as she was concerned.

As Kerendar had spoken in a hushed voice to Shariar, Shariar's face had become even more somber. His hand had clenched on the ruby-studded hilt of his sword. The news that Kerendar brought was not, in fact, very agreeable. Emissaries sent to various parts of the kingdom had returned with the most worrying news. The raising of taxes was provoking disturbances. In certain places, people had gone so far as to maltreat the agents of the revenue. In addition, the peasants were hiding their crops and the merchants concealing their produce, counting on the price increases that famine would produce, its imminence having been advertised. Many inhabitants were leaving the country and several regions were becoming deserted. There was general discontent leveled against a Sultan who spent his nights listening to stories instead of working for the relief of his people.

Scheherazade, who, like all women, had keen ears, did not miss any of what Kerendar said. Thus she learned that a conspiracy had been formed in Bagdad to make an attempt on the Sultan's life. The conspirators were planning to get into the palace, break down the garden gates and finish Shariar off by means of fire and the sword. This criminal company had numerous members, linked to one another by formidable oaths and directed by fanatical leaders. Bagdad was infested by these intrigues, which would have presented a real danger if Kerendar's police had not been watching them and keeping track of the threads of the plot. The grand vizier was in a position to nullify these deadly threats, provided that he did not lose sight of them for an instant, but it would cost considerable sums of money. It was therefore necessary to restrict all the resources of the State to that purpose, and not to employ a single dinar for any other. If he were given the means, Kerendar would answer for everything.

During this speech, Shariar had never ceased tugging the points of his beard, and he had left the terrace with his hand on Kerendar's shoulder, without a glance for Scheherazade, who was not long delayed in retiring to her apartment.

Once she was in her own room and sure that Shariar would not come to look for her that night, she had sent away her women and had lain down on the perfumed leather of her cushions. The nocturnal air had lost a little of its ardor and it was easier to breathe. The murmur of fountains and the scent of roses came in through the windows, mingled with the silvery rays of a belated moon.

The silence was only troubled by the calls of the sentinels who, yataghans drawn, were guarding the garden gates. Briefly, Scheherazade thought about going down there. She sometimes liked to walk there at night and to admire the slumber of the aviaries. The beautiful birds that filled them slept with their heads beneath their wings and Scheherazade was amused by their decapitated silhouettes. She had been deterred, however, by the fatigue of putting on her curved slippers again and had contented herself with thinking about the boastful magpie that had amused her so much when she was a child.

That magpie was the joy of her father's poor cobbler's stall. How it jabbered away, that magpie, while the worthy man hammered and stitched the leather! Scheherazade often thought about her father's stall. It was there that she had grown up, clad in rags that she already arranged coquettishly while sucking a slice of water-melon. It was there that she had heard the various people who frequented the stall talking. The city's news was circulated there, with abundant commentary.

Her father's tongue had been as cutting and pointed as his awl, and he did not disdain amusing his clients with his anecdotes and apologues. It was in that humble and credulous audience that she had acquired the taste for the tales that had played such an important role in her singular history. While very small, she had made her contribution to all that palaver, and her infantile imaginations and inventions had amused that facile popular public.

By that means she had attracted the attention of Ibrahim, the old carpet-merchant, to whom her father had sold her, and who had taught her about love, without her experiencing any for him. Ibrahim had not been her only teacher in that matter, and others had completed his lessons. She had not obtained any pleasure therefrom. The faces that had leaned over her had scarcely shown her youth or beauty, but her complaisance had allowed her to eat better, to dress better, to ornament herself with a few jewels, and enabled her to come to the aid of her family's poverty. In those difficult times she consoled herself for her tribulations by imagining marvelous adventures in which she attributed the leading role to herself.

It had been thus until the day when the rumor reached her ears of the strange proof to which Sultan Shariar submitted the storytellers who strove to distract his insomnia. She had known the bloody risks that the imprudent ran, but had conceived a secret desire to make the dangerous attempt. So, one day, she had presented herself at the palace to be inscribed on the fatal

155

list. It had not taken long for her name to be called. She could still see the high terrace, and the Sultan, attentive to her stories, so astutely interrupted and left in suspense.

She thought about the strange fortune that had come to her. Not only had the trenchant sword not fallen on her neck, but the Sultan's black beard had brushed her face and his heavily-ringed hands had caressed her body. The cobbler's daughter, the little storyteller of the Thousand-and-One Nights, had become the favorite Sultana of the great Sultan Shariar. All Bagdad envied her power, and her own story was even more marvelous than all those she had recounted . . .

While she mulled over that brilliant past, Scheherazade had felt her eyelids grown heavy. Gradually, sleep, long unfaithful, came to her, with the first light of dawn. Soon, poor Shariar would wake up in order to occupy himself with affairs of State, while she, who had no such concerns, could sleep for a long time, idly, as if she were still in the depths of her father's stall, the cobbler's little daughter.

But Scheherazade was not to get much sleep that night. Scarcely had she closed her eyes than she seemed to hear unusual sounds. The palace filled with bizarre noises: running footsteps in the gardens and resounding on the staircases. Soon, those noises were mingled with cries. A strange disorder was manifest everywhere. What was happening? Were the people of Bagdad in revolt? Was there a fire or an earthquake? Had enemies suddenly attacked the city? Was she dreaming, prey to some nightmare? Was it one of her tales, continuing in her sleep?

No! That man standing by her bed, his turban un-knotted, his arms raised, was neither a phantom nor a spirit. Scheherazade recognized that olive complexion, that long nose, those oblique eyes. It really was the grand vizier Kerendar standing before her, haggard, stammering and gesticulating, whose blood-stained hands were dripping red drops on to the marble pavement!

Sultan Shariar had just been assassinated in his bed. His own dagger, with the agate hilt, had been plunged into his breast, and his own sword, with the ruby-studded hilt, had served to cut his throat. His guards lay at his door, their tongues hanging out and cords around their necks. As for the murderer, who had disappeared without leaving any trace, he would never be found.

A muted discontentment reigned in Bagdad, and the death of Sultan Shariar was the proof of it. On entering his master's bedroom in the morning and seeing the tragic spectacle offered to his eyes, Kerendar had attempted to bring help to the Sultan, but all help was futile. Kerendar had only been able to ascertain Shariar's death, and had run to warn Scheherazade.

Scheherazade was very popular in Bagdad because of her beauty and her talent, and Kerendar offered to have her recognized as the reigning Sultana. Nothing was easier, and our man would be able to arrange everything, provided that Scheherazade promised to maintain him as grand vizier and appoint him to govern in her name. If not, power would pass into the hands of the Atabeg of Mossoul, and Scheherazade would be locked up until her dying day in a safe place, unless her days were cut short by other means.

Scheherazade had no ambition, but she liked her comforts. The thought of leaving her palace, her gardens, her summer-houses, her fountains, her rose-bushes and her aviaries was painful. Then again, would not this royal adventure complete her marvelous destiny?

Shariar's death caused her little grief, and the prospect of being absolute mistress of her actions was rather pleasant. Henceforth, she could live as she pleased, without having to distract a doubtless generous but demanding master with her body and her words. She would be able to sleep all night without having to stay up late to amuse her insomniac listener; she would be able to come and go as she liked, rest or remain silent, and above all, not tell tales any more. What a relief not to be obliged to invent those fabulous stories, of which she was beginning to get weary!

All these considerations led her to accept Kerendar's proposition. He took care of everything, with remarkable dexterity. Shariar's funeral was followed rapidly by the coronation of Scheherazade, who soon had the grand vizier Kerendar hanged for the murder of Sultan Shariar, even though no proof had been found of his participation in the crime. A guilty party was necessary, though, and Scheherazade had taken a dislike to Kerendar since he had scared her by appearing so abruptly before her and waving his bloody hands in that ridiculous manner.

※

The first phase of Scheherazade's reign was fortunate—which is to say that the people of Bagdad continued to suffer exactly the same evils, paying the same taxes, supporting the same injustices and the same miseries, but the state of affairs that had caused Shariar to be detested caused Scheherazade to be adored. Peoples are like that. Their lot is uniformly pitiful and their happiness only ever imaginary. Scheherazade thus inaugurated a happy reign.

This was repeated to her so often that she began to be astonished that her own happiness was not equal to that of her people. The disproportion was vexatious. Thus, when Scheherazade had slept for as long as she wished, when she had ornamented herself with all the jewels of Shariar's treasure, when she had shown herself to the people and been greeted with cheers, when she had rebuilt her palace, replanted her gardens, changed the location of the summer-houses, the fountains and the arbors and hanged the grand vizier Kerendar, she perceived that she was no happier than when Shariar was alive. When evening came and she went up on to the terrace of her new palace, something was lacking. She felt idle and uncertain.

Scheherazade had the habit of rationalizing her impressions. Having reflected long and hard, she realized that the stories she had told every evening to Shariar had maintained her mind in a fortifying and ingenious activity. It had been necessary for her to invent a subject and imagine circumstances. Now the game was over, the consequence for her had been a sort of intellectual torpor that was nothing less than a discreet form of ennui. But how could she remedy that condition?

She could not group her retinue and her guards around her to form an audience; she detested their complaisance and was suspicious of their applause. There remained the resource of writing stories, but she knew that stories lose a great deal in being written down. Hers, marvelous as they were, would lack the sound of her voice, the grace of her gestures, the mischief and mystery of her smile and her eyes. Her universal reputation as a great storyteller would be at risk of being lost.

These observations increased her ennui. The days seemed long and the approach of night made her agitated. To distract herself, Scheherazade could have had recourse to pleasures that are no less lively for being silent, but she knew almost all of the pleasures that can be attained from physical embraces, and love cannot be improvised any more by sultanas than by cobblers' daughters. Then again, when all honors are bestowed upon one, when one is adulated, respected and feared, it is very difficult to be loved.

Scheherazade often went to her crystal summer-house—the only one she had conserved from the old gardens—to meditate upon these things. The sound of the water-jets lulled her thoughts and it seemed to her that their fluid voices were telling her an improbable story—but alas, the voice of water is not a human voice.

Suddenly, Scheherazade shuddered. A sudden idea had occurred to her. Would it not be amusing for her, who had told so many tales, to hear them told in her turn? Why not try it? Certainly, unlike Shariar, she would not have boring tellers decapitated; she would content herself with having their ears cut off to punish them for not having charmed hers. Scheherazade was not cruel; she was even slightly repentant about having poor Kerendar hanged. She was wiser now, but wisdom has its hours of ennui. She would definitely summon storytellers. The news would be published in Bagdad the next day . . .

It was, and it had a tremendous effect. The marvelous story of Scheherazade, the cobbler's daughter who had become the favorite Sultana of the great Shariar, had made stories very fashionable, and that fashion had given rise to an infinite number of storytellers. There was scarcely a household in Bagdad in which tales were not being told. The evenings resounded with fabulous stories, full of twists and turns and prodigies. Assemblies, or academies, had been formed which met on certain days to listen to the new compositions of the members of the association. These societies had instituted competitions and were giving out prizes. This resulted in singular vanities, ardent rivalries and animosities that extended as far as hatred. These cenacles were bitterly jealous of one another.

In brief, a veritable literary fury had taken hold of Bagdad. One can imagine the effect produced by the appeal for storytellers launched by the Sultana and the invitation issued to them to come to distract her. The competitors disposed to subject themselves to the proof could have their names inscribed by the chief steward of the palace. The clause about the ears being cut off in case of failure was slightly worrying, but the vanity of Bagdad's storytellers was so powerful that none of them would admit the possibility of having to submit to such an outrage. Was their talent not a guarantee of the fortunate outcome of the adventure? The most modest was convinced that, as soon as Scheherazade heard his tale, she would be impressed and would reward him magnificently. The order in which the storytellers would perform was decided by drawing lots.

The first one favored by the draw was Mardouk. He was a short man, ugly and pretentious. He had an infinite self-esteem, so he did not doubt that when Scheherazade had heard him, she would keep him there and attach him to her person. He was, therefore, full of admirable self-assurance when he presented himself at the palace. In spite of his rivals scorning him and judging him a minor talent, they were nevertheless a trifle anxious. Women have such bad taste that one can never be sure of the justice of their choice, and their caprices foil all anticipations. As for Mardouk, he was certain that he would succeed. That was evident in the fashion in which his twisted legs limped up the stairway that led to the terrace of the palace where Scheherazade was waiting for him.

Mardouk had dressed up for the occasion. He had had the best tailor in Bagdad make him a suit that showed him off to his advantage and he was wearing a voluminous turban surmounted by a spray of feathers. With his hair freshly cut and his beard perfumed, he was animated by a vast pride. In fact, the colleagues in his association had insisted on accompanying him as far as the palace gate, and a large crowd of people had joined them.

It was with this imposing procession that Mardouk presented himself at the palace. When he had been admitted, the crowd had not dissipated. A great animating agitated the groups. Arguments blew up regarding Mardouk's talents. The night had worn on, and the conversations had not ceased—but they suddenly fell silent when the great bronze gate of the palace opened abruptly and Mardouk was seen to reappear. His robe in disorder and his turban unrolled, he was holding his severed ears preciously in a piece of cloth.

Mardouk's example did not discourage his rivals. Every week, the individual selected by lot went up to the high terrace of Scheherazade's palace. She listened carefully to the story he told, but was obliged to recognize that she obtained no great pleasure from it. The marvelous inventions that had delighted her so much when they were born in her own mind appeared to her devoid of interest when she heard them from someone else's mouth.

How monotonous these adventures are, with their marvelous lamps, their enchanted jars, their genies, their monsters, their treasures, their voyages, their grottoes, their magic spells and everything that pleases the poor human imagination! How vain and tiresome it all is! So much so that Scheherazade, after a certain number of trials and twice as many severed ears, became discouraged, and let the storytellers leave without demanding the auricular forfeit that she had the right to claim from them. What good was all that nonsense and trickery to her? Would no one be capable of soothing her ennui?

Wearily, she started sending the storytellers away before they had even unpacked their nonsense. Wounded in their vanity, the latter did not hesitate

163

to attribute their failure to causes that relieved its bitterness. Venomous tongues spread sly and malevolent rumors throughout Bagdad. It was repeated in whispers that the Sultana, weakened in mind and lowered in intelligence, was no longer in a fit state to appreciate the fine tales of Bagdad's storytellers. Comic songs and epigrams were composed on her account, in which she was vilified.

To distract her from these disappointments, Scheherazade wandered in her gardens. They seemed to her to be extremely empty. The sound of footsteps repeated by an echo made her shiver. In vain the fountains launched forth their water-jets, in vain the flowers spread their perfumes, in vain the birds sang. Scheherazade felt melancholy and abandoned. The respect that surrounded her, in showing her the extent of her power, caused her to see its futility. She had almost got to the point of missing the perfunctory and bearded kisses of Shariar, his solid embraces and coarse voice, which had sometimes praised her beauty.

Sometimes, Scheherazade thought about traveling, of touring her realm. Standing on the highest terrace of the palace, she gazed at the horizon. The river flowed through the city, its majestic and monotonous course reflecting the minarets of the mosques. Beyond it, an immense landscape extended all the way to the distant mountains. She watched the eagles soaring in the sky and the flocks grazing the verdure of meadows irrigated by the fertile network of canals. Sometimes, she perceived a caravan on its way to Bagdad. Might it not be bringing, at the rhythmic pace of its camels, unexpected news, a rare gem, a unique presence, a marvelous face?

And she dreamed, regretfully, of the time when life had made misery for her, and the unknown—when, as the little daughter of a cobbler, she had eaten the rinds of water-melons heaped up in the detritus of markets, while vermin pullulated in the rags that covered her young bare skin so poorly.

It was on one of these days of sadness that Scheherazade was notified of the arrival of a great caravan. From the depths of the land of the Garamides, crossing the deserts of the Bogdiane,[1] it had reached Bagdad at the expense of a thousand fatigues and a thousand dangers, to offer the Sultana presents addressed to her by the king of that land. The men who composed it did not resemble those of Bagdad, either in their clothing or in their faces.

Among them was one who had the reputation of a celebrated storyteller and asked to attempt the proof. He was tall, and left his face carefully veiled, like a woman's. He was said to be of a great race and a princely family. He solicited the favor of telling a story to the Sultana. To this request, Scheherazade had shrugged her shoulders. What was the point of repeating a futile experiment yet again? What did the presumptuous stranger expect? This one, as an example, she would not spare. To punish his audacity, she would not have his ears cut off, but his head. So much the worse for the man who was told that she would await him the following day!

---

1 I have left these two terms as they are in the original, although it is possible that the author is thinking of the Garamantes, a tribe once reputed to live in the southern Sahara.

It was a hot and luminous night, like the one on which Shariar had been assassinated. The stars were shining and the moon had risen. Scheherazade, lying on her perfumed leather cushions, listened, as on that previous night, to the murmur of the fountains, while respiring the odor of the roses. She felt strangely troubled. She would have liked to bathe her feverish body in icy water to extinguish its unquiet ardor. As soon as she had finished with the presumptuous stranger, she would plunge into the subterranean swimming bath whose waters came from a spring so profound that they had the sparkling transparency of diamond—but before then, she gave the order for the storyteller to be introduced. He appeared instantly.

He was, indeed, tall of stature, and seemed elegant and robust in his build. An ample robe enveloped him entirely and his face was covered by a veil. Instead of prostrating himself at the Sultana's feet he stood upright before her. She considered him curiously. What words were about to emerge from that secret mouth?

Scheherazade suddenly felt interested. Suddenly, it seemed that the leather of her cushions had become delightfully cool, that the stars were brighter, the moon more silvery. The air had a particular savor. The fountains were murmuring more harmoniously, the roses were more sweetly-scented. Abruptly, in the shadows that were suddenly divine, a nightingale began to sing.

The stranger remained silent, and veiled. Scheherazade was silent too, her heart palpitating, and she lowered her eyes.

When she raised them again, the man had removed his veil and was gazing at her, his face bare, with a finger placed on his lips. He was handsome—as handsome as happiness and the dawn—and he continued to maintain silence; and yet, Scheherazade heard emerging from that taciturn mouth the mute words of the most marvelous of tales: that of Love, spoken in the silence, which contains all the beauty of death and of life.

THE MIRROR

by Jean Richepin

THE old man in whose shop the old mirror was offered for sale had nothing strange about him to distinguish him from so many other old men in whose shops old mirrors are offered for sale.

Like almost all his fellows, he had a hooked nose clad with spectacles, gray wisps of hair under a rabbit-skin cap, a long, dirty and jaundiced beard and a strong German accent.

The old mirror, on the other hand, did not resemble the many old mirrors that so many old men sell.

To begin with, it was not framed, contrary to the custom of all those old mirrors about which the old men say to you, guilefully: "The frame is ebony."[1]

This old mirror had for its only rim the overlap of the sheet of lead on which the glass was set. That sheet of lead was, moreover, quite thick, and as the glass too was thick, the mirror was extremely heavy.

---

1 The shopkeeper's speech is represented in the original by a calculatedly horrible eye-dialect supposedly representative of his thick German accent, but I have made no attempt to duplicate it.

That absence of a frame might have had for compensation the beauty or the dimension of the glass, of which the old man would not have failed to make the most. In truth, he could not, the mirror being scarcely thirty centimeters square and the glass, although thick and very smooth, not having an agreeable tint. One might have thought it composed of green, stagnant, marshy water. That did not tempt self-reflection; it gave you a face worthy of the Morgue.

Like all his fellows, however, the sly old man knew the craft of salesmanship. So he showed, for preference, the back of the mirror, extolling the weight and quality of the lead sheet, and taking particular care to point out a square of paper stuck in one of the corners.

"Very interesting, due to its rarity, for a collector."

And indeed, the piece of paper intrigued and tempted the young man in the process of examining it in a singular manner. The young man had recognized, at the first glance, Gothic characters of a very ancient form, inscribed in very fine handwriting, tracing lines of unequal length, which were probably verse.

"A German song!" said the old man. "A pretty song!"

"In High German, then," said the young man, "for I know modern German, and I can't make head nor tail of this."

The old man took a greasy wallet out of his pocket, opened it, sorted through the papers it contained, separated out one page and held it out to him, saying: "I have the translation and I'll sell it with the mirror." But he held it so as only to be seen at a distance, and did not confide it to the young man, who was already reaching out for it.

"Hold on," the old man continued. "It's thirty francs for the mirror, with the lead and the translation. Thirty francs the lot. An opportunity, a nice opportunity, for a collector, very nice."

The young man paid the thirty francs and carried away the mirror, whose weight occupied both his hands alternately, preventing him from reading the translation immediately, which had been put into an envelope by the old man.

Having arrived home, the young man put the mirror down, propped up against a pile of heavy books on his work-table, and curiously set about reading the translation of the Gothic poem. This is what it said, in bizarre French, probably word for word:

> *Under the glaucous water of the mortal pool where*
> *   prisoner I am, dead alive,*
> *The wrath of the enchanter by his enchantments has*
> *   enchained me.*
> *And I weep here, Undine sealed in the web that is*
> *   my coffin.*
> *Until the day when the clairvoyant and handsome*
> *   Prince I shall see.*
> *Into the clear and limpid running water of the*
> *   river of his homeland;*
> *With me he plunges, the clairvoyant and handsome*
> *   Prince, beautifully enlaced,*
> *And the river of his homeland to the enchantments*
> *   of the enchanter will put an end.*
> *An end too to all the sufferings suffered by the clair*
> *   voyant and handsome Prince.*
> *An end too to this poem, which so many have read*

without reading well (pay attention, you!)
An end too to the song that here I weep, silently,
Undine fixed, alas!
Under the glaucous water of the mortal pool where
prisoner I am, dead alive.

As he finished the final line, the young man looked into the mirror, and saw the face of a drowned man—but that did not astonish him at all; he had had that vision already in the old man's shop, and knowing full well that it was necessary to attribute it to the green tint of the glass and nothing else.

What did astonish him was the pleasure he obtained from seeing himself thus, with the face of a drowned man, and the very long time that he remained in that contemplation, from which he could not tear away his eyes or his mind, delighting therein.

And what astonished him even more, and yet did not astonish him at all, but seemed, on the contrary, to be the most natural thing in the world, was that he soon ceased to distinguish his own face in the mirror, discerning nothing there but a vague green, marshy stagnation—and then he saw, little by little, designed in the floating, melting, scarcely-perceptible features of an apparition on the brink of vanishing, a new face.

It was the face of the Undine. She had water-weed for hair, softly serpentine. Her pupils darted a pale glaucous fire, in which all the gray-green of the ambient water was concentrated. She was weeping—and, at the same time, a furtive smile wandered over her wan lips.

And all of that was very distant, very alien, very deep, gently and infinitely.

171

Where was that distance? Where was that alien place? Deep in what? He did not think of asking himself that. He looked. He saw. He was fascinated. He fell prey to it, gently and infinitely.

"What a singular hallucination!" he said, abruptly coming round.

A hallucination, of course! He could not doubt it. A perfectly explicable hallucination, moreover, he thought. The reading of the poem, the gaze fixed for a long time upon the mirror, the kind of hypnotism that the fixity in question produced, the particular tint of the glass, was more than was required to take account, rationally and scientifically, of the optical illusion succeeding a reverie and amalgamating with it an appearance of reality.

For now, in the mirror, it was certainly himself that was contemplating—with the face of a drowned man, undoubtedly because of the green tint that . . . but himself, certainly, and no longer the Undine, the imaginary Undine!

He smiled at his slight absence of mind. After which, sadly, he said to himself: *It's a pity, even so, that it was only a hallucination. It's a pity, too, not to believe in that sort of legend. To be the clairvoyant Prince who delivers her would be so fine! Simply having the idea that one might be him would be so delightful! But now, now . . . to have such an idea it would be necessary to be mad, absolutely mad!*

Then, more sadly still, with a veritable despair: *They aren't to be pitied, the mad! They're enviable. Oh yes!*

He reread the translation of the poem. He learned it by heart. He repeated it to himself while staring at himself in the mirror. He gave himself the hallucination again. Again the Undine appeared to him. She was always weeping and smiling.

From day to day, her features became more precise. Now, she was no longer content to smile and weep silently. In a very low, very vague voice, like the murmur of a subterranean stream, she said: "You are the clairvoyant Prince, since you have seen me, since you see me."

Every time, before vanishing, in a melancholy fashion, she added: "Why can't you believe them, these truths that you so wickedly call legends? Why don't you love me—me, who loves you?"

And one day, his friends found the young man on a slab in the Morgue. Mariners had fished up his cadaver, retained underwater for rather a long time by the weight of a sheet of lead, which he was clutching in his arms against his breast, gently and infinitely.

Undoubtedly, in rolling over stones in the river, the mirror had cracked and broken. Only a single piece of it remained between the overlapping edges of the lead sheet. The glass was in the river.

Doubtless, too, the water had detached the piece of paper stuck to one of its corners, on which the poem in Gothic letters had been inscribed.

All of it can be explained, as you see, quite naturally, by the madness of the young man.

But perhaps, too, the Undine has been liberated by him, and they are living happily, forever, in a magical palace of azure and emerald.

Are you quite certain of the contrary? Quite certain? Perfectly certain?

I'm not.

THE IDOL

by Frédéric Boutet

Your joyous speech has despotic words;
Your eyes are so powerful, your aspect so strong,
That the kings of the Orient have said in their hymns
That your redoubtable gaze is the equal of Death . . .
Alfred de Vigny.

SINGULARLY wild and desolate was the aspect of that forest in the autumnal dusk.

Jean Falmor, urging his horse along indecisive roads, found himself invaded by sentiments of anxiety and melancholy, which, in the darkness that was gradually taking hold, attained an almost superstitions intensity.

The livid light that still lingered here and there left the distances drowned in obscurity, while things close at hand seemed to grow and take on a particular significance. The traveler was unable, without anxiety, to contemplate the old trunks reaching for the sky with their gnarled and leafless branches in all directions, multiplying, gigantic and similar, as far as the eye could see, with an immemorial aspect, with the semblance of knowing all the mysteries of the night and the woods, or the inextricable tangles of brambles and thorns, creeping toward the roads like unknown enemies—and above everything, the enormous crags, whose forms borrowed a human appearance from the vague shadows that hid them, convulsive stone features beneath their tresses of lactic plants and ivy.

In the trees, the cold wind of the November evening howled without interruption. Heavy fuliginous clouds raced relentlessly over the dark sky, still blood-stained toward the horizon.

The dead leaves heaped on the ground constantly rose up in rapid eddies, some precipitating themselves in unison to the side, while others headed for unknown and various goals, falling slowly back as if too weary ever to set off again—little inconstant things appearing, in their puerile agitation, immediately turned aside, to be feeble creatures in search of happiness.

The centenarian pines scattered their eternal verdure in the wind. Profound groans emerged from the tormented branches, whose stiff and identical movements solemnly cursed the triumph of some unknown enemy. Sometimes, large branches broke. It seemed that the end of the world was nigh.

In the darkness, however, amid the gusts and the melancholy noises, Falmor continued to advance, penetrated by sadness and anguish. Ravines cutting the road obliged him to make continual detours, and soon he could no longer find his direction. Then he wandered at random, oppressed by fear.

He emerged from a profoundly enclosed path and found himself close to a large fire lit against a rock. Several individuals were gathered around the blaze.

175

The traveler dismounted. In the distance, he could see other similar fires, in a line curving to the right. The beings gathered by the fire did not move aside for him; they did not look at him and did not address a single word to him. He saw them, clad in rags, with unkempt hair and beard. A continual tremor agitated them, like that of senile old age, and yet, for the most part, they did not seem to be very old. They all wore the same expression on their faces, of unconsciousness and imbecility. Some were voraciously eating roots or wild berries. Others were asleep and shivering. Several were sitting down, eyes wide, drooling; sometimes, they grimaced odiously against the flames.

Jean Falmor watched them attentively and experienced a strange impression. The features of all those people displayed the image of lost intelligence. It seemed as if a vigorous genius must once have inhabited those heads and enspirited those now-vacant eyes. In spite of their degradation they inspired the respect that an empty temple soiled by the stigmata of a filthy destination inspires in the midst of disgust.

The traveler remained plunged in thought for a while, and finally touched the arm of the man who was closest to him.

Raising his head, the individual allowed a slow gaze to wander over him. He shook his head and resumed eating. The second did not even make a movement; his tearful eyes continued to stare at the flames while a lamentable laugh twisted his face. Another tried to speak, but only proffered disconnected sounds. Finally, an old man whose long white beard was blowing in the wind exclaimed, in a shrill voice: "Oh, I'm cold! Oh la la, I'm cold!" Then he sobbed, brokenly. Two or three of them threw themselves on the ground then, howling.

The traveler, penetrated by astonishment and horror, left them. With the bridle of his horse wrapped around his arm, he marched toward the second fire. Those in its vicinity were just as miserable and degraded. One was singing a plaintive refrain, another was growling dully like an irritated beast; a few, lying face down, were drinking from a pool of stagnant water. Falmor renewed his attempts, but again obtained nothing but silence or incomprehensible words. Several manifested an evident ill-humor, and one of them showed him his fist, with frightful facial contortions.

He went to the third fire. There, near some of the unknown creatures, was an old man, who was studying them. He was dressed in a monastic habit and holding a horse by the bridle. When Falmor approached him the old man took a few steps toward him and asked him what had brought him there.

The traveler told him about his interminable walk through the forest, explaining how he had got lost, and asked the old man to give him, if he could, an explanation of the strange beings they had before them, and then to put him back on his road. He added that he was a good Christian and strongly inclined to recognize, in the deplorable condition of these people, a particularly odious manifestation of the Devil's malice.

The old man invited him to sit down next to him on a fallen tree-trunk, and began by saying: "You're conversing with the monk Marestote."

The traveler greeted his companion respectfully, for the name of Marestote was attached to a man whose profound virtue and vast, clear-sighted wisdom was famous and venerable.

Marestote continued: "I am Marestote. Those who surround us were the intellectual luminaries of all nations." He indicated the creatures sleeping around him like beasts in their lair. "They include saints who have seen God and philosophers whose souls have penetrated the secrets of all ages to create a new wisdom. There are scientists, whose works have driven back mystery, whose words are law in schools. There are artists who were marked by divine genius, prudent and rigorous legislators, erudite doctors who plumbed the secrets of the minds and bodies of human beings.

"I tell you this: those who surround us were the first among men—that is true; as true as it is that they are now the least. All their power has vanished. Nothing remains but the body, deserted by the soul and reverted to the instincts. Nothing exists for them beyond the satisfaction of the primary appetites. The rain falls upon them, the wind lashes them and the cold tortures them. They scratch the earth to find roots and drink from pools. When they suffer, they are content to moan, devoid of the energy to struggle. And they do not even regret what they were, because they have forgotten everything."

Marestote paused, and then continued: "All these men were defeated by the same adversary. The same force broke their prodigious faculties. The same voracious monster has devoured their souls, abandoning their bodies to the condition in which you see them, for the greater power of its fatal power—an eternal enemy, ever vigilant in her perversity: Woman!"

He had pronounced these words with great anger, and Falmor was afraid.

The monk went on: "It is Woman that has made them what they are now. It's her accursed kiss that has vanquished their energies and their thoughts. It's in loving her that they have descended lower than the worst of beasts.

"Alas, since the days of *Genesis*, things have been thus. Why was Man not left solitary? Why that faithless companion, so different and so attractive? Without Woman, everything would be pure and harmonious; voluptuous sobs would no longer trouble the meditations of philosophers and the songs of poets; the perfume of oblations would no longer be combated by the odor of bodies in heat, and the mind of Man would progress in liberty toward the gaze of God without the torment of the flesh.

"Now, the same creature, beast of lust, queen of debauchery, has destroyed all those who surround us. Armed with the lascivious splendors of her body, the perversity of her caresses, the power of her fatal beauty, armed with all the power of love, in the enigma and mystery of her retreat, she has reckoned with their strength . . . and it is her that I, Marestote, a black monk commissioned by the Pope, must combat in her own domain, and vanquish, if it please God!

"The woman in question lives nearby. In a marvelous palace, the infernal glory of her beauty blossoms. A labyrinth surrounds and defends her habitation, and no one, if he does not have a guide, can cross the entanglement of its similar avenues, or even get out of its monotonous maze. However, I'm convinced that I can

179

reach her, for her pride has never recoiled before a power and a challenge. She has a supernatural knowledge of those who travel to see her, and she never refuses to meet them.

"Men have come from all points of the world. Alerted by dreams or by apparitions, armed with the various forces of their beliefs, of their genius, they have risen without fear to the conquest of the kiss, and their souls have been lost. The most celebrated philosophers and prophets of all religions have come from overseas. I have seen fakirs whose spiritual strength was boundless, whose entire lives had been concentrated in thought, and even they were vanquished.

"I know the story of an Arab magician who knew the most terrible conjurations to command material and immaterial forces. He came, served by two enchanted figures who marched before him. He wore a golden breastplate consecrated to the Angel of the Night and presenting his redoubtable emblems. Serpents coiled around it like tresses of flame, and the center was occupied by a magical visage, the gaze of which no one could support. In his left hand was a lamp taken from the tomb of Solomon. On his head, his black and red cap bore of phoenix plume and the pentacle of Good and Evil.

"So he came, boasting of enchaining that woman by means of invincible charms and reducing her to slavery forever, but no artifice was effective against her. The enchanted figures were immediately subdued, the serpents were annihilated on the vain breastplate, where the redoubtable face remained dead—and the magician was seen walking on his hands and knees and grazing the grass like a beast. He joined those she had already enslaved and who retained, in their stupidity, the sole desire not to leave the vicinity of the place where that woman and her souls dwell.

"Thus, she is haunted by her victims, who maintain fires circling her domain by day and night, and their lugubrious fires burn for her triumph, and their smoke rises up like an incense to her omnipotence . . .

"I shall destroy these things by constraining her to obedience, for I have come bearing on my breast the image of my crucified God, carved from the wood of the True Cross—and against that, no power will be able to prevail.

"If you want to march with me, man whom celestial foresight has placed on my path, your presence will be salutary for me; your prayers will protect you from any danger and reinforce mine; you shall witness the triumph of the faith and, with me, you shall purify by fire the accursed seductions of which we shall render ourselves masters. You shall be my companion for the battle and for the glory. God will name you among his elect, and when they speak of my victory, men will celebrate your name with mine, saying: that man has also fought and vanquished for the cause of the Most High!"

The old man fell silent.

"I will go with you," said Falmor. "I too have suffered at the hands of a woman. I will go with you, and I shall die, if necessary, in order to serve God and vanquish the sacrilege."

They mounted their horses.

Side by side they advanced, remaining silent. The wild desolation of the country enveloped them with an unquiet sadness.

They reached the foot of a hill and saw a great red wall extending to the right and the left in a long curve. They went along it and came to a vast open gate. Beneath the lintel, an oval violet flame remained suspended in the darkness without emitting any light. As they approached, it descended to within ten feet of the ground.

"This will guide us," said Marestote.

Going through the gate, they followed the fire, which moved horizontally. They were riding over polished scarlet stone between similar walls, vertiginously high. The sky disappeared behind stormy clouds. Sometimes, the moon's wan light shone momentarily, immediately veiled. Enveloping the riders, a furious wind howled along the walls and eddied in the intersections, but the guiding flame was not tormented by it. Thus, they went along oblique, sheer-sided paths, with innumerable turnings. Similar intersections succeeded one another, in which identical avenues opened. Here and there, bridges traversed the meanders of a rapid river, whose obscure waves flowed between red banks.

After more than an hour, they came into a semicircular area cut by the pink marble façade of a château occupying the summit of the hill and presenting a bizarre and elegant style, with numerous sculptures, delicately-excised battlements, an extended peristyle and sculpted silver balconies that sparkled in the sparse rays of moonlight.

They left their horses behind and, guided by the flame, climbed a huge perron, passed through a silver doorway and then, at the far end of a white vestibule, climbed a similar stairway.

In front of them stretched a spacious gallery illuminated by a multitude of flames of every color, from the
brightest to the softest, the palest to the darkest. They
floated lazily in warmth saturated with musk and attars
of roses, gliding along walls made of ivory, which bore
the encrusted images of enormous sulfur-yellow, mauve
or sea-green flowers, interlaced arabesques, around indecisive blue-tinted pools populated by fabulous birds,
amid lacustrian plants and flowers.

The floor, half-covered in carpets of ermine and
glaucous silk, was tiled with ivory. Large corollas of
the same substance composed the ceiling, displayed
upside-down, attached by their rims, bearing golden
pistils. Most of them held a tiny flame. Along the wall
to the right was an immense divan draped in pale satin.
At the back stood a mirror with three faces, framed
in silver. There was an organ to the left, between high
windows, whose stained glass, reproducing vague land-
scapes of walls, was buried beneath silks tinted like the
carpets.

As they went forward, the two men saw a somber
form leaning against a panel at the extremity of the
gallery, toward which the guiding flame floated. They
recognized a woman draped in a cloak of violet satin.
With her hands, she brought the dark folds back toward the lower part of her face, invisible beneath masses of burnished golden hair, encircled from the temples
to the nape by a silver band terminated by two large
sapphires, leaving the forehead uncovered.

The flame became immobile above her forehead.

The monk marched resolutely toward her. He
stopped, standing up straight in his habit.

"I come," he said, "on behalf of God, the creator of human thought. Woman, I have come to defeat your influence and destroy your power. No adversary, until now, has been able to resist you, whatever his force and whatever his armor. Know that I shall triumph, for I am invincible. I have the chastity of my age; I have the energy of those who count life for nothing; I have the calm and the confidence given by just causes. I am invincible, above all, because I am protected by Jesus, the son of God, God Himself. A piece of his holy and sacred cross, on my breast, reproduces the sign of the Redemption, against which the gates of Hell can never prevail . . . and I fear nothing . . .

"I tell you this: in your palace, which will fall, your glory will be abolished, for you are material, and the spirit of God, which has created you, will destroy you! But it is necessary that the souls that you have enslaved in the bonds of your vices should be liberated. It is necessary that the world's thought be restored to the world. It is necessary to abdicate your hatred and your pride, in order finally to adore the power that you fear and venerate in your rebellious jealousy, which you are avid, above all else, to prostitute, knowing that, alone in the world, it is capable of dethroning the ignominy of your despotism!

"Woman is shame incarnate. Her passions are puerile, her dreams perverse. Promised to Hell, she wants to drag us all thereto by means of the ascendancy given to her by the voluptuousness of her body and the tenderness and cruelty of her heart. She has damned angels. She gives birth to all our dolors and can put them to sleep. There are moments when her embrace becomes the supreme goal. Accursed, and a thousand times accursed are you, prostitute beast, on earth and in heaven!

"For you who are listening to me, the measure is complete. The time of expiation has come. I am your master. It is necessary to obey. Hell burns, life is effaced! Prostrate yourself before the Judge!"

The black monk fell silent.

The woman said to him, with a soft harmonious voice: "I don't understand your words. I only know beauty, my beauty—that alone is important. The souls you demand are not captive, madman! They remain in me of their own accord, in a permanent, every-increasing bliss. They have definitively abandoned their carnal shackles. Various flames, according to their various essences, you can see them floating in this palace—their palace—and I do not want them to leave me, and they do not want to leave me. I can tell you that they are incarnate in me, and also that my beauty is made of their beauty. The weaknesses of the flesh do not exist for us. I am a virgin, and will be forever, and we love one another uniquely. What god would be worthy to move us? What amour could equal our marvelous amours?

"I tell you this: they are speaking to you through my mouth; my beauty is the garden of their delights, and I hold in my hands the keys of Paradise. Do you understand me?"

She raises her head and, parting her arms in a slow gesture, she draws the edges of her somber cloak back to the ivory wall with her fingertips, thus resplendently displaying her naked beauty, her miraculous beauty . . .

The whiteness of her skin is mat and polished, with a gilded roseate translucency. Above her arched feet, resting on a swansdown carpet, the slimness of her ankles elongates and folds back lazily. Then, there is the gracious grasp of the knee and the voluptuous plenitude of thighs; the skin is as delicate as the most adorable silk, seemingly warm and perfumed, and the delight of its touch must be superior to any other.

The polished curves of the abdomen rise above, without a shadow. The amplitude of the hips widens its roundness to diminish on the slenderness of the waist. The torso swells, and the two breasts extend their pure contours, with their rosy and distant tips and their moist cleavage caressed by the curls of her hair. The arms part in a supple movement, developing their tapering lines as far as the small, half-open hands.

The blonde hair is gathered in undulating masses around the throat; allowing nevertheless a glimpse of the gracious bearing of the neck, it surrounds the pale and symmetrical slightly-elongated oval of the face. Of the forehead only a small section is perceptible, blossoming like the profile on an inverted cup beneath the undulation of the tresses circled by the silver headband, whose sapphires reflect sparkling gleams. The straight and slender nose presents nacreous translucencies.

Between the red lips, of an exquisite precision, the enamel of the teeth is scarcely illuminated. The eyebrows are thinly and emphatically arched. The eyelids, half-raised, disclose the unfathomable light of the gaze that attaches to that of the old man.

The eyes are long, perfectly divided, surrounded by serried blonde lashes curved at their tips. The irises have an astral radiance, and the velvet of flowers. They are violet, changing and profound. Their expression is proud and candid, voluptuous and infinitely soft. Nothing can be compared to them.

Flames come in number and form a suspended, swaying aureole around the woman's body and visage.

Thus she poses, divine.

Jean Falmor did not receive the gaze of the eyes, which were pouring all their light into the eyes of the monk, but, torn by a prodigious emotion, he contemplated such superhuman beauty passionately, and, kneeling down without knowing whether it was to pray to God or to pray to her, in the chaos of his soul, he prayed. Meanwhile, he darted a glance at his companion.

Now, the monk Marestote was lying on the ground. His eyes were fixed on the radiant eyes and his hands were clasped, and his voice rose up in a pathetic cry.

"I renounce the World, Man and Christ! You alone exist! You abolish everything before your glory, O Woman, supreme marvel, only God!"

These words, spoken by Marestote struck Falmor with an immense terror. He seemed to find himself at the center of a cataclysm. Without raising his eyes again, he fled. He went down the marble steps and, recovering his mount, drove it into the labyrinth of red stone.

There, he wandered for a long time through the similar junctions, the identical avenues.

It was not until the middle of the following day that, guided by hazard, he reached the gate, still open. Exhausted by fatigue, he lay down on the dry leaves outside and went to sleep.

When he woke up, it was dark. As he detached the bridle of his horse in order to leave, he heard footsteps behind him and saw a human form emerge from the long scarlet maze. It was an old man, marching with a shuffling gait.

Jean Falmor had difficulty recognizing Marestote, the black monk commissioned by the Pope, for the old man's soul had quit his body, in which nothing any longer remained but base desires and instincts. He interrogated him, but obtained no response other than a peevish clucking and vague complaints regarding cold and hunger.

Side by side they walked until they reached the nearest of the fires, and cries broke out because the old man had immediately hurled himself upon one of the miserable creatures to snatch away the root that he was gnawing.

Falmor could not bear to watch the savage struggle. He fled.

He galloped all night, in a delirium and terror of doubt, through the desolate forest, the menacing rocks and the trees convulsed by the wind. As day broke, his mount fell dead, on the threshold of a monastery.

Having fallen unconscious, Falmor woke up in a monk's cell, and, regarding that as an order from God, he never returned to the world of men.

Thus, for having approached the idol that he could not comprehend, he was obliged to spend his life.

Fifteen years later, he died in a state of sanctity, in despair and terror, because, since the very first moment, he had adored with all his soul the woman whose beauty he had seen unveiled, and who had not deigned to take possession of his credulous and uncertain soul.

ENNOIA

by André Lebey

> She has loved adultery, idolatry, lies and
> stupidity. She has prostituted herself to all
> peoples. She has sung at all crossroads. She
> has kissed all faces.
>
> (Gustave Flaubert,
> *The Temptation of Saint Anthony*)

I

A kind of vague mist descended over the city, through which the forms of men and things appeared confusedly. Along the road, in the distance, travelers were hastening, on foot or on horseback, haloed by ruddy reflections that the gradually declining disk of the sun prolonged behind them. The first stars were beginning to appear.

Lights burst forth at the windows of dwellings all along the streets. In the low quarter, the taverns appeared like hearths, toward which everyone was headed. They filled up rapidly and the customers spilled out on to the terraces, with laughter, appeals, cries and the sound of colliding cups and refrains. A whole crowd was sparkling under the gleam of lanterns, distributed in the foliage, standing out, against the illuminated interior of the terrace, as a shifting mass, which the bright dresses of women undulated. They were still arriving. They were coming from the plebeian quarters. Their black, russet or saffron yellow hair helmed their powdered faces; their dresses hanging loosely, without belts, attracted the gazes of men, who called to them with obscene pleasantries and, when they were close by, tipped them over in order to kiss them full on the mouth.

Someone went past the tavern and climbed the steps to the terrace.

A voice departed from one of the groups: "Simon!"

Simon approached the man who had called him and sat down. "I'm going away soon," he said.

"Philosopher," replied his friend, smiling, "you live within yourself too much, and that's bad. Look around you. Some of these women are pretty, and you went past them without looking at them. Here's Falernian wine, and you refuse to drink it! What do you need, then? A night refreshed by the breeze, women, wine, a few friends and songs by good poets, isn't that the dream of life, and is there anything else to desire? Reflecting on that which was or that which is yet to come is a poor way of wasting one's time; what you are pleased to call wisdom is nothing but the dream of your imagination and there is perhaps more wisdom in the nonchalance of my smile than in all your philosophy."

Slightly withdrawn into the shadow, Simon did not reply. Although he had often had occasion to see it,

190

he was astonished by that debauchery, and could not understand what pleasure could be found therein. He judged the life of those surrounding him as insipid and monotonous, without reflecting that his own was equally so, in spite of the extraordinary quality with which it was enveloped. Legend had made him want to learn the marvelous secrets of the strange solitaries who lived in the forests beyond the mountains of Assyria. It was also said that he knew the meaning of all religions and all the sciences, and was able to command nature. No one had ever seen him laugh or weep; his disciples wondered whether he might not be a god.

Because I have never told them what is in my heart, Simon thought, *they have enveloped me with their legends, but if they were able to understand they would see how much I have suffered and suffer still. Yes, I have read the papyruses, I have listened to the doctors, I have classified philosophies and I have tried to build a new one, but sometimes I have looked at the papyruses without being able to read them, I have listened to the doctors without hearing them, and I have toiled over the philosophies; I have looked into the future and I have seen that I lack something. I have searched for the unnamed god and I believe that I have found him, but I have never heard him. The time of exile has been long! There are times when the desire for a semi-slumber invades and one would like to feel the beating of a woman's heart. But women are no longer worthy of being loved; they cannot hear the eternal voice. Time has broken the winged child's bow, his arrows are dispersed who knows where; nothing remains of him but a memory and his empty quiver, with which people play dice.*

The guests were beginning to be astonished by Simon's silence. One of them touched his shoulder and said: "You're too taciturn, philosopher; does your wisdom prevent you from talking?"

"Others might be annoyed by your wit, Nicias," he replied.

"But you don't get annoyed, do you? It's necessary to introduce something into the conversation; already, we don't know what to talk about. But here comes Helen. Do you know her, Simon? We've called her Helen in memory of the one from Lacedaemon, who could not have been more beautiful. Helen!" he called.

The courtesan approached. When she had saluted all the guests she paused before Simon. "Who's this?" she asked.

"Simon, one of our friends."

She sat down facing him, without saying anything. There was a moment's silence, then the wine filled the cups again, and the laughter and conversations resumed.

The philosopher gazed at the courtesan; she stopped speaking occasionally in order to look at him, and immediately lowered her gaze, surprised and confused.

He stood up, said adieu and left.

He was already at the base of the terrace when he saw Helen running after him. She stopped, trembling slightly. "I would like to talk to you," she said, "but I can't."

He looked at her with a certain tenderness, and she thought she saw lassitude in his eyes.

"Lord," she went on, "it's necessary not to be scornful of us. It isn't our fault. There is often sadness in our hearts."

But Simon said angrily: "There has been nothing in your hearts for a long time. You mothers taught you to lie and sold you as soon as you were old enough to couple with men."

The courtesan bowed her head and appeared to be weeping. He waited for something, without knowing himself exactly what it might be. Suddenly, as she raised her eyes toward him, he kissed her on the forehead.

"Ah!" she cried.

But he seemed to run away. She watched him, without having the courage to call to him. Then, when she no longer saw his cloak fluttering over the road, she wiped her eyes.

A woman joked: "One might think you'd been weeping. If your gallant is dead, there are others . . . that's truly too much pity.

II

The taverns extinguished their lights one after another. Couples went by in the shadows. On the thresholds, women lay in wait for passers-by, and when one came along, made signs to him. Gradually, the streets became silent and deserted. The lights were extinct in almost all the houses. The night was so beautiful that Simon did not take the road to his dwelling. He felt full of an extraordinary desire to live, and could not believe that God had withdrawn from the world; the essential thing must be to discover him. Perhaps it was necessary to act; perhaps it was not good to remain in solitude watching others from afar; perhaps duty consisted of manifesting by actions rather than words what one had learned in silence. Perhaps . . . always perhaps . . . and nothing else to guide one but uncertain reasoning. The dream of remaining two throughout life had long been his; having subsequently recognized the impossibility, he had not attempted it, but he had conserved a vague desire for it. The effort of living might then be less difficult, and although Simon knew how dangerous amour is for the meditative, he could not help wishing for it.

And he remembered the prostitute encountered on the terrace of the tavern, with her black veil attached around her neck by a large knot. She had spoken words to him surprising in such a mouth. Why should they not have been true? Dolor is one of the roads to redemption.

And he said to himself: *She has suffered; she is suffering. She remembers the time when amour appeared to her to be the most glorious goal of life, offered as the most infinite and the most magnificent. If she has fallen it was because she did not fund a hand nearby to sustain her, no ear to listen to her plaint, no thoughtful soul to console her. I was brutal; I doubted her: I rejected her. I should have welcomed her. She resembles those who are believed to be no longer pure; not all of them have a banal soul, but those who have not do not want to let it appear . . .*

She is weary of living, but still hesitant; she does not know . . .

While walking at random through the city he arrived at the right bank of the Halya. The river was flowing somberly, speckled here and there with little moonlit waves, and droplets water suddenly sprang up when a fish emerged from the water. Simon sat down,

194

quivering with enthusiasm and delight, as if something extraordinary had happened or was about to happen. He knelt down and commenced a prayer.

The city extended its confused mass, punctuated by the gaps of avenues, from which columns rose up here and there, and then, further away, taller and bulkier constructions. He could also see the temples with their inclined roofs and triangular frontons. On the other side of the river there was a green plain planted with palm trees and bordered on the horizon by an undulation of hills.

When his prayer was concluded, Simon fell asleep.

Suddenly, a distant voice seemed to become audible. He listened.

The voice sang: "Caesarea! Caesarea! You are reposing after the infamy of your debauchery. Your inhabitants have fallen asleep next to women to whom they have given themselves without amour. You have all denied the divine word that you hear within yourselves and the young men have soiled their lips on those of prostitutes.

"Caesarea! Caesarea! Lust has enveloped you in its mortal caress, it has maddened you with the promise of unusual voluptuousness and you have not had the courage to reply that sensualities are as fleeting as the dust of the road carried away by the wind, as ephemeral as the flowers that only live for a single day.

"Caesarea! Caesarea! There will come to Simon the great virtue of God. He will see the matter that suffers; he will follow the prostitute into the brothels, he will take her by the hand, he will listen to the story of her troubles and he will show her the road to the elect."

Simon woke up and raised his head. There was no trace of the angel of Heaven. The stars were going out one by one. White vapors were visible in the orient. It was the morning twilight. The mass of the city emerged gradually from obscurity, standing out against a horizon that was less and less somber. Colors were almost becoming visible. Little pink and yellow clouds were beginning to elongate in the increasingly blue sky. The sun finally caused the gilt of the temples to sparkle, and its rays slowly propagated further and further, like the reflection of a growing conflagration. A transparent mist escaped from the waters of the river, vanishing as it rose into the air. The fatigue of awakening sensed in that scene was gradually finished, until it appeared completely. There was no one in the streets but water-carriers and belated drunkards, who, not having been able to return home, had spent the night drinking more in taverns or snoring against the boundary markers at the crossroads.

III

Nicias had taken Helen home with him. As he had offered a lot of money and she was poor, she had not been able to resist it. She would rather have remained alone that evening.

She went home in the morning. She tidied her room slightly, opened the window, watered her flowers and went to bed. She had no need of sleep, but for reverie; she thought about Nicias' friend, who had said almost nothing, and then had kissed her on the forehead. She did not know why she was moved, but she yielded to her emotion and held out her arms in empty space, crying: "Simon! Simon!"

Someone knocked on the door. She did not get up to open it, not wanting to see anyone now. But the door opened by itself. A man advanced, lowering his head.

"Who are you?" she asked, fearfully.

He took off his cloak.

"Oh, so it's you. I called to you!"

"I heard you," he replied. "I knew that you would call me, and even before you did it, I was coming to your house."

They both fell silent, embarrassed, lowering their eyes. The philosopher was hesitant again; the courtesan felt so small next to him that she did not know what to say, thinking that it was necessary to speak differently to him than to an ordinary man.

He finally approached her.

"Speak," he said to her.

"I'm not yet twenty," she replied. "I've known men for four years, and I've aided my mother with the money they gave me in exchange for my body. It's the fault of the first one I met. One evening, when I was sitting watching the children play on the road he approached me, took my hand and told me that I was beautiful. A nurse had once soothed me with tales of amour, she had spoken to me about one that had my name, and many others I can't remember, because no one since has told me legends or talked to me about the gods.

"The man who had approached me was young. He told me about the coolness of the forests, the calm that falls from the moon, the liberty of the fauns and nymphs; he exalted the joy of loving and promised to love me for a long time. I didn't know that lies were mingled with amour. The night was dark; the forest was quivering under a warm breeze. My father was dead, my mother was in bed. I replied that I loved him already, and that I had distinguished him from the other young men who went past our house to go to the gymnasium. He took me away . . .

"The next day, he assured me that he would come back. He didn't come back, and never came back. I learned afterwards that he had gone to the barbarian lands and had married there. My mother knew what I had done and advised me to become a courtesan. One evening she took me to a populous quarter of the city and sold me to a rich merchant. I was afraid and I wept because I didn't like him at all, and I thought about the other. Like the other, he left me the next day, and like the day before, the next day it was the same thing again. And my life was like that for four years and still is today."

She added: "If I've ever loved a man it was him, the first one. Do you know whether he'll return to Caesarea one day?"

"I don't know him," said Simon, "but I know something else." And he fell silent.

"Say it quickly," she said.

"I hesitate to tell you . . ."

"I'll understand all that you say."

"Listen, then!" exclaimed Simon, raising his hand. "Listen! Before the commencement of the world, when there was nothing but void and darkness, two demons divided the expanse of what didn't yet exist between them. They had both received the mission to create; the one that reigns forever beyond the confines of a silent eternity was to be their judge, but he didn't possess the power to annihilate their future work and could only combine their discoveries.

"One of the demons had a black skin with red glints, the other white skin with blue glints. As they hated the invisible Being, they agreed between themselves to imagine two forces so dissimilar and opposite that their combination would become impossible. The one who had black skin created a being entirely of flesh, bent double, and the one who had white skin created a being similar to the one of flesh, but much lighter and freer, whose shoulders were charged with wings. When the invisible Being saw them he trembled, bowed his head and wept. The demons, who suspected that, even though they couldn't see him, laughed.

"But the invisible Being raised his head again and threw a ball into space. The ball grew as it fell; it finally stopped in the void, became immobile and began to rotate on its axis. Then the demons leaned over the globe. Two little bodies similar to those they had created were moving there. The two demons looked at one another and understood. Then they threw themselves upon one another and fought. They're still fighting, and they'll fight until the globe vanishes. Have you understood, Helen? One had created matter, the other the substance that doesn't die. And they fought because their objectives were so different; and they're still fighting. Helen. They're not as far away as you think; they're inside us."

Thoughtfully, the courtesan said: "And amour, Lord?"

Simon said nothing.

"Isn't that what appeases them?" she asked.

He replied: "If it's amour that is finally singing in your heart, give me your hand and we'll leave. But be careful: there's an amour that you don't know, which is superior to the one you know. You know the amour of bodies, you don't know the amour of souls; it's the one of souls that prevents the body from suffering. The road is less rude then. But it's necessary to neglect the other, because it's only an impurity. Listen. I too have suffered from being alone; we'll be two now to tell people the truth. That's hard because people are wicked. Do you want to follow me along the road and stand next to me when I speak in the towns?"

And when the courtesan laid her head on his shoulder and said: "But you love me, don't you?" he was content to reply: "Helen! I shall call you Ennoia. For me you are the one who has suffered since the commencement of the world, who is suffering and will always suffer. But I shall save you. It's you who caused the ruination of Troy; it's you who cut Samson's hair. But now you shall be the one who is pure, and of whom poets will sing. Weep! Weep! Tears are holy, they come from the most distant part of us; it's God who inspires them in us, to permit us to redeem ourselves."

They went out. They took the road of travelers, but before quitting the city they met Nicias.

What's happening, then?" he exclaimed. "Helen and Simon walking together!"

Helen bowed her head. Simon replied: "Open your eyes and learn to see. Helen is dead; it is Ennoia that you see here. Offer her gold and she will not know what you want with her. She is my sister and no longer has anything in common with you. You can tell the news to those who claim to have known her. You have not known her; there was a secret in her that you have been unable to discover."

IV

Ephraim . . . Issacar . . . Mageddo . . .

They went from city to city bearing the good news. In public squares, while Simon exhorted the crowd, Helen stood beside him silently. She did not understand his words, but she could not remember ever having heard a voice as powerfully soft as his, and she found it admirable. She was glad to be with him and did not ask to understand; she gave the impression of understanding because she had noticed that he was joyful every time she had seemed moved.

She loved him. From the day when he had placed his lips on her forehead, he had appeared better to her; afterwards, she had learned to appreciate what she had neglected: the white roses that blossomed in her window had given her joy in being scented, and she had played with her necklaces, at which she scarcely looked, out of habit. She had followed him fatally, as one follows one's destiny; she had not even debated it a little with herself. She did not think that a day might come when she would no longer love him. She had no one but him in the world; other men were ignoble or insignificant to her.

At dusk they sat down in some deserted corner, preferably in the country. He taught her then. He revealed the mystery of theogonies, the same truth hidden in all religions; he tried to make her feel pity for the human race. He also talked to her about his doubt. She listened without ever making any reply; she only huddled more tightly against him, pressing all of her voluptuous flesh against his and raising palpitating lips toward his pale face. She dared not tell him that she judged amour superior to his teaching, for fear of annoying him; she waited in the hope that he would one day take her as she dreamed of being taken and make her forget by means of his tender caresses the brutal caresses of others that she had had to endure. But the more she enveloped him with desire, the more reserved he became, the more he pretended not even to know what she wanted, the more he exalted her toward the distant idealities to the promise of which she would have preferred the simplest caress.

One evening he talked to her about her past life.

"I dread, Ennoia, that the impurity of your former conduct might rebound upon you now, although you have had the desire to purify yourself. Have you reflected on everything that was abominable in those relationships of a day? You say you believe in love, but you believed then in deceptive amour, the one that only matter dominates, and which is nothing because it has to end, whereas only the other is true because it is immortal and the furthest distances cannot impede it. Believe me, Ennoia, we ought not to love one another as the vulgar love one another; for me you are more than a woman; you are suffering matter and you are *the* woman; you are woman redeemed; it is necessary not to set aside the tiny divine flame that there is within us. That is the condition of your redemption, for, all thought it was unconscious, you have sinned a great deal. Believe me, Ennoia; you ought to give the world the example of a great sacrifice, and the amour that you feel for me, you ought to take further, higher, rid of all mortal attachment, toward the absolute principle, toward God. I ought only to be the means of your amour, the guide of your ignorance. Is that not more beautiful? You are my sister, Ennoia."

And without replying, she had wept on the prophet's shoulder.

And the days and nights had gone by.

And they had gone from city to city.

Meggado . . . Bostra . . . Damascus . . .

V

Outside the tavern, Simon waited. He had returned to Caesarea alone, and for seven days he had not seen his companion; she had left without leaving even a lock of hair, a jewel or a flower. He had been to knock on her door several times, but no one had come to open it. He had thought for a few hours that she was dead or ill, but now he supposed something that he dared not even think. He repeated to himself the rare words that she had murmured, and he refused to believe that they were lies; he remembered her emotion and refused to believe it futile; he had heard her voice.

Then he had come here. He was afraid of seeing her and desired it. His gaze searched all the groups anxiously.

Not perceiving her, he headed toward other places of debauchery with which she had been familiar before their encounter. But he did not find her there either.

He decided to knock on her door one last time. An insurmountable dolor gripped him now, made of anguish, doubt and regret. His soul, weary of impossible idealities, was beating its wings toward a human happiness. Why had he not loved her as others had loved her? Would that amour have been holy, since it would have been more than an ordinary caprice? Was life not that very union, and was not living in accordance with the meaning of that life to serve God? Amour simultaneously ideal and carnal was the reconciliation of the two demiurges, the perfect endeavor.

He was hesitating before the door when he perceived two black shadows along the houses at the end of the street. The moon illuminated the night. A pink fabric appeared beneath a black veil. A clear voice resonated softly.

"It's nearly three months since I had a man."

He retreated into a shadowy corner.

"It's her," he murmured.

She passed very close to him without seeing him, and continued speaking:

"You won't believe me, but it's the truth. For three months I've been living with a prophet who never possessed me in spite of all the desire I had to be possessed and in spite of all my attempts. He turned his head away sadly when I kissed him on the mouth or held him against my breast for too long. He's the man that I loved the most and I'll never love another as much as I loved him, but he offended me and I left. I think he's mad, because he talked to me about incomprehensible things, but I never encountered anyone as strangely beautiful as him."

In front of the door she sighed again.

"Yes, he was mad, because I could have been the happiness of his life and he's passed close to his happiness without perceiving it. But now I no longer love him. Come with me . . ."

The door closed. Simon saw the light filtering under the worn threshold. He sat down and listened.

In the room, first there was laughter, and then songs. He heard the click of necklaces, bracelets and rings thrown into a cup. A silence followed, traversed by the rustle of fabrics, and then he heard amorous words, a sound of colliding flesh, a sigh that gradually rose, a forceful breath that mingled with it, and almost a cry.

Tears came to his eyes at the thought of that future soiled, tarnished forever.

"The courtesan is right. It's necessary not to neglect terrestrial happiness. The flesh is a consoler and it's a sin not to give it what it wants. And I have been punished because I have sinned."

The vision returned to him brutally of the couple that he had heard taking one another. A great sob rose from the depths of his throat. But as he judged tears to be unworthy of a man, he covered his head with a flap of his cloak and returned slowly to his dwelling.

While walking, he repeated the words of the divine voice: ". . . sensualities are as ephemeral as the flowers that only live for a single day."

He murmured: "What does it matter that the flowers are ephemeral? We ought not let their perfume or their beauty be lost; they have not ornamented the edge of our route in order that we should pass them by indifferently. It is necessary to pick all the flowers that life offers us."

And now that he could no longer live, he imagined in a dream the happiness that a misplaced morality had lost him forever.

WEDDING NIGHT

by Catulle Mendès

A livid pallor of dawn slid through the curtains. I was not asleep, gazing at that sad light. A bell rang, violently, redoubled, echoing in the apartment, and a few moments later, Sylvain Brunel opened the door of my bedroom, followed by my domestic, dressed in haste, who picked up the lamp.

"You!" I cried.

My surprise was all the more natural because the day before, Sylvain Brunel had married a beautiful young woman with whom he had evidently been passionately smitten. What was he doing in my house at an hour when he ought still to be ecstatic in the delectable triumph of the wedding night?

My astonishment increased, and became a dolorous anxiety, when I had remarked the pale face of the visitor, his eyes injected with red bile and his lips trembling like those of a fever-victim.

As soon as we were alone, he put a hand on my shoulder and spoke very rapidly, stammering, with teeth that were chattering.

"Do you believe in the impossible? Do you believe in the prodigious chimera of the dead who live, like us, who love, hate, suffer and weep like us? In the miracle of the dead who accompany us in the street, take our arm, sit down at our table, lie down in our bed? If those things aren't true, well then, lock me up—I'm mad!"

While I considered him with an increasing stupor, he let himself fall into an armchair next to my bed.

"Listen," he went on, lowering his voice, his speech slowing, "you know how I love Gilberte, my wife! You can divine with what hectic desire, yesterday evening, I waited for the moment when the two of us would finally be alone? That moment came, so hopefully awaited. Heart melted in delight, I was outside the door of the nuptial chamber; my hand touched the key; I was about to go in . . .

"A frisson ran through me, from head to for, with the zigzag of an icy lightning bolt over all my flesh. What was the matter with me? At first, I didn't understand. The effect had preceded the cause. I had the symptom of terror before the terror itself. But the fear arrived very quickly, sharp and intense. Yes, I was afraid. Why? Because I thought, for no reason, about Madame de Mortales, the poor dead woman who had loved me so much, so close to the dear living one I loved so much! It was like encountering a tomb on the threshold of paradise.

"With the gaze of the spirit, which contemplates past things, I saw her, Laurencia, pale and motionless, in the big bed from which she was not to rise again, having no more life except in the depths of her eyes, where a wild and jealous amour burned; and I heard her repeating to me, with the harshness of her Aragonese accent the words that she had already said to me so frequently:

"'You will never love another woman, will you? No, never? Whether I live or die, you'll be faithful to me, forever? Oh, if you deceive me, Sylvèrte, beware! I'll avenge myself, treason for treason. Resolutely, coldly, if you prefer another woman, I'll deliver myself to another man. Even dead, for I believe that I shall wake from the eternal sleep to accomplish my vengeance.'

"I heard those mad and sinister words yesterday evening, my hand on the key of the nuptial chamber. I heard them confusedly, as if a specter were whispering in my ear. But finally, with a surge of will power, I drove away the chimeras and became master of myself; smiling at my folly, I opened the blessed door. Pale and trembling, in the lace of her peignoir, Gilberte was waiting for me, and became very pink when she saw me. I knelt down before her, like a pilgrim at the feet of a statue of the Virgin and I adored her, full of grace.

"Let those who boast of the vain joys of culpable amours say what they will; perfect intoxication, the supreme delight, is to contemplate the blush of a virgin soon to be a wife, who is frightened, but who wants it dearly. Gently, slowly, as one might touch the wings of Psyche, I had taken her in my arms, and on her lips, scarcely turned away . . .

"Extraordinary thing! To our kiss, it seemed to me that another kiss responded, also tender, distant, like a faithful echo. I looked at her; she smiled, more roseate; she had not heard anything. I was losing my mind, in truth. I hugged her more tightly in the crumpled malines; I felt through the lace the warm and smooth reaction of her delicate body . . .

"God! Who, then, outside that room, simultaneously so far away and so close at hand, had crumpled a peignoir as I had? I looked at her more intently: still smiling; this time, again, she hadn't heard anything; and that open garment allowed the sight of the frail pallor, scarcely blue-tinted by a pale vein, of her adolescent cleavage. The folly of being fortunate carried me away, redoubled by a strange rage—that of being prey, me, a man of sense and firm mind, to stupid reveries. I embraced her, I lifted Gilberte up, astonished by my rudeness, and in the alcove, I said ardent things to her, I bit her with frantic kisses, I enveloped her with insatiable caresses.

"Oh horror, horror! I tell you that those words, another voice pronounced them, down below, almost the same, heard by me alone, that those kisses, other mouths gave them, far away, and yet close by, that another body—where, then? where?—was enveloped by those caresses. There was around us an abominable parody of our amour.

"Have you, by some sad hazard, possessed your mistress one night in one of those dismal hotels near railway stations, where the neighboring rooms, only separated from yours by a thin partition, have welcomed other couples? Add to the annoyance full of shame of a dirty proximity, the irresistible conviction that the noises—the noises that were driving me mad!—were not coming from a bed that as too close at hand, but from some unknown, mysterious, terrible couch, a Sabbat camp-bed in which the damned ferment blood and blasphemy, and you will scarcely understand what I experienced!

210

"I struggled against the terror, always hoping to vanquish it, to drown it in amour, triumphantly to make the frisson of fear into a frisson of pleasure. In vain! In vain! I laughed with ecstasy, I gasped in horror. At one moment, while the words still repeated my words, the kisses my kisses and the caresses my caresses, I even thought, for an instant, that I saw, next to the recumbent Gilbertre, so young and so beautiful, tenderly resistant—yes, next to her, in a narrow shadow—another woman, pale and cold, as Laurencia, embalmed in her tomb, must be at this moment, but loving, resisting poorly, like Gilberte!

"And when, from the vanquished modesty of the young girl-woman, I had extracted, in a redoubling of desire, the supreme confession of the sigh, a different voice, equally tender—alas, where did it come from?—died in the same sigh! Then I leapt from the bed, intoxicated by fear, seating in large droplets, and I grabbed my clothes, and I fled, and I ran through the streets, and here I am, finally. I'm mad, am I not?"

I think that there is no need to spell out the arguments by means of which I succeeded in calming the morbid excitation. I did not succeed in that without difficulty. However, after a long conversation, he consented to recognize that he had been, if not mad, at least hallucinated; that only the memory of Madame de Mortales, perhaps mingled with some remorse, had given rise to that singular aberration; and he left my house almost serene.

It is probable that I would not have thought about that adventure again, and that I would never have narrated the story, if I had not read in a newspaper,

211

two days later, a very horrible article. A warden at Père-Lachaise cemetery—a monstrous brute—had been surprised two nights before as he was violating a sepulcher abominably; and that tomb, said the newspaper, was that of a young Spanish woman, recently deceased, Madame Laurencia de Mortales.

As for the abject wretch, he was tried by the Court of Assizes of the Seine, but he was acquitted, the reports of the alienist physicians having established that the monster was demented. What contributed above all to conciliating the clemency of the jury was the absurd but evident good faith with which he sustained during the trial that if he had lifted the marble slab it was because, as he was making his round, not drunk, shortly before midnight, he had been invited to do so by a soft feminine voice, which had appealed to him, sliding between the stones of the tomb, through the verdure of the yews.

THE BLUE WOMAN

by G. Albert Aurier

A S I searched for the supreme and unrealizable
amour in the obscure maze of the shames of Paris,
I arrived, weary and desperate, on one of those lustful
sepulchers where bare-breasted courtesans prowl.

And I was about to fall asleep in my desperation, as
in a sinister catafalque, when I perceived, leaning on
the white satin of a divan, the impossible woman once
glimpsed in vague aspirations.

A cruel joy suddenly grew within me, and crazy frissons of desire burned my marrow, for I had before my
eyes the beloved stranger, so long an object of hope, the
unique, maddening, marvelous, monstrous, sublime,
seraphic, divine phenomenon: the blue woman.

She let her satin chemise slide to the ground, and
when she was naked, I saw that the flesh of her body
had the pure and soft color of the pale azure skies of
the morning.

Her large eyes shone like pure sapphires; her cheeks
and the tips of her breasts had the joyful and vivid hue
of cobalt.

Her hair was as fleecy over her celestial neck as the ultramarine of African seas, and her speech had the ineffable blue tint of forget-me-nots.

And when, on the satin of divans, I had embraced the blue woman for a long time, when I had learned from her monstrous kisses unknown on earth, I planted my trenchant teeth in her azure neck, in order that no one else would ever savor that superhuman sensuality; I saw the fuming indigo of her blood flowing over her flanks as caressant as the pale azure of a morning sky, and I saw her soul, as blue as the flame of sulfur, fly away toward the eternal blueness.

And since then I have wept, in the banal alcoves of white women, for the irredeemable loss of my life.

ORIANE VANQUISHED

by Jean Lorrain

Oriane the fay was the shepherd's alarm
Vaguely glimpsed in her blue-tinted rooms,
She put to sleep, weary and charmed
Knights helmed with eagle's plumes.

THE moon penetrated into the cavern, spangling the mica-incrusted walls of rock with blue-tinted gleams. A moving cascade of ivy obstructed the entrance, dotted here and there with large clematis flowers, like stars: an inextricable and supple mesh of foliage and corollas, through which the clearing of the forest appeared, all white with the flickering light of the star on the pale tops of the chestnut trees.

Supported by three pillars of basalt, the grotto was sunk in a half-light of dream, invaded on all sides by mistletoe, honeysuckle and tall ferns whose dentellate leaves shone strangely; everywhere, from fissures in the vaults, and crevices in the pillars and the ground, vegetation had sprouted. There were brambles, eglantines, trailing hops, foaming hemlock and broad burdocks with glaucous velvet leaves; and all of that was entangled, climbing and falling back, plants gripping one another and crawling over the moss, palpitating vaguely with the tremor of stems and the vitality of sap, under the blue moonlight slipping in from outside.

Sometimes, in the chestnuts of the clearing, a slight noise whispered, which was the respiration of the dormant forest; then the breeze went further, to torment a few nests in the thickets, and a great whinnying tore through the silence; a herd of wild horses passed by at the gallop, their rumps shiny in the moonlight filtering between the mobile leaves.

The forest was full of those herds of mares and unbroken stallions; they furrowed it in all directions, with a loud noise of broken branches. They wandered at random, their breasts white with foam and their manes flying, assembled around the oldest stallion of the herd, and, on spring nights, in the mating season, they fought furiously until dawn, biting one another in the belly and whinnying; the nests in the bushes were alarmed, and the roe deer in the thickets; and the forest was impenetrable because of the innumerable wild horses that guarded it, prompt to charge any human being and trample him.

In the cavern, the brambles and the tall ferns continued to slumber, and silver droplets pearled on the moonlit honeysuckle leaves. In the mesh of ivy the clematis flowers seemed to open more widely; and bloomed like shiny flakes of frost in the clumps of brambles, under which red-gold and steely glimmers now lit up; and from the tangle of thorns and burdocks sprang a magical efflorescence of épées.

There were Celtic swords with enormous hilts, Gothic two-edged swords, all straight, Saracen swords with curved blades, Anglo-Saxon lances, and even medieval Frankish spears. Also surging forth here and there amid the branches, as if left behind after a battle, were the drawn bows, quivers and pointed arrows of hostile flowers, and the brambles were now swinging bucklers and helmets, which reflected the moonlight like mirrors; the petals of charmed eglantines were detached there, and beneath that iron flora, the faces of sleeping warriors slowly emerged, ecstatic in the shadows.

Clean-shaven craniums and heavy blond curls, the snub-nosed profiles and fleshy smiles of bold pagans with bronzed skin, the long eyelids allowing blue gazes to filter through, forever immobile, of some son of the Norman race, the thickset shoulders of warrior Goths, the thin and muscular torsos of Saxon cavaliers, the white beards of old campaigners and the beardless, pink faces, almost angelic, of young pages, there were a good hundred of them asleep there in the grotto with metallic reflections, beneath the steel flora of their arms, captives forever of the ivy and the brambles, knights and barons, paladins and pirates, Christian kings and miscreant dogs, blond-haired ephebes and aged equerries: the same dream enchanted their closed eyes and haloed their faces with ecstasy.

Extended in their various poses, some lying on their backs others face down with their heads under their arms, all had retained the same gesture of adoration and delirious prayer, for all their hands were joined, and one sensed that they must all have fallen asleep with their eyes fixed on the same vision, with their lips imploring same name: *Oriane.*

And now, finally evoked and rendered tangible by the desire of her lovers, Oriane appears in person in the shadows of the ensorcelled grotto, and illuminates it with her presence.

Standing in an aureole of milky and quivering gleams, like the halo that circles the moon on rainy nights, she leans the nudity of a fay on the transparent fractures of a cathedral of ice; stalactites surround her and three crystal steps display their glaucous humidity at her feet. Everything about her has reflections of snow and nacre; the pale and heavy hair that hangs down to her heels has the imperceptible hint of gold with which the fires of dawn brush the frost, and her entire naked body shines like a pearl, a fabulous pearl that the orient has painted pink, sparkling from the nipples of her breasts, the nails of the big toes and the tips of the fingers, enlivening their rosiness, to the flowering rose that opens at the location of her lips, where lies the kiss.

Captive of their desires, as they are captives of her beauty, Oriane arches her back and moves slowly beneath her moonlit mane, stretching voluptuously, and then leans, dazzled, toward a small oval mirror that she holds in one hand, a mysterious opal in the depths of which the prayerful faces of each of the warriors appear, one by one.

For how many years has Oriane retained them, motionless and mute, retrenched from life, almost turned to phantoms in the brambles and hemlock of her lair? Some a hundred years, others only fifty; there are some there who have been asleep for twenty winters, others for a month. There is an entire century of amour and reckless covetousness asleep there, in the depths of the forest, vaguely appeased in a dream that suppresses the world for them but forbids them death.

Each of those who lies dormant there, ecstatic, with hands clasped, arrived on some fine April morning or lukewarm autumn evening, helmet on the head and hope in the heart, to knock with the flat of his blade on the threshold of the cavern; there they have dismounted, tied their horse to some holm-oak, and then, stammering words of amour, entered.

And the weary horse, tired of waiting, after having stripped the foliage from the trees and the grass from the ground, has broken its tether and fled into the forest, becoming wild again, and, the mare of the adolescent having encountered the palfrey of the knight there, the herds of mares and stallions now gallop, whinnying, their rumps shiny in the moonlight, through the nocturnal forest, awakening the loud breakage of dead branches.

On this beautiful night in July, in the midst of the reverie of the forest in flower and the slumbering adoration of her lovers, Oriane is sad; in the distance the herds of mares have whinnied loudly, she knows that the forest is no longer impenetrable and that times have changed. An incorruptible hero, brought up by monks in the hatred and horror of women, a proud adolescent with a grim heart and pure hands has just entered it. He has already crossed the edge of the forest and, firm in the saddle, helmed and armored in mat silver, sad and sullen beneath the moon, sullen itself, he is advancing slowly but surely through the short grass of the pathways and the wild oats of the clearings, the embalmed clearings of her forest, where the bees will

219

no longer flutter at midday and the dragonflies at dusk, for the cruel ephebe is bringing deliverance in his right hand and death in his left.

Deliverance for them, death for her—worse than death; old age that is the real death of women and fays, since it extinguishes amour and destroys desire.

And Oriane leans over to smile one last time at the opal mirror that is already becoming tarnished by rust and disjointed; and yet, what has she done to those monks? She, the charm and enchantment of gazes and the joy of nature, how radiant she has been, corolla, vibrant wind or woman, what has she done for anyone to excite this harsh conqueror? The times have changed, and against him, all her traps will be vain! Oriane knows that in advance, for he is coming towards her, hardened by hatred and ablaze with rancor, an avenger and administrator of justice.

He detested and abhorred her beauty, which had made the others slaves, and it is not so much to liberate them as to punish her that he had made this perilous voyage, for in the depths of his heart, he is scornful of those heroes that a woman had been able to vanquish, and his hatred for her was further exasperated by his scorn for their laxity; and the cruel adolescent was getting closer by the hour. A complicit owl was guiding him through the wood, flying before him from tree to tree.

Standing on her throne of ice, in the depths of her grotto, Oriane could hear the frightful nocturnal bird ululating; she heard branches drawing aside, the pommel of the sword bumping against the saddle; and every footfall of the horse resounded in her heart.

To be sure, she would have been able to lead him astray by means of subtle mirages, illusions and vain appearances, slowing down his progress through sudden inextricable thickets and unexpected marshes; she could have hidden herself in some fleeting form, a wild animal, bird or flower, but what would be the point? Times had changed; she was vanquished in advance. It was Christ who was marching with that child, Christ the enemy of joy, sensuality and amour. He it was who had excited against her that executioner with the visage of an archangel—and now two tears were pearling in the pale eyes of the fay, and the shiny face of her mirror was entirely tarnished.

The sweet Oriane knew that she was defenseless; she loved her vanquisher.

At that moment, an immense light irrupted into the grotto. With the trenchant edge of his blade a man had just ripped through the moving curtain of ivy that guarded the threshold.

As if laminated with silver by the moon, a slender silhouette loomed up against the clearing, a helmeted silhouette, on which a living owl perched on the summit deployed two great wings: Amadis.

Then, having put his aurochs-horn trumpet to his mouth, Amadis blew three times with all the force of his lungs, and, taking his épée by the blade, holding it like a cross in front of him, he came into the lair.

"By the omnipotent Christ and Our Lady the Virgin, let the scales fall from the eyes that the Accursed One has troubled, and let the Christian heroes retained asleep by the weight of her spells rise to their feet, finally free."

And, the bodies lying there having risen to their feet, with a great clanking of iron, Amadis saw that, beneath their rust and disjointed armor, the beings that appeared among the flowers and the plants all had the green-tinted faces of cadavers or gleaming skeletons— and he could not help stepping back.

With a sinister rattle of tibias hooked on to femurs, fleshy shards scraping with a soft sound in the grip of clenched desiccated fingers, and a nauseating odor of carrion, the atrocious vision only lasted for a moment. After a vain struggle to stand upright, the larvae of the knights had fallen back into the brushwood; now the cadavers were slowly liquefying. Amadis' exorcism had only awakened the putrefaction of those who had long been prey to the worms, and the broken spell had allowed, like a broken dyke, a humanity ripe for the tomb to flow freely. One alone, a skeleton, remained propped in a sitting position, sniggering mute laughter in a ray of moonlight, its vertebrae caught in a flowering eglantine.

Standing in the middle of the charnel-house, Amadis felt mortally sad.

Then Oriane said: "What good has your courage done? They were dreaming, and living their dreams. That one knew full well what he was doing in bringing you here." And with her tremulous and wrinkled hand, which had already become the hand of an old woman, the fay pointed at the owl. "You have prepared his pasture for him."

Then Amadis looked at her. Poor Oriane! Her hair had become gray, and, shriveled, toothless, coughing, bent double and broken, looking like a specter herself with her skin the color of ash and her eyes white with cataracts between bloody lids, Oriane, that nudity nacreous as a pearl a little while before, extended a long Sibylline arm toward the hero and in a doleful voice, said:

"And me, what have I done? I had the age of their illusions and their desires made me young. Beautiful in their amour, I smiled at their dream and my smile protected them against death by smiling at them. Today, the number of years forgotten in my presence and the weight of their regret is overwhelming me, their awakening has aged me by a thousand years, and now I am condemned to live for a thousand years, hideous and sad, the life that each of them might have lived down here. Oh, misfortunate child, the last illusion that those men still had flourished in these woods, and it is you who have killed it."

In the time required to hear that, she had vanished.

In the clearing, day was breaking. A sad light illuminated the cadavers heaped pell-mell in the grotto, and, perched on the head of a dead man, the owl was digging curiously with his beak in the place where two eyes once full of azure had been, now two black and filthy holes.

LISBETH

by Gaston Danville

WHEN the blonde young woman with the low-cut dress came forward to the edge of the stage there was a laudatory tumult from all sides, a long salvo of applause, pattering like a rainstorm peppering rooftops; canes struck the iron tables, where the saucers and tankards leapt up.

She bowed.

As soon as I saw her eyes through the mist, floating in the thick atmosphere—her unforgettable eyes, by virtue of which I recognized her—an irrepressible frisson of anguish vibrated along my nerves.

While she sang, and the audience listened attentively, I studied her at greater length, and my conviction was affirmed by that examination. Not very pretty, her face—a trifle bony, in fact, and very pale—the ceruse mask emphasizing its habitual lividity even more; but with a strange grandeur, the dark blue, almost black irises of her eyes gleaming with an unsustainable gaze in the middle of a vaguely blue-tinted sclerotic, seemed like two abysses of infinity dotting the perhaps-banal face: two gulfs gaping over an alluring unknown, toward which one felt oneself drawn involuntarily.

Ordinarily, the lashes imprinted them with a gilded shadow, veiling their glare, but when she raised her eyelids, they appeared, with that disquieting expression of fatality, initially surprising, and then imprinted with so much charm, such a languorous tenderness, that one forgot the unfavorable impression, surrendering entirely to the enchantment of their caress, drowning in a contemplation replete with ecstasy.

It was definitely her, and the shock that struck me in the heart could not leave me any doubt on that score.

Thrown into confusion by the sudden flux of memories, I left; the orchestra thundered with all its brass instruments, and the shrill trills of the mocking, woodwinds, rising above it, laughing sardonically, exasperated me with a stabbing sensation.

Outside, I remember, there was not a breath of wind to agitate the meager plane-trees of the avenue. In the sky, like diamonds scattered in a casket lined with dark velvet, the stars were shining, and darkness spread its calm and benevolent serenity over the sleeping city, only rarely troubled by occasional pedestrians or the rumble of a belated carriage.

A carillon sounded an hour that I did not hear. In front of me loomed up the resurrection of the past, the lamentable and funereal past, the murderous past— and what a swell of thought growled confusedly at that bleak invocation!

Finally, hazard—how I blessed it that night!—put me in the presence of the Woman who, I was sure, without having any material proof of it, without even

225

any clue that could encourage me in the belief, had, as a secret, still latent presentiment affirmed, played a definite part, and bore an intimate responsibility for the death of my poor Jean, who had been so dear to me. I had never encountered, among the crowd with whom one is obliged to rub shoulders, another soul similar to his. He had been—yes, I do not hesitate to affirm it now—my only friend, the only human being worthy of that name, so often lavished wantonly, prostituted many times over, on those with whom a temporary or accidental communal interest, a vague similarity of tastes, or identical aspirations, seem to unite you in some way.

While he was a lieutenant in the light infantry, Jean de Sancey had met Elisabeth, the girl with the mysterious eyes, in the little provincial town where he was garrisoned. Subsequently, she had been able—by means of what spells?—to inspire in him one of those passions that hold the entire being in a jealous and perpetual servitude.

Already, the unknown woman who thus took the best part of Jean away from me, stealing him from my affection, had inspired an instinctive sentiment of repulsion in me, to which were added vague thoughts of danger—which, alas, were realized only too soon. So, I had always refused to become more closely acquainted with the woman who had separated us in that fashion, and whom I considered as an enemy, when I learned one day that Sancey had killed himself, without there being any explanation for the unexpected suicide. The other had not been seen again.

That story, never forgotten, returned now, with an abundance of precise details that revived my grief and my hatred; and immediately, I made a resolution to do everything possible to discover the key to the enigma. Since the sphinx with the mute eyes had reappeared to me, I would be able to interrogate her and, if necessary, constrain her to yield her secret to me.

In the distance, the sea extended, streaming with light beneath the sparkling kiss of the moon. The placid and mute waves bathed the white strand with a feeble surf. A lighthouse, far away, bloodied the misty horizon with its red light. Phantoms of odors drifted in the warm air, but the foliage was scarcely stirring. Before the tranquil peace of the décor, the fever burning my temples abruptly fell away, and the consoling influence of the pale and beautiful things surrounding me soothed the bitterness of the initial violence. The night bandaged my wound with the delicate and obliging womanly hands.

One night, I obtained the favor of seeing her home. Oh, all the way to the threshold of her apartment, we only exchanged banal conventional remarks, and noth-ing—nothing at all—gave me any hint of the scene that was about to unfold. While she lit the candles on the mantelpiece, she fixed me via the mirror—I was standing behind her—with an indecipherable stare, and, at that moment, I almost lost all consciousness of the surroundings, abandoning myself to that black and white reflection, the enormous circle of which suspended me in terrifying anguish, in the feverish expectation of an unsuspected future.

"Bonsoir, Monsieur de Rèce," she said. "You've come to talk to me about Jean, haven't you?" Then, softening the tone of her voice, she added: "I haven't forgotten the poor boy, I assure you."

As if in a cruel nightmare, I saw her take off her mantle and her hat; afterwards, a phantasmal smile fluttering over her bloodless lips, she raised her head, and fascinated me for the second time with her wide open eyes. It was impossible for me to turn mine away—oh, the frightful torture I endured!

Was I then, the victim of a frightful hallucination, or was I not rather the spectator of the drama whose memory she was evoking internally? I watched, terrified and impotent, the scene that I had been unable to divine, but which must, in reality, have occurred between *her* and *him*.

In the little room to which I had come so often, Jean, his brows furrowed, a malevolent crease barring his forehead with an unaccustomed wrinkle, was marching back and forth, with the haggard expression of a madman. Brief and unintelligible words were emerging from his pursed lips. Evidently, he was prey to the haunting obsession of some evil idea. Then she came in.

"Lisbeth," he said, in a low voice, his tone veiled, but pierced with an ill-contained anger, "do you know that what you're doing is vile . . ."

"What's that, my friend?"

"It's futile to pretend. Lisbeth, when I met you, you were poor, an orphan, abandoned by everyone, and all by yourself. I vowed to you, that day, a love such that it was only through you that life was sweet to me, and you agreed to go with me. I gave myself entirely to you, without restrictions, making you the mistress of my soul as well as my body—oh, I'm not complaining; I've been entirely happy—but in return, and you freely agreed to the pact, I asked you for just one thing: to remain faithful to me no matter what might come.

"And that was, for me, as you know full well, an illusory oath, for I did not think, even for an instant, that you could be lying. In that love I had placed all my hopes, and also, alas, all my illusions; it had become for me the supreme refuge and the ultimate joy, beyond which there was nothing but oblivion . . . but you did not see it as anything but a momentary folly, a temporary caprice. Tell me, why have you done me so much harm? I have always been submissive and very affectionate toward you; I was eager to realize the slightest of your desires before you expressed them . . .

"Was what I had dreamed of so impossible, then, and, my God, what have I done that you should punish me so cruelly? Just now, criminal ideas came to me; I would have liked to crush the two of you together, as one does with vipers that bite. I've seen you again . . . and I'm weeping . . .

"Lisbeth . . . Lisbeth . . . one word, and I'll forgive you . . ."

She tapped the floor nervously with her heel, and said, pitilessly: "I don't understand, my poor friend, and if you're going to go on like this for much longer, I'll leave . . ."

"You shan't leave!" howled Sancey, in a hoarse voice. And he placed himself before the doorway, furiously.

She had lowered her veil, and came forward.

"Let me pass!"

"No!"

"Let me!" And she tried to reach past him and take hold of the doorknob—but he grabbed her wrists, and threw her down in an armchair.

She got up almost immediately, beside herself.

Holding on to the curtains in order not to fall over, staggering under the frightful combat in which his crazed ideas were engaging in his brain, he made a movement, extending his right hand, which encountered the butt of his service revolver in the panoply.

"Threats!" said Lisbeth, sniggering. "You wouldn't have the courage to kill me. Well, yes, I've deceived you, you hear . . . so fire, then, *coward!*"

That word made him turn red, as a bellows does a fire; he pressed the trigger, having turned the barrel toward his head.

When the blue smoke had dissipated in heavy spirals, undulating like a light fog in the room, Lisbeth saw the lieutenant's body lying there, his blond moustache twisted in a final rictus, his hands clenched, with a little hole above his eye, which was gazing vaguely, already vitreous.

On the carpet, a thin trickle of blood was coagulating, making a red stain; the buttons of his uniform jacket were shining . . .

A cold sweat bathed my temples. I seemed to see everything around me dancing, the eyes immeasurably dilated, while demonic laughter burst out in my ears.

They were laughing, those eyes, in truth, they were laughing . . .

I fainted.

When I came round, Lisbeth, with a bottle of smelling-salts in her hand and her eyelids lowered, asked me, ironically: "What's the matter with you, my dear? Such sensitivity! I was almost afraid . . ."

The slut!

So, I knew what had happened, and my just desire for revenge had never been greater. But so invincible was the power of her gaze—her horrible gaze, which seemed to be reading my mind, and simultaneously dominating it—that she became my mistress.

Yes, I committed that sacrilege, that frightful profanation, and I tried in vain to escape the yoke, to recover my self-possession; her evil influence held me captive as securely as the heaviest chains—not that thoughts of rebellion did not come to me.

One night, I got up without making any noise—a spider spinning its web could not have done better. On a table, a pair of scissors was gleaming faintly. I took them, and slowly—very slowly, I assure you—without my footsteps sliding over the parquet being audible, I came back to the bedside, holding them open in my hand.

How my heart was beating at that moment, and what joy illuminated my features! Silently, I sniggered . . .

Finally, I was about to be able to break that infamous union, appease my remorse, chase away impious sensuality and find repose! Since her eyes, her magical eyes, her vampiric eyes, were all of her strength, a single thrust of that frail weapon, and it would all be over.

Leaning over the dangerous sleeping woman illuminated by the alabaster night-light, holding my breath, I was about to strike . . .

Damnation!

In the pale face, with an almost automatic movement, the waxen eyelids were raised, and, drinking my soul, pitiless suckers, the enamel eyes of the ghoul commanded; she extended her lips to me—the thin red ribbon of her lips, which burned me with a kiss that only the eternal victims of Hell ought to receive . . .

And that passion endured, endured, seeming not to want to end.

Another time, I contrived to pour a narcotic into her glass—poison repulsed me. She raised the glass, smiled at me satanically, and then put it down on the table so abruptly that the crystal broke and shattered.

Other attempts failed in the same way.

Meanwhile, that ignoble perpetual compromise and my unworthy weakness made me ashamed—but in her presence, all resolution disappeared within me, like a flock of clouds rapidly dispersed by the wind. Every day, I promised myself to break that vile bond; every night saw me lavishing my caresses on the terrible fascinatrix.

No, no, the tortures that I experienced then are not among those that can be imagined, and it is still a subject of astonishment for me to recall that time of extreme suffering and to see that I have survived it!

This is what happened.

Every evening, I waited at the exit from the public place in which she was singing. That time, firmly decided to accomplish the act, at any price, I had equipped myself with a hunting-knife; it was open in my pocket, and on the way I caressed the cold blade. I was very witty, very cheerful. She did not perceive anything; I avoided, moreover, meeting her gaze, for she would certainly have guessed everything that night, as she had always done before.

I recall the whole scene very well. I let her go in first, into the corridor, which was not lit at that time of night. Then, whistling a tally-ho, overflowing with delight, I slew the beast, with a firm hand, cutting her throat.

She oscillated, without uttering a cry, her head almost separated from her body, and then fell forwards, with a dull thud. I heard the blood gushing from her arteries against the wall, and also the raucous sound of the air, vainly aspired by the breathless lungs, in a supreme effort.

Carefully, I wiped the blade, and the next day, very calmly, I left for America,

And now that I've told you everything, Father, decide whether you can absolve me . . .

THE SAURIENNE

by Renée Vivien

THE sun is terrible. The sun is more terrible than the plague, the wild beasts and the gigantic black serpents. It is more terrible than the fever. It is a thousand times more terrible than death.

The sun has burned my nape and my temples and my cranium; it has desiccated and blanched my hair like the grass, during heat-waves. Another man than me would have gone mad after long marches in the desert. It seemed to me, at times that molten lead was running over my brow and along my limbs. Ha ha! Another man than me would have gone mad, but I have a solid head and body. I've seen men howling and gesticulating like demons after long days of marching in the desert. The sun, hammering their imbecile brains, had given them strange ideas, But me, I've always been tranquil and reasonable.

The sun is terrible.

Toward the end of an afternoon, when long rays of light were still raining down, as sharp as javelins, I encountered a bizarre woman. I'm not a coward, but that woman scared me because of her frightful resemblance to a crocodile.

She had a rough skin, like scales. Her little eyes frightened me. Her mouth frightened me even more, being immense, with sharp teeth, also immense. I tell you that the woman resembled a crocodile.

She was gazing at the water when I had the courage to approach her.

"What are you looking at?" I asked her, curious as well as slyly frightened.

She posed her terrible little saurian eyes upon me.[1] Instinctively, I recoiled.

"I'm looking at the crocodiles," she replied. "I'm somewhat akin to them. I know all their habits. I call them by their names. And they recognize me when I go along the river bank."

She was speaking in such a simple tone, so naturally, that I shivered with glacial fear. I knew that *she was telling the truth*. I dared not stare at her skin, as rough as scales.

"The king and the queen of the crocodiles are my intimate friends," she continued. "The king lives at Denderah. The queen, who is as powerful and even crueler than him, preferred to go forty leagues higher up, in order to reign alone. She wants power without division. He also likes independence, which means

---

1 The word *saurien* does not have the same implication in French as its English equivalent, referring to the order of reptiles that includes crocodiles, caimans, etc. rather than to dinosaurs, so a pedantic translation would render this word as crocodilian and the artificial feminine derivative as crocodilienne, but it seems more esthetically satisfactory to employ the transcriptions.

that, while remaining good friends, they live separately. They only come together at rare intervals, for the act of amour."

I saw a gleam of libidinous ferocity in her pupils, which made my teeth chatter. I'm employing that banal expression deliberately, all the force of which, and all the horror of which, I understood at that moment. The frightful sun was oppressing me and crushing me, like the weight of a giant. Liquid fire, it was burning me. And yet my teeth were chattering as if it were winter, when the great frosts make your blood torpid.

"I believe you," I panted.

She drew closer to me, with a gauche movement that was heavily insinuating . . .

The simpering of that monster was even more terrifying than her deformity.

"No, you don't believe me. What is your name?"

"My name is Mike Watts."

"Well, Mike, I affirm to you that I can ride crocodiles mounted on their backs. Do you believe me?"

I was sweating even more abundantly, but this time it was a cold sweat that chilled my limbs.

"Yes, I believe you."

And, in fact, I did believe her. I'm not mad. I've never been mad, even in the desert, even when I was thirsty. But I believed her, and you would have believed her, as I did.

She sniggered odiously—which is to say that she opened her mouth. She opened her abominable caiman's mouth very wide, and showed me her teeth, silently. A frisson caused her body to undulate, and that was all, O God who invented Hell!

"No, you don't believe me," said the Saurienne. "But I'll prove to you the truth of what I'm saying."

She scrutinized the yellow river, which was carrying sand and mud.

"Here's one," she said. "Stand back."

I didn't wait for her to reiterate the order. I ran away as fast as I could. Some distance from the river, however, I stopped, suddenly fettered by something even more peremptory than fear.

At the moment when the crocodile unclenched its jaws I saw her hoisting herself up on to its back and, for the duration of a nightmare, I saw her riding on an alligator . . .

I'm not rambling. I have all my reason. Nor am I lying. Lies are for the civilized. We never lie. We hate complications.

The Saurienne came back toward me, leaving the crocodile thrashing around heavily in the brackish water. She came back, her eyes shining with triumph . . . and something else . . .

She was looking out for an exclamation of approving surprise. But I was tottering like a drunken man and stammering incoherent syllables . . . *ba . . . be . . . bou . . . bi . . .* And I was drooling like an idiot.

She looked at me with the libidinous and ferocious pupils of a monster in rut.

"Come," she commanded.

I tried to follow her. I could not. I made the strangled gestures of a lunatic restrained by a straitjacket.

A few paces from where we were there was a clump of very long grass, and trees whose branches resembled giant snakes. She squinted at that shelter from the corner of her eye. I had no difficulty divining what she wanted from me.

It would be difficult for me to explain to you what I experienced at that moment. All sorts of ideas were galloping through my brain, like an enraged dog-pack. I understood that it was necessary to kill the Monster, but how? How?

Bullets and blades would slide over her carapace without doing her any harm. Come on, isn't there even one vulnerable point? No . . . yes! The eyes . . . THE EYES!

I was seized by a joy of fever and delirium, the joy that is only known to shipwreck victims finally returned to land and invalids who see the dawn dissipating the night of their horrible hallucinations. I danced; I made my saliva hiss. I even stammered a few stupid amorous words to my redoubtable companion.

I emptied my water-bottle in a single draught. The thought of my imminent deliverance flowed through my veins with the beneficent warmth of brandy. I would thus have the strength to accomplish the murderous task . . .

And while the Saurienne, her gaze capsized beneath intoxicated eyelids, awaited the carnal satisfaction, I took my knife . . .

I took my knife and, striking the monster wallowing in the grass, I put out her eyes . . .

I put out her eyes, I tell you. Oh, that's because I'm courageous, me. You can complain on my account, but you can never claim that I'm a coward. Many men would have lost their head in my situation. Me, I didn't hesitate for a second . . .

And as I went away I turned round to see, one last time, the yellow river that was carrying sand and mud.

THE KING OF PERSIA

by Maurice Magre

THERE was once a small boy who was full of good sentiments; but he had a light mind. He thought about a host of good deeds to accomplish, but he forgot them readily, because of the facility he had in changing his ideas.

His name was Lucas and he was the son of an old mariner. His father often took him fishing with him; but the years were beginning to curb his back and make his arms tremble. He no longer had much strength to haul in the sails and the nets.

"Father," Lucas often said, "I'll help you fish today, and when we come back, I'll hold the tiller and you can lie down in the bottom of the boat and watch the seagulls passing overhead."

He had every intention of doing that, but when he was at sea, he contemplated the foam, the faces of the fish gliding around the boat, he thought about a little girl named Annalik, and he forgot to help his father.

The latter threw the nets, took the tiller, and was glad all the same about Lucas's good intentions.

One day, when they were sailing together, they encountered a big ship whose crew made signals addressed to them.

"Hey!" cried the captain to Lucas's father. "Are you a good pilot and can you guide us to the nearest port in France?"

"Certainly," he replied. "I'm a good pilot and this is my son Lucas, who, if he would take the trouble, would be the best mariner known. I'll gladly guide you."

The ship came from Persia, and the captain had been charged by the king of that country to bring back a handsome young Frenchman to marry his daughter and mount the throne.

That's what I need! the latter thought. *What's the point in looking any further?* "We'll take you back to Persia," he said to Lucas, "and you'll be king."

And Lucas threw his cap in the air and was very joyful.

"Father, I'll send you a ship laden with embroidered garments, delicious wines and a thousand bags of gold. Later, I'll come back to my native land with warships and Persian soldiers. Where our humble house stands I'll have a marble palace built, and the richest ship-owners in the city will salute you, because you'll be the father of a king.

Lucas's father was proud to see his son succeeding to such dignity, but he was saddened by the idea of being separated from him. As the Persian vessel was going to depart immediately he descended into his boat again.

"There will also be dresses for Annalik, and I won't forget a diamond pipe for you!" shouted Lucas.

And, speaking thus, he swore, in his heart full of generosity, to send all those things.

Lucas's marriage was celebrated with great magnificence. Fêtes were held throughout the realm of Persia. There was a solemn ceremony at court in which the king placed a golden crown on Lucas's head. Then he went through the streets of the capital in a chariot, beside his young wife.

The Persians cheered, and Lucas saw envy and admiration on their faces. He rejoiced in his power and the beauty of Ximena, the king's daughter, whose skin was brown and her eyes blue-tinted and child-like.

While the cries of the people rose up toward him, Lucas, who had keen hearing, perceived the words of an old woman, who was saying to her neighbor: "Better to be a mute slave's dog than the King of Persia."

He was greatly astonished, judging that remark to be almost devoid of sense.

It had sufficed for Lucas to see Ximena to love her and forget Annalik; as I said, he had a light mind. Ximena was a charming beauty; she seemed to be entirely ignorant of life, and when she smiled her ingenuousness was so evident that everyone was ashamed of his own thoughts. She responded with modesty and timidity to Lucas's words, and the latter was charmed by so much grace. He noticed that during the feast that was held at court on the evening of his marriage she did not take any nourishment. He attributed that to the emotion she must be experiencing and the amour that he had doubtless inspired in her.

When they were alone in their apartment, Lucas pressed the charming princess to his heart. But she pulled away, blushing, and told him that before abandoning herself to him she desired, because of a vow that she had made, to pray to the Persian god of amour in a solitary place in the palace. As she said that Lucas saw her teeth shining between her child-like lips, and it seemed to him that they were longer than was appropriate to the just proportions of a face.

That was a temporary impression. Two negro eunuchs were waiting at the door for the princess, and she left.

Lucas was beginning to be troubled by that absence when Ximena returned, with so much tenderness in her gaze that all dread vanished.

He knew the happiness of amour, and when the sun appeared he congratulated himself on his high destiny as much as the admirable spouse who was asleep next to him.

Months passed. Lucas reigned. He thought about reforms to make in the realm. He saw great injustices committed around him; he suffered from that, but temporarily, like a man who does not meditate his thoughts very much.

He began a letter to his father. He never finished it. He thought about sending the promised ship laden with garments, wine and gold. He gave an order to a jeweler to make a diamond pipe. The latter executed the order and brought the pipe to the palace. Lucas's prime minister, having seen it, asked him for it and

Lucas, generous of heart, gave it to him, forgetting that it was for his father.

Every evening, Ximena quit the nuptial chamber and went out, under the pretext of a vow, preceded by two negro eunuchs. That intrigued Lucas greatly.

It's necessary that I clarify this mystery, he thought. But Ximena came back afterwards, with arms that enlaced around his neck so tenderly that Lucas no longer thought about the enigma, or put off his research until the next day.

One evening, however, he saw a red patch on the young woman's shoulder, a bloodstain; and her teeth seemed even longer than usual that evening.

He waited impatiently for the following day, and when Ximena went out with her two negro eunuchs, he set out to follow them. The palace was deserted.

The princess went down a spiral staircase that led to a deep cellar. There Lucas perceived a young adolescent attached to a stake. One of the negroes pierced his heart with a knife, the other detached his limbs one by one, deposited the pieces on a golden platter and presented them to the princess. And Lucas saw with horror the companion of his nights seize those morsels avidly and devour them.

He fled. He felt a great dolor, and he was not accustomed to dolor.

Anything is better than suffering, he told himself. *Let's not think about it. I'll see tomorrow what I ought to do.*

He welcomed the princess in his arms, as usual; he rejoiced in the caresses, the puerile brightness of her eyes and her fresh skin, adjourning the sadness and horror that he ought to feel at the idea of the spectacle that he had just seen.

I'm the husband of an ogress, Lucas said to himself. *That's a terrible affair. That state of things can't go on. I'll put things in good order, but not until tomorrow. I want to know one last night of the love of that woman, savage and cruel in truth, but delectably amorous in my arms. I'll punish her tomorrow.*

And the days went by. The taste for the happiness of every evening forced Lucas to reject his good thoughts when they presented themselves to his mind. And as that happiness diminished his will, he no longer thought about reforms to be made in the realm, presents to send to his father, or the letter that he had begun.

Tomorrow, I'll act as reason advises; I'll think about it tomorrow.

And tomorrow never came.

But one day when he was leaning on a window sill he heard the two negro eunuchs chatting in a palace courtyard.

"There isn't a single adolescent left in the whole city for our mistress," said the first.

"So we'll be obliged to kill the king, her husband, tonight."

Lucas had heard enough. He took a dagger and headed for Ximena's apartment.

She was lying on cushions, and when she perceived him she had a naïve and spontaneous movement of joy. Her eyes were pure and soft, and Lucas dropped his weapon and ran away.

He left the palace and ran all the way to the sea. A ship was departing for France. He embarked on it and gave the captain all the money he had on him.

They were already within sight of the shore when a fishing boat crossed the path of the ship. Lucas recognized his father under the sail. He had the boat hailed and he was deposited in it.

His father fell into his arms, shedding tears of joy.

"How is it that a King of Persia is returning thus, without a cortege and without honor?"

Lucas said to him: "Welcome a forgetful son. Don't talk to me about the thousand bags of gold, or the diamond pipe. I've only ever been able to have good intentions, for the lightness of my mind has always prevented me from realizing them. I've never thought enough to act well, but I've been able, thanks to that, not to be unhappy. Let me sit down beside you in your boat, without thinking about anything. Perhaps another ship will come to search for me in order for me to be king of another country. I'm of the race of those who watch the seagulls fly overhead, and it's necessary not to ask any more of me than that."

THE RENDEZVOUS

by Maurice Renard

To the memory of Edgar Poe

Paris, Boulevard de Clichy
Tuesday 10 March 1908

To the Public Prosecutor

DEAR MONSIEUR,
Before reading this letter, you will have been informed as to how it was found, and you will have learned that I am dead. I will, in fact, have killed myself.

Nothing, doubtless, will contest the fact that I am my own murderer. I desire that with all my heart. I hope that the house will be found in good order, as it is now, and that I myself will be a very discreet, banal and obvious suicide. That is probable and rational—but not, alas, certain. For there is one thing capable of surrounding my end with tumult and mystery—so hideous a thing that one might die in order no longer

246

to know that it exists. For no more than that, I can assure you!

That is not, however, the only reason for my death. If I kill myself, you see, it's also in the hope of killing *it*—the thing—with the same blow . . . do you understand? Except, you see, that I'm not *sure* of destroying it along with myself . . . so I thought it would be best to tell you my secret. It will explain any strangeness—if there is any—and prevent you from suspecting a murder.

Oh, above all else, don't accuse anyone! I've already done so much harm! Don't accuse anyone, if some-one—someone bizarre—is keeping company with my remains. Don't accuse anyone of anything, even if the terror of a supernatural agony is recognizable in my features, and my crazed eyes are wide open, staring at the broken door. But no! Not that! That's impossible—because, you see, at the very moment that I depart, I shall be saved! I shall kill myself before that, you see, even if I have to tear out my heart with my fingernails in order to die in time.

The clock marks half past one; that will, therefore, be in three hours time. My God! No more than three small hours! And so many things to say, so many long explanations to give!

To abridge the story, though, and to avoid describing the people involved, I've attached two photographs to my letter: one of a group of young people, and a portrait of a young woman. Would you care, please, to examine the former. That's not a battalion of lunatics. It represents the pupils in the studio of Montgény, the architect, in 1896. It was taken one Sunday in the courtyard of the school. It's a burlesque; everyone in it is showing off the key attribute of his particular talent, the emblem of his most characteristic habit, or making a gesture that symbolizes them. Very Latin Quarter, as you can see, but also not very witty—and now so sad!

I call your attention to the group on the left. In the second row, the young man in spectacles, furnished with a palette and crowned with a diadem of turnips, is the water-colorist Guillaume Dupont-Lardin, whose name you will surely recognize. The turnips have been put on his head because "turnip" and "water-color" are synonymous in studio slang, and because good old Guillaume was already thinking of nothing but painting water-colors. His family, however, demanded that he should be an architect; he had given in, but he only worked hard enough to pass his exams and obtain his diploma, in order to set out subsequently on his chosen career. He is the best, the only friend I have ever had. I knew him there, at Montégny's, where he was student-treasurer in '96.

My turn now. I figure, with two comrades, in the scene of hypnotism that you perceive beneath Dupont-Lardin. I'm neither the little pale fellow who is sitting down nor the fat bearded one who seems to be sprinkling him with magnetic passes. I'm the tall dark one with the hooked nose. The other two, Juliot and Salpêtrière, really were a medium and a hypnotist, and their exhibition was the principal turn at our parties. For my part, being a mere amateur in that kind of exercise, I had never been anything but Salpêtrière's assistant. I did it, moreover, without enthusiasm, and my master was disappointed in me, claiming that, with my gaze—"more hooked than my nose"—I might have been the greatest magnetizer in the world. It's possible, I suppose . . . but I've always found the process unpleasant. Those one puts to sleep flutter their eyelids so hectically, their faces are so utterly stripped of all expression, that it frightens me; it's as if one were crippling them . . .

Let's pass on to the second print. That one, Monsieur, I beg you to burn once you have studied it sufficiently. Do you place any credence in the religion of memory and the cult of objects? If so, I have no doubt that the poker will tremble in your hands when you mix the ashes of that photograph with the embers of a fire. I have never been able to separate myself from it since I stole it . . .

Oh, Monsieur, if things were worn out by gazes, if our tears were able to dissolve images and our kisses able to erase them, you would not have Gilette's portrait in front of you. Instead of that . . . she is no longer very elegant, my relic. One might think that it had rained on her all night long. Wretch! You were able weep upon a portrait every night; what more did you want? You possessed the sole sensuality that did not fade away of its own accord, and you have ruined it! You enjoyed indefatigable Desire, and you have satisfied it! Do you no longer know, then, where regret, repentance and remorse originate? Imbecile! There are ancient, rotten desires, which gratify as they decompose!

I've been stupid and criminal, it's true. But look at her! And yet, you can only perceive her as a silent, motionless form. You'll say to yourself: "She's a pretty girl, of the Scandinavian type." And you'll think about something else. Oh, if you only knew!

When I saw her for the first time it was evening, in a twilit drawing-room. Suddenly, it seemed to me that a light emerged from the shadows. She was like a stained-glass queen coming toward me, so white and pink and blonde, with her young flesh as resplendent as a spring dawn! She looked at me quite frankly, her lengthwise-narrowed eyes full of grey light. I was dazzled.

An unexpected voice caused me to start. I had not seen Guillaume behind her, I heard him pronounce my name, then say: "This is my fiancée."

Then, Monsieur, I felt the Earth turn upside-down, and the stars appeared to me through the ceiling. I was lost. Oh, Gilette, Gilette!

That evening, I should have gone away, without wasting a minute—but it seemed to me that a precipitate departure would cast an equivocal shadow over the joy of the betrothed couple. I told myself that everyone would draw conclusions, and that it would be better to delay my flight until the day after the marriage. Was that the real reason? I wonder now whether, in staying, I was a hero or a coward.

Whichever was the case, I stayed. Then they demanded—oh, how reckless, how blind, they were!—that I built their house! Guillaume had bought an old property to demolish, in the Boulevard Clichy between the Place Pigalle and the Place Blanche, near the corner of the latter. It was their favorite quarter, and it was there that they wanted to live, in a house designed by me. You know what engaged couples are like—they brook no resistance. Anyway, how could I refuse? What reason could I give? That would have been to betray myself, wouldn't it? And then, of course, it suited me: to work for her, to build her home, to make her a house as one makes someone a dress, to create the décor of her gestures and the landscape of her beauty, to put my signature on the site of her life—I reckoned . . . well, was it not, so to speak, to complete her according to my own tastes, to couple her grace with my artistry, and to marry something of her with something of me . . . ?

Nonsense! Silly talk! Words, words! Mere wordplay! So be it! So be it . . .

Meanwhile, I dreamed about that house, amorously. I didn't want it to be a temple for my divinity so much as an embrace around my beloved. I also wanted everything therein to be in accord with her northern splendor, and that the dwelling should become as an edifice what she was as a woman: a sort of emanation of her being. The ceilings in its rooms were to be appropriate to her height, and the dimensions of its doors in harmony with her passing and momentary silhouette. The walls behind her would require colors varied in accordance with the different rooms, but also as if a subtle painter had brushed each of them into the background of her portrait. I promised myself an orgy of attentions: the door-handles would bulge, beneath her hand, with welcoming roundness and immediate familiarity; the positioning of the furniture would be becoming to her poses, and each of the windows would seem the ideal frame for her to lean out on her elbows.

My task wasn't difficult, for Gilette was radiant everywhere, and her presence illuminated her surroundings with a mysterious personal light, the bizarre result of which was that everything seemed dependent on her, and embellished by her proximity. People and objects seemed to be effaced by her supremacy, and when she was there, the entire world seemed secondary.

No, no, my task wasn't difficult . . . pooh! What did I build? Go and see! Have yourself shown around the house! One might call it a Norwegian chalet, or Russian, or Danish, or anything else! It's banal and pretentious. My comrades nicknamed it "the isba".[1] Oh, *the isba*! Woe! Oh, our dreams, our dreams . . . !

But time's passing. I hear the ticking clock measuring it out behind my back. My hour is drawing near, and you don't know anything yet. Let's get on with it.

The construction of the isba was a cause of frequent meetings for us. The criticism of the plans, the examination of the estimate, the choice of details, and then the surveillance of the work multiplied our meetings and brought about an intimacy between Gilette and me, which the collaboration tightened. That didn't help to cure me. My lust was excited by it, until it became a sort of unbearable fever. When the house was finished, I perceived that it was too late to fight it, and that it could only be extinguished by death or satisfaction. Unfortunately, I didn't want to die without having tried my luck.

Then I descended, one by one, all the steps of ignominy.

Far from going away, as I had previously resolved to do, I moved closer to the Dupont-Lardins, renting this apartment in the Boulveard de Clichy, two hun-

---

1 An isba is a primitive Siberian hut made of wood and turf.

dred meters from the isba in the direction of the Place Pigalle. Guillaume and his wife rejoiced in my proximity. It was decided that we would see one another every day. A place was set for the "worthy architect" every morning and evening in the dining-room that he had constructed, on the table that he had designed.

They loved one another madly. Tell me—should that not have discouraged me, driven me to despair? Bah! Their affection only exasperated my desire, and filled my heart with jealousy. Furthermore, I was convinced that they were completely mistaken in loving one another, and clung to this absurd argument: "Nature has not fashioned them for one another. They're making a mistake. They're wrong to love one another. What right do they have to do so, since Gilette is destined for me alone? What other body could be more exactly adapted to mine? Her arms, I'm sure, would not be able to join together in empty space without designing the contour of my torso, and the adjunction of our lips would be the perfect kiss . . ."

In brief, never had there been two better spouses, in my view, than Gilette and me; we were truly two halves of the same whole. Stupid and banal, isn't it? "It's necessary, however," I said to myself, "that things should be as they are; how else could I suffer, because of her, this almost superhuman passion?" Is the violence of my lust an excuse for my sin? Maybe. It's all the same to me. I leave it to you to judge, Monsieur. The fact remains that I loved Gilette in an exceptional, unique manner worthy of celebration, as Leander loved Hero, as Tristan loved Yseult . . . as everyone, doubtless, has loved his beloved, since the Lord created humans and created them male and female.

Three o'clock! Three o'clock is already chiming behind me! How quickly the hours rotate today! I haven't said anything yet. One might think that I'm retreating in the face of what must be said. Come on!

For more than two years, Monsieur, I was parasitic upon the Dupont-Lardins, and I had no other concern than to bring about intimate meetings with my hostess. They were rare, Guillaume working until nightfall in his studio and his wife staying by his side. After that, they went out together . . .

You can imagine all the stratagems that it was necessary to contrive to separate them, without seeming to. What villainies! What turpitude!

There was only one day a week, unless chance intervened, when I was assured of finding myself alone with Madame Dupont-Lardin for a couple of hours. That was on Tuesday, between five and seven. On that day, Guillaume had agreed to teach a course in the History of Art at a great institution for young ladies on the Left Bank. That tells you that Tuesdays were my true Sundays, and that I regularly took advantage of that godsend to go to the isba. Sometimes, there was no one there: "Madame has gone out." Sometimes, too, some unwelcome visitor came to disturb the charm—for me—of our solitude. But most of the time, things went as I wished, for Gilette had no reason to avoid my proximity, by virtue of liking to spend as much time as possible at home, and she received few visitors outside of her appointed day.

Yes, Monsieur, for thirty months I was only really alive for two hours a week, and not always then. For thirty months I was the ridiculous, odious, but unsuspected suitor of Madame Dupont-Lardin. She and Guillaume, absorbed in their own happiness, didn't notice anything.

Oh, if only I had clearly distinguished Gilette's indifference, perhaps I would eventually have shaken off the yoke—but by virtue of wanting her to be well-disposed toward me, I gradually acquired the certainty that she would become so. And yet, I admit, to my shame, in spite of my expectations and assiduous care—which she did not even suspect—no word or movement ever escaped her that might have motivated an avowal on my part. In spite of that, I was the victim of a mirage, like so many other forsaken wretches. Soon, Gilette could not do or say anything without my interpreting it in favor of my covetousness. I translated her slightest gestures as good omens: a fleeting glance became a wink of connivance; any phrase whatsoever concealed an allusion; simple politeness became complicity. I was hallucinating, I tell you! And one day, a lovers' quarrel having come between her and her husband, I thought that the propitious moment had arrived.

It was a Tuesday—and I was able to converse with her in private.

I declared myself.

At first, she did not grasp what I meant. Then, when she had understood, she tried to laugh it off, pretending to think that it was a joke. Finally convinced of the gravity of my words, Madame Dupont-Lardin manifested as much sadness as amazement, and spoke

to me very kindly and softly, but also quite categorical-
ly, without my being able to discover a single word of
hope in what she said.

The mirage dissipated; it was as if there were a great
darkness behind it. I listened to Gilette as one listens to
a delirious individual. I had immediately made a decision to kill myself, that same evening, as soon as I had
left the isba. I could no longer live in hope, you see . . .

She didn't know that; she read nothing in my eyes;
she gave me advice, maternally. My God! We were
sitting very close to one another face to face, in a tranquil manner. Her voice was almost unemotional. No
one could have guessed that she was pronouncing my
death-sentence. As for me, Monsieur, I looked at her
. . . oh, I looked at her with all the strength of my
existence. I was looking at her for the last time.

Vaguely, I heard her reasoning and moralizing: "My
poor friend what you have done is not good, aestheti-
cally or morally. It's not entirely your fault, however . . .
I should have seen it . . . Guillaume too. But how could
you suppose . . . ? Oh, it's not nice, not worthy! You've
been slightly mad, haven't you? But it's over? You can
see reason now? Oh yes, when I think about it, it's
obvious that you weren't yourself. Guillaume admires
you so much—and you love him, too! What would he
have made of this business? What were you thinking?
Don't look at me like that. What would Guillaume
have made of it?"

"Guillaume?" I replied, regretfully, knowing that
my reply would make her indignant. "He would never
have known anything. Nothing, therefore, would have
caused him pain. I swear to you"—and this was true,

Monsieur!—"that I would give my blood to spare him . . . even the slightest anxiety."

"But your cynicism and contradiction are frightening!" said Gilette. "Please, my friend, say no more. I no longer recognize you. Listen: I don't want any rupture, any quarrel. No, Guillaume would be too upset, and might even conceive suspicions. You'll find, I hope, sufficient strength to stifle . . . your desires, without going away. Forget them, my dear, if they're not already forgotten. As for me, I no longer know what happened. Upon my word, nothing has occurred. I have no memory of your declaration; you don't recall my rejection; neither of us is aware that you have doubted my constancy. Isn't that the best solution? What do you say?

"Come on—let's resume our customary existence, me without rancor and you without bitterness. Except . . . if you recommence . . . then, what do you expect? Guillaume will be told. To listen to you twice would require your banishment and would be unworthy of his wife. You think so too, don't you? Well? Shall we forget? Is that a promise? Answer me."

On, Monsieur, how I pitied her plans! The future? The future was for others, not for me. I looked at her; that's all. I looked at her unrelentingly. She was the only light in the bosom of the great darkness. She opened her frightened eyes wide, which seemed to be magnified, and to be considering me with anxiety and curiosity . . . and I would never see them again! Never again!

"Come on!" she continued. "You're frightening me! You're not listening. Is it a promise? Swear! Give me your hands, honestly, as if I were a man. There. Swear to me never to speak to me again about today's subject. Swear to me that you'll cure yourself, that you'll no longer be unhappy or . . . dishonest. And, for my part, I swear to you on oath that . . ."

Monsieur! In the middle of that sentence, she broke off! Oh, it was extraordinary! In a matter of seconds, her voice had become lower and lower. She had become grave, voiceless and languid. Think of a phonograph whose spring is running down, about to stop—it was like that, odd and painful. At the same time, a stony indifference had frozen her features into the neutral appearance of ancient statues, the zero of expression. Her eyelids, having fluttered dolorously, had ended up becoming motionless, similarly petrified. She had arched them immoderately, revealing excessively staring eyes with enormous whites, like glass eyes . . .

And this was why Gilette, in the middle of her suddenly decelerated sentence, had fallen silent: I had looked at her too intently. She was in a trance.

I had noticed all that at once, you see. When her hands touched mine and her eyes began to allow themselves to be caught, I had seen it—oh, with alarm! But it wasn't my fault! No, not my fault! Open any manual of hypnotism: who would ever have the absurd idea of entrancing an unconsenting subject? It was an exceptional, almost miraculous case. I was fascinated by it—but I had perceived all the advantage that I might obtain from the circumstance.

The great darkness that enshrouded my soul had been illuminated by an abrupt and diabolical dawn; nasal trumpets were blaring in my ears. And, instead of freeing the poor fluttering eyelids, I had tightened the magnetic vice of my gaze upon them. Then, within myself, insistently, I had commanded: "Sleep . . . ! Sleep . . . ! Sleep . . . ! Sleep . . . !"

And now she was asleep, Monsieur, sitting in front of me, cold, pale and cataleptic, like her own marble stature.

And her entire future was at my discretion.

But it was necessary to act without delay; someone might come in unexpectedly, and then what a tragicomedy there would be! Rapidly, I sought to formulate the orders that Gilette was about to receive and would be clearly imposed on her mind. I wanted them to be brief, precise and complete, quick to deliver, easy to retain and exempt from all ambiguity, incapable of giving rise to any misunderstanding by false interpretation.

After a minute, I believed that I had composed adequate terms, and I hastened to operate the suggestion, for fear was hovering over me—the fear of being surprised, and another . . .

I've already mentioned it: the company of the hypnotized frightens me. I have an aversion to their conversation. They're mysterious interlocutors. And the isolation in which I found myself, in a very perilous situation, with a patient whom public opinion would have labeled a "victim", redoubled my alarm.

I began with the traditional interrogation.

"Gilette! Are you asleep?"

In a blank and mechanical voice, she replied: "Yes."

"Are you prepared to obey me?"

" . . . "

"It's necessary. I wish it. Will you obey me?"

" . . . Yes."

"Good. Remember this: Every Tuesday, from next Tuesday on, at five o'clock, you will come to my home and"—I added in a hoarse tone, with a kind of sob—"you will be my mistress, as ardent and delighted as the most spirited, the most enraptured of mistresses. At seven o'clock you will leave, and you will lose the memory of our rendezvous and our relationship until the following Tuesday. In the same way, when you wake up, you will forget that I have put you to sleep. Is that understood?"

"Yes."

"Repeat it."

She repeated the infernal orders word for word, without inflection, impassively and automatically, in the manner of a schoolgirl reciting a fable, and she articulated her promises of love as she had once intoned "holding a cheese in his beak."[1] An odious scene. I hastened to bring it to an end.

I woke her up. Fortunately, everything progressed normally. Beneath my transversal passes I saw the color and animation return to her cheeks, her eyelids fluttering and her eyes blinking, and Gilette's pose relaxed, while a low-pitched murmur escaped her lips, accelerated, rose in pitch, acquired cadence, and became her clear habitual voice, resuming in the middle of the interrupted sentence: ". . . I will never say anything

---

1 The full line from Jean de La Fontaine's fable "*Le Corbeau et le renard*" [The Crow and the Fox] is "*Maîte Corbeau sur son arbre perché, tenait en son bec un fromage.*" [Master Crow perched in his tree, holding a cheese in his beak] It is one of La Fontaine's most oft-quoted lines, thanks to the various metaphorical connotations that can be inferred from or imposed on the word *fromage*.

to Guillaume. If not, I shall be forced to tell him the truth. Oh, come on, tell me that it's a promise!"

"Yes, I promise," I replied, cheerfully, my throat full of nervous laughter. "Yes, you're right: I was mad. But it's sufficient, to be mad no longer, to know that one is. And you have demonstrated that I was, Madame, in such peremptory fashion that I ceased to be, at the exact moment when you persuaded me. Oof! It's good to be able to joke about it a little! Ha ha ha! I'm now cured, permanently. Of course we should forget all about it. I agree with you—let's forget it. To hell with the nasty story! Let's never mention it again!"

"Ah!" cried Gilette, in a triumphant tone. "Ah! Finally! You are, therefore, still the honest man that I was already mourning. What a nightmare you gave me, my poor friend! And what a relief too!" She took her head in her hands as she concluded: "But forgive me . . . such a shock . . . I ask your permission to take my leave, my dear; I've suddenly come down with an atrocious migraine . . ."

I spent the week that followed in a deplorable state of overexcitement. I don't know what terrors sometimes seized me by the neck and strangled me. Then there were crazy fits of joy and morbid hope, which shook me with an evil hilarity. Would she come? For a whole week, that was the only question I asked myself. Would she come?

Scientifically, I could not doubt it; but the hosts of the isba led so peaceful and joyful an existence that it would have shaken God's conviction. Mine was almost annihilated at times. An opportunist hypnotist, a sort of sorcerer's apprentice, I had played like a vicious child with something too immense, too sacred, too mysterious . . . and now I remained confounded by my terrible work, to the point of mistrusting the most natural effects.

Gilette's insouciance in the meantime constituted a proof of my success, but I could only see it as evidence to the contrary, and I tried in vain to discover, in the depths of her pure eyes, the suggestion that I had implanted. I could not glimpse anything, any more than Guillaume could, with his husband's eyes behind myopic spectacles. The need to be certain haunted me. For that critical week, I established a calendar analogous to those the soldiers fabricate for the duration of their service, and just as they erase the days one by one, one by one I struck out the hours.

At the end of their litany, the Tuesday presented itself. It was the first of October.

At hazard, I made my bedroom into a veritable hothouse, filled with precious flowers and rare foliage— and when the moment arrived, I went down to take up a position beneath the arch, in order to meet Gilette, if she came, and lead her to my second floor apartment without being able to make any mistake.

My belief that she would come had dwindled away by degrees, and I consoled myself as best I could by imagining all the humiliation of such a success. Even supposing that she would soon be there, what would she be? A simulacrum, a mannequin set up by me. What pleasure could an automaton of that sort provide?

262

When I saw her in the distance, though, clicking the pavement with her little heels, insubordinate and decisive, smoothing down her skirt with coquettish artistry, so white and pink and blonde, so light in spite of her furs and so graceful in spite of her haste—so alive, in sum; get on with it!—I could no longer think of her as an automaton. There was nothing jerky about her unconstrained gait, I can assure you!

She drew nearer. Her eyes were laughing at the escapade. They were not the eyes of a sleep-walker. As she passed me, she put her sleeve in front of her mouth and said: "Go back in quickly! What imprudence!" And she ran gaily toward the staircase.

Lord! One might have thought that she was springtime disguised as winter!

I rejoined her with a single bound, and I went ahead of her, taking her hand. Her perfume rose up in front of us, effluvia of orchards in flower and renascent gardens, filling the old stairwell.

On the threshold, Gilette enveloped me with all her crazed flexibility, plunged her gaze passionately into my eyes, and then whispered, through a kiss from which I thought I was about to faint, stammering with emotion: "At last, my love! At last! At last!" And desire made her lascivious pupils squint slightly. We slid toward the bedroom, interlaced.

Here I shall pause. What would be the point of accumulating all the superlatives necessary to describe all the maxima and all the apogees? The time passed like an Edenic breeze. Only a few vague reflections and attempts at analysis disturbed my blissful joy—but every time I questioned myself about Gilette, I was forced to recognize the naturalness to which her actions and language testified. There are things that cannot be contradicted. Furthermore, she manifested impressions that I had not ordered her to feel. On that day alone, her luminous young body awoke to primal delights. It struck surprised and confused attitudes; and, charmingly, she was glad that it was so profoundly astonished, and was agitated in spite of her in a scarcely modest fashion, which caused her to redden all over in rapture.

Such is the contradictory mind of man, though, that I started, abruptly, to think that it was *too* natural. A comedy, of course! It was by *feigning* being entranced that she had enjoyed it! Ah! Little poison! Little mask! She had wanted to keep the better part and the finer role for herself; to preserve for herself, in case of a possible scandal, the absolving excuse of suggestion!

Yes, Monsieur that was what I thought. It's curious, is it not? Confronted by the enormity of my crime, I refused to believe in it, and did not want to admit my victory in the presence of its magical character and colossal dimensions!

Gilette took responsibility for calling me back to reality. Suddenly, she shuddered and said in a curt voice: "It's time. I feel it. I have to go." Then she got up.

I tried to pull her back with the end of a ribbon, but in order to detach herself she made a movement so sharp that the ribbon remained in my hand with a scrap of lace. And I observed an impulsive fatality in that retreat, which forced my respect and my credulity.

I helped her to get dressed.

Her farewells were tender and desolate. In tears, she repeated: "A week! A week without seeing you! How shall I be able to wait so long? But what can we do? It can't be helped. *Au revoir!* Until Tuesday! *Au revoir . . .*

Her plaint weakened my firmness. That week of solitude, which had to be endured, appeared to me as a desert to be crossed, interminable and tenebrous. As I watched Gilette going down the stairs, I experienced a mortal anguish, like that of Hell itself.

She turned round on the final step and directed a broken-hearted smile at me. "Until Tuesday! Until Tuesday, above all . . . !"

Then, having studied my agony as I leaned toward her, she said: "Poor dear! It's time! It's time! Goodbye!"

She escaped.

I inhaled, until the last suspicion, the breath of April in which her presence lingered. And her absence commenced . . . a terrible and singular absence, in which Gilette was exiled as Madame Dupont-Lardin; in which the woman who loved me emerged from the other and went into the unknown, further away than anything else: nowhere!

I was not without anxiety, however, with regard to the consequences of our rendezvous. I feared that it might have left some confused vestige in Gilette's memory, and, the following day, I rang the doorbell of the isba.

I received the usual welcome there, cordial and informal. Guillaume, however, seemed worried. His wife, he said, had tired eyes and drawn features that presaged nothing good. He had found her thus after returning from his course the previous evening. And Madame Dupont-Lardin deigned to confide in me that she felt weary and languid, without being able to discover the reason.

Left alone with her for a moment, I took the opportunity to ask her, in the manner of a clownish magistrate: "What did you do yesterday, from five o'clock to seven?"

"Yesterday?"

"Why yes," I continued, in the bantering tone. "I came to offer you my compliments, and you weren't here. Who, then, deprived me of the pleasure of seeing you? The dressmaker? The milliner? Or the adulterer?"

Madame Dupont-Lardin burst out laughing. "Insolent fellow!" she replied. "You're overly curious. For your punishment, you shall know nothing!"

She had said these words in a very cheerful tone— but her forehead immediately became pensive, and she fell into an obstinate reverie from which I could not divert her. I understood that she was trying to remember how she had spent the time from five until seven, and that she could not.

Afterwards, I went home, tranquilized and without having extended my visit, for it was particularly disagreeable for me to converse with an indifferent Gilette, the stranger who, a week before, had snubbed, scolded and humiliated me, and considered me as nothing more than a camp-follower to be put back in my place.

The following Tuesday, my lover, faithful to her mission, re-emerged from nothingness and, delightful and punctual, brought me that weekly paradise of which I had assured myself.

I've just consulted the clock . . . it's five to four. Another thirty-five minutes to live! Oh, why didn't I write this letter sooner? I really need to collect myself somewhat!

So . . . oh, *I don't know any more! I don't know any more!*

So, that was how things stood at the beginning of October. And the weeks of darkness followed the dazzling Tuesdays.

The people of the isba saw less and less of me. I was reproached for that coldness. Madame Dupont-Lardin gently gave me to understand that my delicacy was overly reserved. She had "forgotten my indiscretion days ago, and took pleasure in chatting, as in the past, with Guillaume and his old friend". Oh yes! I too would have like to see more of her, but enamored, voluptuous, and not negligent! And I now deplored the scruples that had prohibited me from suggesting to her a pure and simple love, without intermittence, and a resolution to run away with me . . . and I cursed the fear that made me tremble at the thought of hypnotic sleep, and prevented me from putting Gilette to sleep again in order to be able to dictate a new law to her.

Oh, that frightful sight of a medium in catalepsy! Periodic acquaintance with the magnetized had not succeeded in vanquishing it. I shivered at the thought that, one day, an event would occur that would force me to plunge that woman into a trance again and intimate some command or counter-command to her. And now that I had sounded the psychic mystery, oh, ever since then, in that redoubtable shadow where thought treads on tiptoe, among the uncertain and formidable mechanisms that I had had the audacity to bring into action, everything frightened me! To obtain the results

I had obtained, I had set in motion the most enigmatic machinery—and now I feared that the secret engagement of those gears might bring about unforeseen conclusions and irreparable consequences.

Now, the bizarrerie of the effects that I had brought about did not reassure me with regard to those that might yet be produced. The inexorable fatality of its phenomena is a terrible face of hypnotism. The obedience of the subject to the commands of the magnetizer has something blindly mathematical about it, which impresses you beyond all expression.

Several times, impelled by the genius of perverse frissons, I gave myself the squalid spectacle of Gilette reduced to the state of a magnetized thing. Once, as we were saying farewell, I said to her: "Stay with me. Don't go away again." And I placed myself in front of the doorway, with my arms extended.

Her face contracted painfully. She did not say a word in an attempt to appease me. She did not even try to duck under one of my arms. She simply went past. Wildly and impetuously, like a Herculean athlete, suddenly equipped with an irresistible force derived from who knows where. The shock knocked me down.

Another Tuesday—having premeditated this second test—I went to her house a little before five. It was the standard "old friend's visit". We chatted about frivolous things—but Gilette, suddenly and without any formality, broke off our paltry duet and rang for her chambermaid.

"Give me my hat and coat, quickly," she said. Then, turning to me: "You'll forgive me . . . there's something I have to do. I'm absolutely obliged to go out. I'll see you soon, won't I? No, don't accompany me—I'm going to the Devil!"

Not knowing how to put it better, it was thus that she abandoned me in order to go to meet me.

Oh, what a strange mistress I had! Sometimes, Monsieur, remembering that it was my will that ruled over her, I experienced an abominable sensation of being possessed myself!

And yet, is love ever anything other than that? In every miserable pair of lovers, is not one always dominated, victim of the other's suggestion? And when it is the man who is fascinated, does that not seem to you to be monstrous, as if the woman were then usurping the prerogatives of the male? What do you say? In sum, our lusts—Gilette's and mine—were merely a transposition into the experimental domain of what happens in nature. I had done nothing but reproduce a natural phenomenon artificially, and my crime blends into a laboratory experiment. Perhaps it would not even have been a crime, if I had committed it in the name of humanity! What is it, all things considered? It's psychological serum therapy, that's all. I've inoculated passion, in the same way that one injects a virus.

God makes consumptives, just as he makes lovers; in the former instance, tuberculosis forced on rats and guinea-pigs replaces it adequately; personally, I have achieved the second replication. Replication? Get away! I have parodied it as a man might do. I have aped it in a burlesque fashion. And I was not long delayed in recognizing the inferiority of my work by comparison with His.

Gilette's health deteriorated. From one week to the next I followed its slow but inexorable decline. Always lively and radiant when she came to me, I heard from Guillaume, during one of my appearances at the isba, about the long unjustified meditations and the cause-less depressions that took hold of her for hours at a time, while she sat huddled up in a savage mutism.

That day, Guillaume begged me to come back more often, to cheer them up . . .

I did nothing about it. I was perplexed.

One morning, near Christmas, Guillaume present-ed himself before me, causing me a keen apprehension. They had consulted the celebrated Dr. B*** with regard to Madame Dupont-Lardin's condition—but B*** had pronounced from the outset that Madame Dupont-Lardin was suffering from acute neurasthenia.

At that announcement, my fears dissipated.

"Well," I replied, "neurasthenia is treatable—and curable!"

"I know, I know. The doctor has prescribed capsules, wines, injections, douches. But the principal medica-tion—would you believe it?—Gilette has refused. She refuses to submit to it."

"And of what does it consist?"

"Oh, it's nothing much. It consists of spending two months in the sun, in a verdant and pleasant country, by the seaside. Walks; rest; distractions . . ."

"Yes. But she doesn't want to?"

"She says that she can't; that it's impossible for her to leave Paris. And when I ask her why, she replies: 'I don't know, but it's impossible.' And then she resumes meditating, her eyes lit up, her cheeks on fire, and her head in her hands, as if she were hunting for the solution of an indecipherable problem! The doctor claims that this obstinacy is a further proof of the neurasthenia." Guillaume paused, then went on: "Listen, old man, help me, I beg you! Let's try to convince her, both together. She's followed your advice so many times! Her mother owns a villa near Saint-Raphael; if Gilette spends two months there, she'll be cured, she'll live. Otherwise . . ." He made a childish gesture of discouragement, sniffed, coughed, and ended up bursting into sobs.

"What?" I cried.

"The doctor . . . won't guarantee anything . . ."

Emotion made my reply tremulous. "You can count on me Guillaume! We'll convince her, I promise you. You did well to come. But she mustn't be left alone. Go now, old chap, for the time being. I'll follow you. I'll be there."

When the brave fellow had gone, wiping his eyes and his spectacles by turns, I tried to gather my confused ideas.

Without the permission of her "soul director" Gilette would not want to embark for the South. Now, her life being at stake, whatever the cost, she must go. Thus, the duty was incumbent upon me to put her to sleep and to grant her, if not her liberty, at least a few weeks of respite. The operation would be effected in my home, on the following Tuesday. Three days remained for me to simulate, in her husband's presence, the pressing objurgations that would legitimize, in his eyes, such a change of mind.

My program was completely full.

On the thirty-first of December, having gathered my courage in both eyes, I summoned Gilette to the hideous torpor.

A beautiful temptation offered itself to my consciousness: to say to her, "It's over. You'll never come again. Resume your independence."

That was the infallible remedy, the magic words! I did not pronounce them. I loved her too much. I preferred my pleasure to her happiness. And this, in its concise form, carefully prepared, was the decision of which I notified her, and which, by the same token corrected the faults of the earlier order:

"You will let nine Tuesdays pass without coming. On the tenth, at five o'clock, you will be here. After that, every Tuesday, there will be a rendezvous on the previous conditions—except that, if I happen to be near you, don't go looking for me elsewhere, and come to find me wherever I might be."

That same evening, she told Guillaume that she had decided to go and stay with her mother for two months, since he wanted her to go to the country so ardently.

Guillaume was exultant. He did not know how to thank the advocate of his cause enough. One thing, however, grieved him. Retained by the annual exhibition of his works, he could not leave Paris before the fifteenth . . .

He had the good sense not to avoid the issue, though. The decisions were taken; Gilette was to leave without delay, and he would join her in Saint-Raphael later.

*

On the first of January, at nine a.m., the Côte d'Azur express carried Madame Dupont-Lardin away.

It was the first time that Guillaume had been separated from his wife. It made him very melancholy and, dreading the desolation of solitary evenings, he pressed me to dine at the isba every day. Even sadder than him at the prospect of a longer separation, I accepted his offer gladly. At least, in that fashion, I would have news of Gilette, and someone who would talk to me about her. That helped me to endure the eternal days—especially the Tuesdays: those nine Tuesdays that were advancing very gently from the depths of the future; Tuesdays of fasting and abstinence, now as empty and black as the other days, like all those nights that all those days had previously seemed to me to be . . .

The first of them fell on the seventh of January.

Tuesday the seventh of January, 1908! I expected it to be one of those ordinary, uninteresting days whose anniversary recalls nothing to make you weep . . . but it was a terrible day, Monsieur! And I know more than one person who will sob on the seventh of January every year of their miserable lives!

It was ten o'clock in the evening, or thereabouts. I was about to take my leave of Guillaume. He had received a letter from Gilette that morning, redolent of cheerful serenity, and, in order to celebrate what he called "his dear invalid's recovery", he had wanted to open a bottle of champagne.

That little orgy had dissipated my spleen and accentuated his optimism—and we were exchanging some rather roguish repartee, I can tell you, when a telegram was brought in.

He read it through. I saw him turn pale, and sit down heavily in order not to fall, At the same time, it seemed to me that my blood turned to cold water, and I felt my lividity like a glacial coating . . .

Guillaume was panting, as if he were out of breath.

"Bad news?" I said, in a strangled voice.

He began to shake his head, and stammered: "Very . . . bad news. My wife . . . very ill . . . I've been told to go . . . out there . . . without delay . . . without delay . . ." Rising to his feet with a single motion, he added: "She's dead! I'm sure of it. You know these cautious, circumspect telegrams. 'Come without delay' means 'you'll arrive too late'. Come on! I have to leave."

I reckon, now, that his calmness was more frightening than tearful and moaning despair, but I had so much difficulty mastering my own distress that I could not see it—nor could I measure how much more elevated his great and pure suffering was than my fear.

Perhaps he was mistaken, though. Why would the telegram not reveal the whole truth? I tried to convince him of that, and to persuade myself of it—vain efforts. Guillaume departed into the night with his funereal certainty, and I remained alone, facing mine—and the conviction that I was an assassin.

I strode back and forth in my room until dawn, covering league after league in an endless shuttle, which wore me out completely but achieved nothing. I had thought hard, to be sure, but had been unable to establish anything, save for useless suppositions. But Monsieur, the only evidence that imposed itself on my mind tormented it: Gilette, doing well until then, had fallen victim to a serious accident on the very day of our rendezvous and, to judge by the timing of the telegram, in the late afternoon—which is to say, at the time she was accustomed to spend with me.

Had I failed to efface from the tables of her soul the primitive injunction obliging her to come to find me between five and seven? Was it a matter of a morbid accident, or a mental catastrophe? Or had she fallen under some carriage as a result of a somnambulistic precipitation? Had she been run over by a train?

To all these conjectures I raised thousands of objections. A bitter argumentative battle was fought inside my head; different voices launched their invective against my reason, my conscience and my egotism. I thought I could hear their altercation.

And that lasted until morning.

The light of the sun gave me confidence. Doubt gradually equalized the good chances and the bad risks. Toward evening, I did not even believe any longer that Gilette was dead.

At nine o'clock, a telegram arrived:

All over. Guillaume.

No explanations. No details. No consolation. "All over." I knew neither the exact time nor the circumstances of the event. And I dared not telegraph to obtain the story . . .

Then the torture of the previous night began again—and this time, two dawns rose without brightening my interior life. I asked myself, with persecutory

275

obstinacy: *How did it happen?* And while my interrogated consciousness could do nothing but confuse me, my questioned memory offered no worthwhile reply. I never left off repeating in every possible tone what I had instructed Gilette to do, turning my imperative formulas in every sense; no ambiguity revealed itself that might indicate the solution to the mystery. As time went by, however, my guilt was affirmed by my judgment. The exact manner in which I was responsible for the calamity was something that still escaped me, but that I was its author, at the end of three days of anguish and insomnia, I could not doubt.

"You've killed her!" I shouted that at myself, Monsieur. "You've killed her! You've killed her!" And since then, I have been unable to impose silence on myself.

Beside the coffin that he had brought, however, Guillaume told me how Gilette had died. He told me about the absurd crisis of appendicitis that had come upon her like a thunderbolt, the necessity of an immediate and hasty operation, in the most unsuitable conditions, and her death under the chloroform at two o'clock in the morning. He told me all that, which should have soothed my soul. Well, do you know that I thought? "You've killed her! You've killed her!"

It was too late, you see. It was an obsession. "You've killed her!"

But no, it wasn't me. I'm innocent!

Go on! You know perfectly well, deep down, that it's you who killed her. You've killed her, I tell you. Ah! Ah!

Shhhh!

You've . . .
Silence!
. . . Killed . . . !
Oh! It's a curse!

✳

It was at the exit from Montparnasse cemetery, following her burial, that I was subject to the first temptation
to suicide. The state that Guillaume was in prevented
me from giving way to it. To leave him in pain seemed
to me to be deserting a post confided to me. I understood my duties as a consoler and I gave myself the task
of accomplishing them before disappearing.

The widower's grief bordered on dementia. His fine
initial stoicism had given way to the furies of rancor.
He cursed love, fate and everything. He wished that he
could believe in God, in order to hold Him responsible
for his distress and blaspheme against him effectively.

I succeeded, however, in putting his pencils and
brushes back into his fingers, in bending him over his
sketch-books from morning until evening, where por-
traits of Gilette soon succeeded one another, page after
page, until the work exhausted him. He resumed his
Tuesday course. Round-shouldered, jaundiced, mute,
darting fearful glances behind him, he was no longer
the same man, alas—but at the end of the day, he was
still a man, and had it not been for me . . . who knows?
If it is not his life, it is, at least, his reason that he owes
to my solicitude.

But how much trouble he had given me, at the beginning! The cemetery, too, was not far from the isba.

It was such a quick matter to run to it! One crossed the Place Blanche, went along the boulevard, and the first turning on the right, the Avenue Rachel, was a short dead end on to which the gates of the necropolis opened. Three days on the run I found him there, in the little Dupont-Lardin family chapel. On his final escapade, he had lifted up the flagstone of the vault and was about to go down the stairway! I extracted a promise from him that he would only come back once a week, and that he would let the stone rest in peace.

He had the strength to keep his word. It was a good sign. After that, I was not long delayed in perceiving that he was getting better and better, and had no further need of a helper.

My role came to an end sooner than I had hoped. However brief its duration had been, though, Monsieur, it had been sufficient for me to live for one single month with my remorse to get used to its company. A crushing grief, an infinite sadness, rendered existence more sepulchral than death, but for the moment, the courage to get out of it had abandoned me. I was incapable of the slightest effort. My job as an architect disgusted me. Any labor exhausted me. I would have liked never to leave my bedroom, and that it should be carpeted in black, like a catafalque. The window remained closed. I held myself prisoner there to the extent that hunger did not drive me from it, and Guillaume, surprised by such an affliction—and perhaps suspicious—decided not to draw me out of it. I hated everything that interrupted my lamentable intercourse with the memory of Gilette. The joy of others offended me. A burst of laughter from a passer-by was sufficient to irritate me.

The Carnival, which produced a festival hubbub in the streets, brought my anger to the point of paroxism. While it reigned over Paris, I tried to stop up the window by means of a carpet and a mattress—wasted effort; the rumor of the people in a jubilant mood filtered through the stuffing, albeit muffled, and also reached me via the neighboring rooms. Songs, howls of merriment and tunes played on toy trumpets escaped from it like rockets, and I understood, from ambulant music and explosions of noise that the floats of a cavalcade were filing along the road.

No longer able to bear it, I formed a determination to go in search of silence and peace in a more tranquil quarter. I went out.

The cavalcade was drawing away in the direction of the Place Pigalle. I fled in the opposite direction.

A scattered crowd disseminated its strollers across the entire width of the boulevard. The popular gaiety was reinforced by a plague of confetti. It was hurled energetically into every open mouth, but it only cut short obscenities and bestial cries, for the populace had borrowed the voices of a herd of livestock, braying and lowing in pleasure. Paper whips, lashing out frenetically, outraged suddenly-frightened faces. Serpentine lassos seized necks and, for a second, linked up a group within the multitude. A few poorly-costumed people in masks were parading or performing imbecilic buffooneries. Oh, what a herd of donkeys! What a herd of goats! Idiots lecherous for *amusement* in that vale of tears! Joy! Misery! *Joy!* What an atrocious folly!

I hastened my steps.

279

It had rained that morning, but the day was ending in a fine winter evening, already mingled with lukewarm and perfidious languor. The setting sun lit up the puddles with stained-glass gleams. A shabby Paillasse was stamping in the muddy pools in order to soil the citizens' Sunday clothes. As I made a detour to avoid him, someone slapped me with a handful of sordid confetti. I became annoyed. The witnesses guffawed. I made off even more rapidly.

The boulevard became unbearable. Bordered by taverns with baroque shop-fronts—*Le Ciel, L'Enfer, L'Araignée, Le Chat Noir, Les Porcherons*—fronted with misshapen and sinister statues, it was a grotesquely ugly frame entirely appropriate to that proletarian masquerade. I was on the point of taking refuge in Guillaume's house, but the dread of still being able to hear the howls of the Carnival there dissuaded me.

Everything grated on my nerves. *Le Moulin Rouge*, a few strides from the holy place where the dead lie, seemed to me to be the shame of Paris.

As I crossed the Avenue Rachel I saw that the gate of the cemetery wasn't closed. Should I go in? Alas, why? To hear rabble amusing itself beside Gilette's mausoleum! Such a prospect sent me back into the crowd, with my head bowed.

As I went on, the crowd thickened. I experienced increasing difficulty going through it. I felt that its *joy* was hostile to my despair, and its slowness opposed my progress. Gradually, I was forced to slow down. People looked at me curiously. And in the Place Clichy, the mob—and especially the *joy*—became so violent that I was obliged to turn back, jostling elbows and bumping shoulders under a deluge of confetti, streamers and invective.

I had to resign myself to it. The simplest thing was to return to the house. That was what I tried to do.

The flow diminished. The idlers were circulating with greater discretion—but I saw, without pleasure, that the masks were multiplying. The imminence of darkness was doubtless encouraging their wearers to venture outdoors, with their tawdry finery. They were pouring out of all the side-streets into the carnivalesque boulevard, dolled up in rags, made up with flour and ink, disfigured by ignoble painted grimaces—all pitiful and all *joyful*. They emerged from the gloomiest back streets, the darkest cul-de-sacs, and even from the Avenue Rachel, which led to the sepulchers! Yes, even there, people dwelt who wanted to dress up and claim their share of the *joy*, of the madness.

Two clowns came out of it in front of me. They had false noses made of cardboard, lustrous smocks parti-colored in yellow and blue, and were *joyously* singing the latest popular song. A woman, dressed as a laborer, with a pipe in her teeth and a moustache on her upper lip, followed them, laughing alone. Then came another, indefinable mask. Man or woman? Odalisque or Roman? Dirty toga or improper burnoose? It was impossible to tell what it was. But incontestably, its wearer was drunk, and had to lean on the walls in order to walk. In truth, it was a challenge! The most wretched wanted to rejoice today, in order to annoy me! This one's feet went *flip flop* on the damp asphalt; the peplum, which trailed in the mud, certainly hid nothing more than old slippers, but the filthy wretch

281

was wearing a disguise and the brute was drunk! Oh, that *joy*, that *joy* everywhere!!!

I was indignant, and I swiftly overtook the drunkard, averting my eyes. That travesty of misery in a festive mood incarnated for me the unanimous revelry and the universal *Joy*, to such a point that it was odious to me to hear the drunkard's footsteps floundering behind me. All the sadness of the world had taken refuge in my soul. I aspired to solitude with an unhealthy ardor. A church bell, which slowly chimed the hour, seemed to me to be sounding a funeral knell.

I reached my house as one gains a place of sanctuary.

Relieved to have fled the enlivened throng, I climbed the staircase unhurriedly, and I had reached the first floor when a disagreeable sound made me go more quickly, attacking the climb. It was a halting *flip flop* on the floor-tiles of the hallway, which soon died away on the stair-carpet.

Oh, damnation! The carnival mask that was now climbing up! *Joy*! The *Joy* was pursuing me!

In four strides I was on my doorstep, searching for my keys and not finding them, because of the urgency of my desire to find them and to hide myself from the view of that *Joy*, you understand: the *Joy* that was coming along the landing with its laughter and its hiccups, making fun of me!

Finally, the key slid into the lock—and I felt liberated, victorious, able to mock.

"May the Devil take Mardi Gras!" I said. "Hold on—Tuesday! It's Tuesday . . . it's today . . . alas! It's today that *she* was supposed to . . ."

And all of a sudden, Monsieur, my teeth began to chatter, and my bones began to dance the Dance of the Dead. I was in front of my open doorway, without being able to go through it. I heard the mask climbing up—the mask from the Avenue Rachel. I heard it stumbling against the walls in the semi-darkness. *An exhalation of the morgue preceded it!*

It surged forth, hanging on to the banister. It was not a burnoose, or a toga, but a parted shroud that enveloped it. What I saw, by the light of the setting sun, could not be described. It was neither masculine nor feminine, and it was not drunk. It was a creature of quicklime that was coming toward me . . . an obscure and slimy monster that touched me . . .

It embraced me with its cold and sticky rigidity. And this is what its death-rattle tried to say: "Come! Come quickly! Our two hours are curtailed; I had so much trouble getting out . . . I'm late. Come, my love! Oh, I'm suffering a martyrdom . . . but I love you even more than I feel ill. Come!"

I allowed myself to be drawn, stupidly, uncomprehendingly—*and my late mistress dragged me to the bedroom.*

The blocked window created a precocious night there. Night was also falling inside my head. I was entranced by stupor. An abject kiss on my cheek suddenly woke me up. I stood up straight and pushed the amorous cadaver away, so brutally that I heard it fall over along with a chair. My hand sought a familiar object of its own accord; I turned something mechanically; an electric lamp lit up.

283

The dead woman had already got to her feet. Standing up, she rearranged the folds of her shroud. In the pitiless light, it was a sight to drive you mad, a spectacle to kill you, a horrible prodigy to which it was necessary to put an immediate end!

But how? What secret law of hypnotism had prolonged the effect of my orders beyond death? I didn't have time to think about that. Only one expedient offered itself to my confused mind: to put that thing to sleep and command it to return to its coffin and remain there, lifeless, until the end of time . . . yes! But was that material specter able to go to sleep? Were the dead magnetizable? Could those who were no longer awake become drowsy? Could someone asleep be put to sleep? And what about me? Could I be bold enough to plunge my gaze into those two ignominies . . . having not dared to do so when they were the stars in my sky?

I made a great effort.

"Gilette," I began—oh, these diminutive names do not suit the dead, and how false that one rang! "Gilette . . . sit down. It's been such a long time since I last looked at you . . . No! Don't look into the mirror! I implore you! I forbid you . . . !"

Her death-rattle groaned dully. "It's abominable to know that one is dead . . . to feel oneself suffering thus . . . and f . . ."

"Mercy! Mercy!" I begged.

"Why ask for mercy? Are you guilty of something? I love you; that's all that matters. Come, my darling! Oh, I need so badly to be your mistress, as ardent and delighted as the most spirited, the most enraptured of mistresses . . ."

She pronounced the last words emphatically, and, with her arms raised in an atrociously coquettish pose, she extended her winding-sheet like a screen behind her miry nudity.

"Gilette!" I stammered, retreating to the doorway. "I told you . . . that I wanted . . . to look at you . . . for a while. Take this armchair . . ."

She obeyed meekly. Outside, a shrill steam-valve released an incessant incoherent shriek.

I tried to influence Gilette then, but I could not succeed in obtaining the condensation of my will-power, and my listless gaze vacillated. Besides, from a distance, without touching the patient, nothing can be achieved. Would it be necessary, then, to place ourselves hand-in-hand, knee-to-knee?

Just as I was preparing to submit myself to this new torture, a fortuitous occurrence plunged me even further into the gulf of horror. Someone in the antechamber exclaimed: "What! All the doors open! Oh, that odor! What a stench! Well, where are you?"

Guillaume!

What? Come again? *Guillaume was there*. It was Mardi Gras—a holiday; he had no class!

The scene that was about to unfold, Monsieur, unfolded in my imagination with a rare promptitude. I saw in advance, the satanic *flagrante delicto* in which the widower surprised his deceased wife in amorous conversation with the family friend—and I attained the depths of terror.

The cadaver stood up, tottering and bewildered, and went to hide behind the bed-curtains. With a flick of the wrist I put out the light and I ran to meet

Guillaume, to grab hold of him, to drag him away, to take him downstairs so quickly that he only recovered his power of speech outside. I made no reply to his questions. I gripped him firmly and I forced him to run through the crowd, to run faster and faster. Where? I didn't know. We were going at top speed. At every moment, over his shoulder, I scanned the space that we left behind us—but, thinking of the vigor of the hypnotized and the injunction: "Come to find me wherever I might be," I stopped the first motorized cab that was free.

It took us to Montrouge, then to Vincennes, then somewhere else. It drove us through all the suburbs. I still kept silent.

At seven o'clock, however, I consented to go back to Montmartre, and, after having deflected Guillaume's insistence with the aid of a story I had invented and which he seemed to believe, I deposited him in front of the isba.

As I had expected, my bedroom was deserted.

As a precautionary measure, I shook the bed-curtains. No one was hidden there any longer. Besides, oily footprints were discernible on the clean carpet, in which the departure of the impure thing was inscribed, along with its impatient stamping and its arrival. But its sojourn in my home was eternalized in a nauseating fashion, and I had to air the place in order to expel Gilette entirely.

Then I began to reflect . . .

And I've been reflecting for a week.

"Every Tuesday, from five to seven, a rendezvous on the previous conditions" and "come to find me wherever I might be."

Thus, I have inflicted the haunting of a revenant upon myself! Every week, the dead woman will return, becoming more repulsive from week to week, for long years. I shall be visited at first by a filthy creature, then by a shapeless mass of little moving things; a skeleton will follow, whitening with age; and finally there will be a cloud of dust . . . but that cloud is a long time off . . . it will have to descend into to the depths of my own tomb, every Tuesday . . . *if the phantom is capable of surviving me . . .*

I could go far away . . . America. Nothing could rejoin me there, in two hours. But is it not necessary, by Divine Mercy, to attempt the impossible to in order annihilate that which I have formed? Can I allow that profanation of Death to continue without trying to put a stop to it? Then again, who knows? No one noticed Gilette because of the Carnival and the masks . . . but how can she pass unnoticed on other occasions?

It's necessary to put a stop to all that. Yes. However— even if the thing were practicable—I'll never be able to put her to sleep again. I'm too frightened. And do you know, I can't even see her again, or hear her, or . . . oh, no, no, no!

Tuesday. She'll be coming soon.

That's why I'm going to kill myself.

I'm going to kill myself, above all, because it's the only means of rendering myself blind and deaf, of separating myself from touch, smell, taste, memory and everything that allows us to perceive, to know, to recall . . .

And I'm also going to kill myself—pay attention, now—because I have a definite hope of destroying, along with my will-power, that fragment of it which

287

I slipped into Gilette's body and which, remaining alive, governs her on the appointed days and lends her, dreadfully, an intermittent and fateful soul.

I believe that. I'm not certain of it, for here I run into the unknown of science. Nevertheless, I shall kill myself before half past four, before she is reanimated, out there, before she can lift the li . . .

Oh! Who's ringing my doorbell? So forcefully? So persistently?

Who's knocking, so urgently?

My God, how dark it is! What time is it, then? Four o'clock! Still four o'clock! But . . . God in Heaven! The pendulum's no longer moving. The pendulum has been stopped since four o'clock! And how many lines I've written since!

The knocking's louder! The door's caving in! Oh! Oh! Oooooh! Gilette! One second! I'll open up! Wait a second!

Quick, my revolver! In the name of the Father, the Son and the Holy Spirit . . .

ACKNOWLEDGEMENTS

"La Fée Lubantine" was first published in *La Comtesse de Morlane* by Catherine Durand in 1699; the translation was first published in the anthology *The Origin of the Fays and Other Stories*, Black Coat Press, 2019.

"Le Séminariste" by S. Henry Berthoud was reprinted in *Contes et traditions surnaturelles de la Flandre*, Lemesle 1831, where it is dated 1830; the translation was first published in the Berthoud collection *The Angel Asrael and Other Legendary Tales*, Black Coat Press, 2017.

"La Morte amoureuse" by Théophile Gautier was first published in *La Chronique de Paris* 23-26 juin 1836; the translation is original to the present volume

"Les Willis" by Alphonse Karr was reprinted in Contes et nouvelles, Michel Lévy 1856; the translation is original to the present volume.

"Vielle histoire" by Charles Barbara was first published in the *Bulletin de la Societé des gens de lettres* in 1853;

the translation was first published in the Barbara collection *Stirring Stories*, Snuggly Books, 2021.

"Titane" by Jules Lermina was first published in *Le Figaro, supplément littéraire de dimanche* 25 avril 1885; the translation was first published in the Lermina collection *The Secret of Zippelius and Other Stories*, Black Coat Press, 2011.

"Le Veuvage de Schéhérazade" by Henri de Régnier was first published in *L'Illustration* Noël 1925; the translation was first published in the Régnier collection *A Surfeit of Mirrors*, Black Cost Press, 2012.

"Le Miroir" by Jean Richepin was first published in *Le Journal* 29 juin 1899; the translation was first published in the Richepin collection *The Crazy Corner*, Black Coat Press, 2013.

"L'Idole" by Frédic Boutet appeared in *Contes dans la nuit*, Chamuel, 1898; the translation was first published in the Boutet collection *The Antisocial Man and Other Strange Stories*, Borgo Press, 2013.

"Ennoia" by André Lebey was first published in *Le Centaur*, tome 1, 1896; the translation is original to the present volume.

"La Nuit de noces" by Catulle Mendès appeared in *Le Rose et le noir* (1885); "Wedding Night" was first published in the Mendès collection *The Exigent Shadow and Other Strange Obsessions* (Black Coat Press, 2019).

The original version of the "The Blue Woman" by G. Albert Aurier appeared as the first of three "Proses sans titre" in his *Oeuvres posthumes*, Mercure de France, 1893; the translation was first published in the Aurier collection *Elsewhere and Other Stories*, Snuggly Books, 2019.

"Légende d'Amadis et de la fée Oriane" by Jean Lorrain was first published in *La Revue illustrée* 1 juillet 1896 before being reprinted as "Oriane vaincue" in *Princesses d'ivoire et d'ivresse*, Ollendorff, 1902; the translation first appeared in the Lorrain collection *Masks in the Tapestry*, Snuggly Books, 2017.

"Lisbeth" by Gaston Danville was first published in the *Mercure de France* janvier 1892; the translation was first published in the Danvillle collection *The Anatomy of Love and Murder: Psychoanalytical Fantasies*, Borgo Press, 2013.

"La Saurienne" by Renée Vivien was first published in *La Dame à la louve* (1904, signed Renée Vivien); the translation was first published in the Vivien collection *Lilith's Legacy: Prose Poems and Short Stories* (Snuggly Books, 2018).

"Le Roi de perse" by Maurice Magre was first published in *Messidor* 17 février 1907; the translation is original to the present volume.

"Le Rendez-vous" by Maurice Renard was first published in the *Mercure de France* septembre 1909; the translation was first published in the Renard collection *A Man Among the Microbes*, Black Coat Press, 2010.

A PARTIAL LIST OF SNUGGLY BOOKS

MAY ARMAND BLANC *The Last Rendezvous*
G. ALBERT AURIER *Elsewhere and Other Stories*
CHARLES BARBARA *My Lunatic Asylum*
S. HENRY BERTHOUD *Misanthropic Tales*
LÉON BLOY *The Tarantulas' Parlor and Other Unkind Tales*
ÉLÉMIR BOURGES *The Twilight of the Gods*
CYRIEL BUYSSE *The Aunts*
JAMES CHAMPAGNE *Harlem Smoke*
FÉLICIEN CHAMPSAUR *The Latin Orgy*
BRENDAN CONNELL *Metrophilias*
BRENDAN CONNELL *Unofficial History of Pi Wei*
BRENDAN CONNELL (editor) *The Zinzolin Book of Occult Fiction*
RAFAELA CONTRERAS *The Turquoise Ring and Other Stories*
DANIEL CORRICK (editor)
    Ghosts and Robbers: An Anthology of German Gothic Fiction
ADOLFO COUVE *When I Think of My Missing Head*
QUENTIN S. CRISP *Aiaigasa*
ALADY DILKE *The Outcast Spirit and Other Stories*
CATHERINE DOUSTEYSSIER-KHOZE *The Beauty of the Death Cap*
ÉDOUARD DUJARDIN *Hauntings*
BERIT ELLINGSEN *Now We Can See the Moon*
ERCKMANN-CHATRIAN *A Malediction*
ALPHONSE ESQUIROS *The Enchanted Castle*
ENRIQUE GÓMEZ CARRILLO *Sentimental Stories*
DELPHI FABRICE *Flowers of Ether*
DELPHI FABRICE *The Red Spider*
BENJAMIN GASTINEAU *The Reign of Satan*
EDMOND AND JULES DE GONCOURT *Manette Salomon*
REMY DE GOURMONT *From a Faraway Land*
REMY DE GOURMONT *Morose Vignettes*
GUIDO GOZZANO *Alcina and Other Stories*
GUSTAVE GUICHES *The Modesty of Sodom*
EDWARD HERON-ALLEN *The Complete Shorter Fiction*
EDWARD HERON-ALLEN *Three Ghost-Written Novels*
RHYS HUGHES *Cloud Farming in Wales*
J.-K. HUYSMANS *The Crowds of Lourdes*
J.-K. HUYSMANS *Knapsacks*
COLIN INSOLE *Valerie and Other Stories*
JUSTIN ISIS *Pleasant Tales II*

www.ingramcontent.com/pod-product-compliance
Lightning Source LLC
Chambersburg PA
CBHW020359110726
47899CB00006B/1784